THE MUSICIAN AND THE MONSTER

JENYA KEEFE

RIPTIDE PUBLISHING

Riptide Publishing
PO Box 1537
Burnsville, NC 28714
www.riptidepublishing.com

The Musician and the Monster

Cover art: Shayne Leighton, parliamentbookdesign.wordpress.com
Editors: Carole-ann Galloway, Stella Li
Layout: L.C. Chase, lcchase.com

ISBN: 978-1-62649-887-7

First edition
September, 2019

Also available in ebook:
ISBN: 978-1-62649-886-0

THE MUSICIAN AND THE MONSTER

JENYA KEEFE

RIPTIDE
PUBLISHING

For M, always

TABLE OF
CONTENTS

CHAPTER ONE

"You're selling me to the elf-lord?"

This house, the one Ángel Cruz had grown up in, looked exactly the same as always. A small, old house in Jacksonville, it was shaded by the serpentine branches of oaks and had last been decorated in the early 1980s. It was immaculately clean and redolent with Ángel's childhood memories.

But nothing was the same, not after the bomb his father had just dropped.

Both his father and mother were present, which was alarming enough. Ángel hadn't seen Victor Cruz and Abigail Barrington in the same room together since his high school graduation. And then there was the stranger—a red-haired white man—occupying Victor's chair at the head of the dining room table. Victor never ceded that chair to anyone.

And for a third—they were selling him to the elf-lord. Ángel was dumbfounded.

"Don't be melodramatic, Ángel." Victor could have patented that sigh, the one that said, *Why is my son always so tiring?* "Sit down."

Ángel sank into a chair. He'd been summoned up from his apartment in Miami for an emergency family meeting this morning. After his grueling six-hour drive he was sweaty, smelly, and tired.

He caught the red-haired man glancing between him and his father. People often did because they looked so much alike: both small-boned, skinny, and brown. Nervously Ángel toyed with the woven rainbow bracelet on his wrist, guitar-string calluses catching in the threads.

He'd been prepared for a confrontation, but there was no way he could have prepared for this.

Victor said, "This is simple. Your family has generously supported you for your entire life. You have been provided with the best of everything, including an excellent education that you decided to throw away. You chose to waste all your opportunities and live like a child. Now your family has money troubles, and for the first time, you're being asked to contribute a little."

"Money troubles?" Ángel glanced at the man who sat in his father's chair, and then back to his father. "What does the elf-lord want with me?"

"He prefers not to be called the elf-lord," said the stranger, fussing with the cuffs of his good gray suit. "He is the cultural envoy from the Otherworld." At Ángel's baffled stare, he added, "My name is Neil Jeremy. I'm a senior special agent with the Department of Otherworld Relations. The envoy is not fond of the term 'elf' in general. He prefers 'fae.'"

Ángel nodded.

"The trouble," continued Agent Jeremy, casting a scalpel-sharp glance at Victor, "is that Mr. Cruz has been indicted for attempting to run a Ponzi scheme on the cultural envoy from the Otherworld, and is now facing a prison term of up to fourteen years, not to mention liquidation of all assets to partly recompense the losses of his victims."

Ángel stared at him. Then he looked at his father, who didn't meet his eyes. "Excuse me?" Ángel said.

Agent Jeremy explained, tersely, that the FBI had been gathering evidence on Ángel's father's financial crimes for quite some time. A few months ago, Victor had contacted the envoy from the Otherworld with promises of extraordinary returns on a risk-free investment, and the envoy, apparently not an idiot, had alerted the DOR.

And now here they were.

The DOR agent said, "The envoy pledges that he will personally contribute ten million dollars in restitution to the other victims of your father, and the most serious charges against him will be dropped, if you, Ángel, are willing to live with and work for the envoy for six years."

Ángel reeled back in his chair.

His father, a crook? It was inconceivable. Sure, Victor Cruz was a proud man, and sometimes a bitter one. He could be bad-tempered and judgmental. His divorce had dealt a blow to his pride that he'd never recovered from, and certainly his son's open homosexuality had not brought him joy. But he lived by the immigrant's ethic: hard work, education, Church, and family. Take faithful care of those, and the American Dream would fall into your hands. It had never occurred to Ángel that Victor might be *dishonest*.

"Ten million dollars?" Ángel's voice squeaked when he was finally able to speak.

Jeremy said calmly, "Your father stole over seventeen million dollars from over thirty different investors."

Ángel glanced around the room. The house was nice—everything worked perfectly, his father made sure of that—but no one had poured seventeen million dollars into this house.

Victor said tiredly, "Just cooperate, Ángel."

"What would the el— What would the envoy want me to do?"

"The fae live communally, in large groups of family and friends," said Jeremy. "As the only fae on Earth, the envoy is—well, he's lonely. He doesn't have anyone to talk to. You would be his companion. There would be a salary, of course, and room and board."

The silence in the room was deafening.

After a moment, Ángel said, "He's paying ten million dollars for *company*? Is he angry? Will he— Is he going to punish me for what my father did?"

Victor scoffed. "Now you are being absurd. The envoy is a man of honor."

"Perfect target for a thief, then, no?" flashed Ángel at him. "*Absurd* was you trying to rip him off. And now you want me to save your ass."

Agent Jeremy said blandly, "Six years is less than half the minimum prison sentence your father could expect for fraud."

"I'm not the one who committed fraud," said Ángel, standing up.

"Ángel," said his mother. "Please sit."

He looked at her. Abigail Barrington had married a short Cubano electrician in a burst of adolescent rebellion, and then, thinking better of it, had divorced him and moved back to Savannah, leaving her son behind. She looked out of place here in her ex-husband's Jacksonville home—pale and blond and slim.

He sat.

He'd spent summers with her other family in Georgia, where he'd always felt, at best, like a guest; at worst, an embarrassing reminder of an episode everyone would prefer to forget. But he did remember happy times too. She had taught him to dance in the dining room of her house. They'd pushed the table and chairs up against the wall and turned up the radio to waltz to "She's Always a Woman" by Billy Joel. She'd laughed as they danced.

She wasn't laughing now. "No matter what you do, your father is going bankrupt. His business is gone. He's going to lose this house, and his retirement account, and the money he put aside for you. He'll be publicly disgraced before all his friends. He'll lose friends, the people who trusted him."

This was horrifying. In spite of himself, pity for his father rose up in his throat. He still couldn't believe that Victor would ever do this—his father wouldn't know how to contact the envoy from the Otherworld.

But he bet his wheeler-dealer stepfather would. "Did you know?" he asked. "Were you in on it too?"

"But if you step in," she went on, not answering him, "that's where the damage stops. Your father won't go to prison. They won't come after my family, or your brothers. Ned won't lose his home, Michael will be able to stay in school—he'll need to get loans, but he'll be able to do it. Think of Ned and Michael. Think about Ned's children."

"You did know." He stared at his mother. "I bet it was Bill's thing all along, wasn't it?"

"That doesn't matter now."

God. His mother was married to a man named Bill Harrington, who'd made bank in Hilton Head real estate development, who talked big about money and deals and how you had to spend in order to make. Maybe he'd lost his shirt. Maybe that's where the seventeen million had gone: into Barrington's pockets. Rescuing his ex-wife from her husband's financial disaster—that would appeal to Victor. But then someone had gotten stupid, gotten caught, had brought them all down. "Doesn't it? I might pay for Papá's fuckup, but I'm not going to pay for Bill's."

Agent Jeremy said, "Bill Harrington hasn't been indicted for these crimes. The evidence points to Victor Cruz."

His mother twisted the knife. "It's not as though you have a career or a family of your own."

I do. Ángel didn't say it out loud though, just stared at her, seeing only the lack of love in her blue eyes.

His father loved him in his way, or had once. When Ángel was outed at seventeen, Victor had raged, wept, begged him to pray for forgiveness and change his ways. But his mother had simply turned away, with a coolness that suggested she never had loved him. Whatever happy memories she cherished from his childhood weren't happy enough for her to keep in touch.

He had defied them both. He hadn't changed his ways. He'd quit college to make a living as a musician. He would rather play and sing for *los turistas* at the Manatee Bar in Ormond Beach than pursue a career in engineering or medicine, like his brothers, or to become an electrician and work for his father.

He'd somehow cherished the hope that his parents still loved him. That they would someday come to accept him. Their queer boy, their session musician.

Now those hopes tasted as bitter as aspirin dissolving on his tongue. *This* was his parents' assessment of his actual worth. His life, his relationships, the career that he'd been building, held nothing of value to them. He was expendable, and they'd sacrifice him to save themselves.

But he couldn't just abandon them.

He turned to Agent Jeremy. "Two years."

"Four," said Jeremy instantly.

Ángel sighed, looking again at his family: his mother, blonde, with her family's sky-blue eyes, so lacking in warmth. His father like an older mirror image, brown and lean.

Neither of them quite met his eyes.

"Done," said Ángel.

An imperceptible sigh of relief from his parents. Maybe from Agent Jeremy too. Then his father said gruffly, "Thank you, *retaco*."

"You haven't called me *retaco* since I was seventeen," he snapped. "You don't go back now." He transferred his glare to Agent Jeremy. "Four years. And after this, all debts are paid. We are done and *done*."

Agent Jeremy snapped open his briefcase and pulled out a fat contract. "Have a look," he said, passing it across the table. "Let me know if there's anything else that you'd like us to change." Ángel began to read, heart breaking, eyes burning. He vowed that he would never return to this house, or speak to these people, ever again.

CHAPTER TWO

"So is he dangerous?" Ángel asked Neil Jeremy.

They were in a helicopter, high over the mountains in northern Montana, speaking through noise-canceling headsets.

"No, don't be silly," said Jeremy.

Legends told that the fae were *very* dangerous: amoral, pitiless monsters, to be feared and placated and, above all, avoided. One absolutely did not voluntarily go live with them.

Ángel had heard the elf-lord's music, of course. He'd released several albums: fae music transcribed for piano and orchestra. It was wild, incomprehensible music, full of strange harmonies and eerie, unearthly sounds. Ángel didn't understand it, but it was enormously influential. In fact, most of what he knew about modern-day elves came from the lyrics and websites of elf-obsessed alt-metal musicians. Which seemed to justify Victor's comments about Ángel's squandered educational opportunities, but anyway.

Once, centuries before the birth of Christ, the beautiful and strange people of the Otherworld had moved freely across the magical veil. Then, for reasons that only the fae could know, that veil had become an impenetrable wall, and the fae had disappeared from the Earth, leaving behind only myths and tales: Tuatha de Danann. Daoine Sidhe. Tylwyth Teg. Fairies and djinni and demons; the peri, the yōkai, the Seelie and Unseelie Court. Monsters of all sorts.

The tales said that they lured people into bogs to drown, lured ships onto rocks to be destroyed. Stole people's money and replaced it with autumn leaves, stole people's babies and replaced them with monsters. Seduced people with their beauty, cursed them with their magic.

"Why did he come here?" he asked Jeremy.

"Stop worrying, Ángel. You won't be in any danger."

Jeremy had an annoying way of not really answering questions.

Sometime in the twentieth century—so Ángel had read—the veil had thinned enough for the fae of the Otherworld to begin studying humans. Watching them in magical ways, learning their languages, studying their culture.

Then, four years before Ángel was born, the fae had sent a gift through the veil. A previously ordinary beech tree in Springvale Park in Atlanta had begun to glow and emit an intoxicating scent. Crowds had gathered around, drawn as if by magic to the shining tree; then a rift had opened up, revealing a wooden chest full of objects that had been immediately taken into custody by the federal government.

The chest had contained several discs—exactly the same technology as vinyl phonograph records, although in a kind of clear, organic resinous material that Earth didn't have. Someone had had to reverse-engineer a player that spun the discs at the right speed. The message on the discs had been in four languages: English, Mandarin Chinese, Hindi, and Arabic, all correct and fluent. They had promised that the people of the Otherworld meant humans no harm. The fae claimed to be scholars and artists, not warriors. They wanted to learn.

The box had also contained beautiful textiles and carvings; plant specimens that had gone straight to biologists for analysis, but which (it turned out) had been intended as food; jars of liquids—perfumes, ointments?—that chemists around the world were still trying to figure out; and more of that haunting music.

Entirely new fields of study had sprung up across the globe, just from the contents of that chest. The United States had established a new Department of Otherworld Relations.

And then, eight years ago, another tree had begun to glow: a crepe myrtle on the Georgia Tech campus. And an elf-lord had stepped from its branches. Alone, naked but for blush-colored crepe myrtle blossoms, and the veil of his long hair.

The elf-lord had been arrested by freaked-out campus police before the DOR had swooped in and established him in a new position: cultural envoy. Since then, Ángel had seen pictures of him on the internet and in magazines. He was tall, humanoid, fluent in English. He was a musician. He said he was a scholar. He only wanted to live on Earth and exchange information. He sometimes gave concerts and little talks about the Otherworld, or at least he used to; Ángel couldn't remember the last one. He was pretty sure that he'd consulted with the scholars who were trying to understand the gifts that had been sent. For a while he had been a frequent guest at the White House. He'd once played a piano recital at a state dinner for the British Prime Minister and his family. Chopin.

Ángel stared out at the strange landscape beneath him. "If he's lonely," he persisted, "why doesn't another elf come through to be with him? Or why doesn't he just go back home?"

"The veil doesn't work that way. Well—we don't actually know how it works. But he says no one else can come through. It was just that one time."

"And you believe him? Maybe there are other elves in, like, Africa, or China, and we just don't know about it."

"We would know," said Jeremy.

Ángel wasn't convinced. The elves were tricksters—everyone said so. It was in supermarket tabloids and Facebook memes, in newspaper editorials and Twitter posts. People discussed "the alien problem" on Fox News and MSNBC. Some were terrified that the envoy was luring humanity into a false sense of security with his apparently harmless ways, the harbinger of a magical invasion. In eight years the invasion had failed to materialize, though. As far as Ángel knew, the envoy was nothing but a piano player.

The only other thing Ángel really knew about the cultural envoy from the Otherworld was that he always seemed to wear exactly the same outfit: crisp black button-down shirts tucked into tailored black pants, polished black leather shoes. *"Like he's trying to be as boring as possible,"* Ángel's best friend Marissa had said. *"Like an elf-lord could ever blend in."*

Down below the helicopter's curved window, an endless deserted vista of mountains flowed by under a sunlit blue sky. He had assumed that the envoy to the Otherworld lived in or near the Department of Otherworld Relations headquarters in Atlanta, so he had been surprised, this morning, when the DOR jet had taken him nonstop from Miami to Missoula, Montana. From there they'd boarded this helicopter and flown north. They were now somewhere up near Canada, and Ángel couldn't have felt farther from home if they'd been on the moon.

There was nothing down there. Nothing but huge mountains and deep valleys and cliffs and rocks and trees, and streams like shining steel guitar strings, and occasional narrow, winding roads with no cars on them.

Who knew there were parts of the country that were this remote? Ángel shivered and wondered if it ever snowed up here. Did the envoy from the Otherworld like it? Did the Otherworld have mountains? Did it snow there?

"Look up ahead," said Agent Jeremy's voice in his headset, and Ángel followed his pointing finger to see a large grassy hill in a valley, cleared of trees, with a tall wall around it and a large pink house in the middle.

The DOR agent said, "The house was built by a software tycoon in the nineties. I guess he thought it was picturesque up here. Didn't take long before he realized he didn't want to live in the middle of nowhere after all, and moved back to California. He donated it and all its furnishings to the DOR."

"Does the envoy like living in the middle of nowhere?" asked Ángel.

"It's very secure," said Jeremy. "You're one of about twenty people in the world who knows where the envoy lives. The locals think a reclusive novelist lives here. If you tell anyone, we will be annoyed."

"Oh."

As they got closer, it became clear that the house was in fact a mansion, very ornate, faced with some sort of gleaming salmon-colored stone, with white fluted columns, round-topped windows, and curving balconies. Ángel's mind groped through the lessons of a half-forgotten undergraduate architecture class, and came up with "plantation/rococo" to describe the style.

The mansion was encircled by a rolling lawn, late-summer brown, which was protected by a high spike-topped cinder block wall, which was surrounded by miles and miles and miles of dense forest, dark green under aching blue skies. In the distance stood ranks of purple-and-white mountains. The helicopter lowered itself toward a concrete pad just outside the wall, where an octagonal pink mini-mansion guarded the gates. "The security detail lives here at the gatehouse," said the DOR agent. "No one lives in the main house except Oberon, and now you. Nearest town is Stahlberg, about twenty-five miles away."

"Is he really called Oberon? I thought that was made up by the press."

"Oh no, that's his name."

Ángel glanced at Jeremy, eyebrows raised. "Yeah? 'I know a bank where the wild thyme blows' Oberon?"

"No, of course not. No one can actually pronounce his real name. He accepts 'Oberon' as a reasonable substitute. Here you go."

The helicopter touched down. Ángel took off the headset, gathered up his backpack and guitar, and hopped down onto the concrete pad, instinctively cowering away from the deafening concussion of the still-spinning rotors. He glanced back through his blowing hair and saw that the DOR agent had not followed him.

Ángel stood alone as the helicopter leaped skyward. Agent Jeremy gave him a little wave. Ángel swallowed, his mouth dry, watching the helicopter dwindle into the distance.

He walked across the grass to the gatehouse. Waiting there was a young woman in a professional-looking navy pantsuit. She was tall and straight, and carried herself with a competent air that spoke of the military. Her black hair was pulled back in a sleek ponytail. She did not smile when she greeted him.

"Ángel Cruz. I'm Chandler Evanston of the DOR, chief of the envoy's security. Please put your bags, shoes, and the contents of your pockets in this bin, and step through the metal detector."

Evanston oversaw a staff of navy-suited goons who apparently weren't content to let the metal detector do its job. They searched his backpack and guitar case, poking a sort of periscope inside the instrument's sound hole to view its interior. Ángel thought that was funny until they turned their attention to *him*, patting him down with alarming thoroughness, checking inside his mouth, running fingers through his hair and behind his ears, and impersonally exploring his crotch through his jeans. When they discovered his cell phone tucked into his sock, the chief of security frowned. "You were told no computers."

"It's just my phone," he protested.

"No computers." She pocketed it. "Did you disobey instructions in any other way?"

"Will I get that back?"

"No," she said, glaring at him. "Strip."

"What?"

"Strip, or we'll strip you."

He stripped. A goon rotated him by the shoulders and bent him over a table. "Gonna do a cavity search, *guapo*?" asked Ángel, his voice high and trembling despite his bravado. "Hope you got some lube."

The goon let go without probing further. "He's clean."

"That wouldn't have been necessary if you hadn't demonstrated your willingness to disobey instructions," said Evanston, handing him his clothes.

"So it was punishment, not security," gritted Ángel, still shaking as he pulled his jeans up over his hips. "Got it."

"I don't think you do," she said. "Mr. Cruz, have a look at this."

He pulled his T-shirt over his head as she turned on a TV. She showed him footage of a large crowd of angry people, assembled in front of a bank of skyscrapers. There must have been five hundred people there, chanting angrily but incomprehensibly, waving homemade magic-marker signs that said things like *SAVE OUR SPECIES* and *HUMANS FIRST*.

"This was last week," said Evanston. "On the eighth anniversary of Oberon's arrival. Chicago." She pushed a button on the remote. "This one's in Dallas." A protester waved a sign that said *DEATH TO MONSTERS*.

"Las Vegas." The signs read *GOD HATES ELVES* and *KILL THE ELF-LORD*. A brick sailed over the heads of an array of cops and bounced impotently off the gleaming surface of the Luxor Casino.

"Since Oberon's arrival eight years ago, there have been thirteen credible assassination attempts," continued Evanston. "He has been poisoned, shot at, and targeted by explosive-bearing drones. He has been injured four times, once quite seriously. Just last April a bullet missed his head by about six inches when he was in New York for a UN meeting."

"Right," said Ángel, tugging his hair out from the collar of his shirt. "That's really scary. But it doesn't have anything to do with me. I didn't seek out this position. He asked for me to come."

"I know," she said. "He was determined to bring you here. I advised against it. My job is to keep him safe. I do that by controlling every aspect of his environment, and that includes you."

"Well, good to know where I stand," sneered Ángel. "Can I have my phone back?"

"No. You cannot have your phone back. From now on, any communication you make with anyone outside this estate will go through me."

"But—"

"No buts. You signed a contract in which you agreed to submit to any and all measures deemed appropriate by the envoy's security staff. Learn to live with it, Mr. Cruz. And don't lie to me again—you'll find I don't like liars. Gather your stuff and my men will take you up to the house. Oberon is waiting for you."

CHAPTER THREE

Two of the goons walked with him out across the dry lawn toward the house. They were brawny and fit in their navy suits. They might be carrying guns.

In the distance, at the top of the hill, the tall form of the cultural envoy from the Otherworld stood silhouetted against the sky, his black clothes and famous white-and-green-streaked hair fluttering a little in the breeze. Ángel took a long, shuddering breath of cool mountain air.

The goons exchanged a glance and stopped. Ángel stopped with them.

"Go on," said one of them, waving him on.

"Aren't you coming?"

"Oberon will take care of you," said the same goon, with fake heartiness. He waved a hand in greeting to the distant envoy. "Go on. Call us if you need anything."

Ángel swallowed and kept walking.

Behind him, he heard the other goon mutter, "Better him than me."

"Me too. Damn, it gives me the willies."

"Fuck me," whispered Ángel.

He was on. He could do this. He forced his feet to move, kept his chin high, his shoulders loose. Pretended he was stepping onto a stage. Giving a performance. He looked taller when he was performing.

He met his audience on the brow of the hill.

The elf-lord said, "Good afternoon, Ángel Cruz. Welcome to my home. I am Oberon. Am I pronouncing your name correctly?"

"Yes," said Ángel. No sound came out. He cleared his throat and tried again. "Yes."

"May I carry your guitar?" The elf extended a languid hand.

"Oh. Yes, thanks." Ángel was very careful not to touch Oberon as he gave him the guitar case.

Side by side, they walked back toward the pink mansion.

He felt like a rabbit taking a stroll with an Alaskan malamute. His blood was rushing with adrenaline, his mouth dry, heart thumping. Sweat pooled in the small of his back, ran coldly down his temples to his jaw. He had to force himself to take each step forward, to not break and flee back to the gatehouse, to beg Chandler Evanston and the goons to protect him.

Just stay cool, Ángel.

He kept his eyes forward, but examined Oberon with his peripheral vision.

In photographs—and on the internet, and on the cover of his bestselling album *Fae Seasonal Song-Cycles*—the cultural envoy from the Otherworld appeared, essentially, to be a man: a strange man, with a serious, high-boned face. A tall and slim man, with large eyes, pale skin and hair, clad in black. Accounts of his first appearance from the tree said he'd had long hair, but it was short in every picture Ángel had ever seen. He seemed odd, not normal, but not necessarily inhuman.

In person?

He was utterly, utterly inhuman. He didn't look or sound or smell human. He was white and weird and frighteningly beautiful, more beautiful than any human. Now he glanced at Ángel, catching him studying him, and Ángel flinched, heart in his throat.

"This estate is very large," Oberon said. "You will be comfortable here."

His voice was deep, a velvety bass-baritone. It sounded inhuman too, as if the organ from which it emerged were different from a man's larynx. He spoke slowly, but with an unimpeachable North American accent, more neutral than Ángel's own Cuban-inflected English. His expression didn't change as he spoke: it was impossible to imagine what thoughts or emotions were happening behind his shining green eyes. The curve of his wide mouth looked contemptuous. Or cruel.

He was a walking Uncanny Valley—almost human, but every tiny difference was just different enough to make Ángel's scalp prickle.

What the fuck have I done? How am I going to live with this thing for four years?

They crossed a broad tiled patio, past an out-of-commission fountain of frolicking dolphins, toward the house's porticoed front entrance. The house was sided in big sheets of pink-veined marble, like raw pork belly. It must have been ruinously expensive to ship all that stone up here. Above each roman-arched window was a circular white frieze, featuring a flying cupid in gilded bas-relief; above the door was a fan-shaped stained-glass window depicting a baroque angel, clothed only in her pink hair and surrounded by purple morning-glory flowers. Ángel mouthed a silent *Wow*.

They approached the house, Oberon moving with inhuman grace, turning a simple walk into the lazy stalk of a hunting cat, boneless and deadly. The big door was opened, as they approached, by a petite woman wearing jeans and an embroidered shirt. "Ángel Cruz," said the envoy, "may I introduce Lily Va. She does the cooking and cleaning for us." He gave her Ángel's guitar.

She was human, middle-aged, Asian. Short and sturdy, a bit of silver in her black ponytail. He wanted to stare at her all day, rather than look at Oberon. She said, "I'm here every day. Let me know if there's anything you need," and reached for Ángel's backpack.

He reluctantly surrendered it to her. "Thanks," he said. "I will. Um, do you live here too?"

"No, sir, I live at the gatehouse. My husband works for the security team."

"Oh, please don't call me sir."

Oberon said, "Tell Lily your food preferences, or if there is anything you don't eat."

Ángel nodded. Oberon and Lily stared at him expectantly. "Oh. Now? Um, no allergies. I don't really like zucchini. Or veal, veal is gross. That's all."

"Good," said Oberon. "Come, I'll give you a tour of the house."

He led the way, and Ángel followed, casting a longing glance back at Lily. She nodded at him gravely.

The house was decorated within an inch of its life in shades of pink, purple, and turquoise. The living room had a sectional sofa of dark-pink leather like sunburned skin. The sofa curved around a fieldstone fireplace large enough to roast an ox. A gigantic mural of mermaids and seahorses shone on the opposite wall. The dining room featured lavender paneling, a white lacquer and gilt table that seated twenty, and a mirrored chandelier the size of a Volkswagen Beetle. "I usually eat in the kitchen," said Oberon.

The more Ángel saw of the big house, the more unreal it seemed. He associated elves with nature—they liked woods and forests and . . . natural fibers. Right? Surely the creatures that inspired everyone from Spenser to Tolkien wouldn't live in this glossy kitsch mansion?

"Did you decorate?" he ventured.

"No, these are the original furnishings. I have changed almost nothing. It seems rather ornate to me. Do you agree?" Oberon turned to Ángel so suddenly that he nearly startled.

"It's a little, yes," he stammered.

"Here is the music room. I know you are a musician." Oberon gestured with a liquid hand around the small, surprisingly cozy room with a piano, an electric organ, and several other instruments. "It has the best acoustics in the house. It's a good place to play or sing. And my office is through here."

The office was someone's dream of manly power: dark wood paneling, a huge mahogany desk like an altar, flanked by big burgundy leather wingback armchairs.

One object stood out: a big plain ceramic pot by the window, in which grew a plant: glossy dark-green leaves, sturdy thorny stems bearing silver-white roses. Ángel had never seen a rose bush indoors.

"That didn't come with the house," he guessed.

"No, the roses came from home. I spend most of my days here in the office. You're welcome to join me anytime."

Ángel risked a sidelong glance at the envoy's inscrutable face. *God.* He imagined himself hanging out here while Oberon worked, and suppressed a shiver.

Oberon must have seen it. "You're tired," he said. "I'll show you your room; you can rest before dinner."

To be alone, away from the envoy, for a little while. The idea almost made Ángel light-headed with relief. "That would be nice."

"First, though, you must see the security system." Oberon crossed to a panel of monitors built into the wall. "Most rooms have one of these terminals," he said, pushing a button. A live video image of the living room appeared: empty fireplace, pink sofa. "Push this to scroll through the feeds." He flipped through images: the gym, the dining room, the music room, all empty. The kitchen showed glittery granite countertops, stainless-steel appliances, and Lily, slicing vegetables. The office showed Ángel and Oberon.

Ángel looked up, trying to find the camera amid the crown molding. He couldn't see it. "All the rooms have cameras?"

"Yes. These household terminals show the rooms we use most frequently. There are several rooms I never go into—guest bedrooms and so on—and of course the security team at the gatehouse monitors those feeds, but they don't show here. You can add them from this menu, if you wish."

"Oh."

"You have full access. Feel free to watch whenever you like." The way he spoke was pleasant, and Ángel found himself baffled as to how to respond. *Why would I want to do that?* seemed rude.

"Okay."

"Your room is upstairs. This way."

Oberon led him up a curving staircase, fingertips trailing on the wooden banister. "Do you like this house?"

"It's very nice," said Ángel politely.

"This is your room," Oberon said, opening a door. The room was big, dark, decorated oppressively with a peacock theme: vibrant blue-green walls, curtains, and bedspread. "There is a bathroom through there. There are ten bedrooms, and they are all the same size—you may explore the others and pick a different one, if you prefer."

"Thank you."

"Mine is at the end of the hall, on the left. You are welcome to come there whenever you wish."

Ángel's mouth went dry with terror. "Thank you," he managed to say again.

Oberon turned to look at him, eyes wide and expressionless in the dim room, and without warning placed a palm on Ángel's cheek, fingertips tracing his ear.

Ángel startled like deer at the sound of a gunshot. The elf's skin on his face—it was inhuman, it was *wrong*. He flinched away, tripped over his own feet, and started to fall. Oberon caught him, strong hands gripping his upper arms, and Ángel's strained nerve broke entirely. He wrenched himself away and crashed to the floor, his head bouncing hard off the peacock-feather rug. Oberon made another swift move to reach for him, and Ángel scuttled backward. He fetched up against the wall in the dark, dusty space under the bed.

There was a long pause. Ángel curled his legs up against his chest, pressed a hand over his mouth, panting.

The envoy stood motionless by the side of the bed for several long moments. Ángel stared at his well-shined black shoes.

Then Oberon turned and silently walked out, closing the bedroom door behind him.

CHAPTER FOUR

Lily came to fetch Ángel a few hours later.

"It's almost dinnertime," she said, kneeling by the bed and lifting the peacock-colored dust ruffle to peer at him. "Are you going to come out?"

No. I'm going to stay right here for the next four years.

He was the product of a Cuban and a Southern upbringing, though, and one thing both cultures agreed upon were firm ideas about courtesy and hospitality. It was the duty of a guest, not just to behave well, but to ease any social awkwardness by displaying pleasure with the accommodations. The host made the guest comfortable, and the guest assured the host that he was comfortable by enjoying himself. Hiding was unacceptable.

But what was his role here? Was he a guest? An employee? . . . Something else?

The envoy is *lonely*, the DOR agent had said. The envoy had paid ten million dollars and a generous salary for four years of Ángel's time.

Ten *million* dollars.

Did the envoy expect him to be his lover? Had he been on the lookout for a vulnerable cutie he could pay to supply sex? Was Ángel the world's most expensive fuck toy?

If so, did his parents understand what was expected of him? Had they knowingly pimped him to the elf-lord?

They wouldn't have. Never. For God's sake, Victor was a devout Catholic. But then Ángel remembered the way his father hadn't met his eyes.

"Is he angry with me?" he asked.

"Oberon won't hurt you."

"How do you know?"

Lily shook her head. "I've worked here for years," she said. "He's very strange at first, but he's nice when you get used to him."

Maybe you're not his type. "You don't sleep here, though."

"You can't hide under there forever."

Can't I?

No, actually, he couldn't. He needed to pee. "I know," he sighed "Um. Does he want me to come down?"

"He told me to make enough dinner for you both."

"Okay." Ángel chewed his lower lip. "Tell him . . . Tell him I'll be there in a few minutes."

She left, and he crawled out from under the bed and went into his bedroom's attached bathroom. It was tiled in radiant turquoise dichroic glass, and the fixtures were golden and shaped like sea turtles. There was an enclosed shower and a pink enamel claw-foot tub.

In the vast, impeccably clean mirror, Ángel looked at his hollow-eyed reflection. His curly dark hair had glued itself into rat tails around his face; his shirt was wrinkled, streaked with dust, and he smelled sour with fear-sweat.

"Get a grip, *mongo*," he whispered to himself.

Oberon was a nonhuman creature from a different world. Less closely related to human beings than starfishes or palm trees. His beauty wasn't the beauty of a good-looking man; it was fluid and graceful and toxic, like a jellyfish.

Elf-lord. Demon.

But he was Ángel's housemate for the next four years. So Ángel was just going to have to learn to live with him.

He took a fast shower, brushed his hair and teeth. Back in the bedroom he found that Lily had unpacked and hung up his few T-shirts and jeans in one corner of a walk-in closet that was nearly the size of his childhood home's dining room. Dressed, he steeled himself and headed down to the kitchen.

He hesitated in the doorway.

The fae was perched on a stool at the granite-topped kitchen island, dressed in his black shirt and pants, eating with chopsticks. Under the electric lights of the kitchen, his face was white—not the white of a white man, but the white of fresh cream, faintly golden on his lips and under his huge, tilted eyes. His skin was poreless and faintly lustrous, more like extremely high-quality suede than human skin. His hair—translucent, fine as corn silk, streaked in shades of wheat-blond, ivory, and pale green, was shoulder-length and tucked behind ears that came to an infinitesimal point.

Oberon looked up and regarded Ángel. His eyes were large, shining, green as leaves beneath winged green brows, and utterly without expression.

Wordlessly, he gestured to a stool.

For a moment, Ángel remembered the legend: don't eat their food or you'll be trapped. Well, he was already trapped, and he would need to eat. Ángel climbed onto a stool. Not the one right next to Oberon. Lily handed him a bowl and a pair of chopsticks: brown rice, stir-fried vegetables, some kind of white fish. A goblet of ice water. Clumsily, Ángel managed to pick up a snow pea and bring it to his mouth. He tasted ginger, garlic, the crisp greenness of the pea pod. Lily folded a dishtowel, gave him an encouraging nod, and left the room.

He picked at his food, studying the envoy with a kind of horrified fascination. In general outline, Oberon was human: the structure of his body, the arrangement of his limbs. It was the little details that disconcerted: his hands seemed extra long, perhaps because the fingers were all the same length, straight across, pointer to pinkie. And, of course, there was that strange white skin.

The more he looked at the differences, the more his heart thumped. His skin felt tight and cold, and his stomach fluttered.

"You are shivering," said the envoy.

After a moment, Ángel managed to reply in a shaking voice, "Sorry about that."

The expressionless voice was polite. "Did you hurt your head when you fell?"

"No, no," he said. "The rug is thick. So's my skull."

"I upset you," said Oberon.

It was an observation, not a question. Unnerved, Ángel said, "Do you think I could use a fork? I'm not actually very good at eating with these."

"In that drawer." He waved a white hand, a gesture so impossibly elegant for such a mundane situation that Ángel wondered if it was some kind of mockery.

Ángel hopped down from the stool and went around the island to find a fork. Then he found himself unable to go back to his seat. He remained where he was, hands braced on the cool stone counter, the island between himself and Oberon, eyes lowered with humiliation.

"Will you accept my apology?" asked Oberon.

Surprised, Ángel looked up and met the fae's eyes for the first time. They were luminous green shot through with gold and amber, fringed with straight, sweeping gold lashes.

He nodded. "It's fine."

"Why do you say it is fine when it is not fine?" asked Oberon calmly. "Right now I think that you're either about to attack me or run away."

"No, I—" Ángel consciously relaxed his grip on the countertop, stepped back from the island. "No."

"This afternoon, as I was showing you to your room, your heart rate was elevated, as was your breathing. You were emitting a signal that I misinterpreted. I thought you were . . . happy. Excited. I was plainly quite mistaken, and you might have been injured because of it. I am sorry."

What did *emitting a signal* mean? "Can you read my mind?" asked Ángel.

"Obviously not."

Part of what was most disconcerting about Oberon was the lack of expression on his face, the stillness of his body as he spoke. His voice, however, was flexible; its timbre changed on words like *happy*, changed again on *sorry*. It wasn't quite an accent, just a subtle shifting in the color of his voice.

Oberon said, "Are you going to eat your dinner?"

"Yeah." Ángel pulled his dish of stir-fry toward him and speared a piece of fish with the fork. It was good, but his stomach ached with tension.

Courtesy. Courtesy was a performance, as much as playing a concert. It had its rules, its proper moves. Ángel couldn't bring his heart to this performance, the way he should, but he could follow the rules.

He said, carefully, "Of course I accept your apology. You have been very kind. Thank you for making me feel at home."

"You are welcome," said Oberon, in the exact polite tone that Ángel had used. As if he, too, were just following the rules of courtesy.

Or mocking him.

After dinner, Oberon said, "Would you like to see the house's music system?"

"Sure."

He led Ángel into the music room and sank into a chair shaped like a swan. He was slim and graceful in his concealing black clothes. If you didn't know he was an adult male, he would look as much like a tall boy, or a strong tall woman, as a man. Maybe he wasn't a man, not the way human men were men. Maybe gender wasn't the same for his people.

"There are speakers in most of the rooms," said Oberon, picking up a tablet and tapping the touch screen. His hands were long and weird, but graceful as they moved across the screen. "Very good ones. You can listen to music wherever you are. Here."

He handed Ángel the tablet, which showed a list of pieces of music.

Ángel sat cross-legged on the white rug, his interest engaged despite himself. "You have a lot of stuff," he said, scrolling. The list seemed endless.

"This is one of the projects I'm working on," said Oberon. "I'm sending Earth music back to the Otherworld, along with transcriptions and annotations about the historical and cultural context of each piece." He leaned over Ángel's shoulder, causing chills to skitter up Ángel's spine; Ángel kept his eyes on the screen.

Everyone knew that the elf-lord sent information back to the Otherworld—but how? And why music?

"You see," continued the fae, "the ones with the yellow dots are the ones I've decided to send."

"What's the blue dot mean?"

"It means I've listened to them, but I'm not sending them. Red means I haven't decided."

"So no dot means you haven't listened to it yet?"

"That's right."

Ángel thumbed through the endless list. Oberon was a musician himself, of course. But while he had played Chopin at the White House that one time, Ángel had never pictured him listening to *human* music.

No surprise Oberon hadn't gotten to it all—there was *so much* music on here, in every possible form and genre: symphonies, operas, chamber music, folk music, dances, country, jazz, pop, rock. Fascinated, Ángel scanned the enormous collection, trying to find any organizational principle or logical pattern. Blue dots for the Violent Femmes and Anton Bruckner. Yellow dots for Bob Marley, Richard Strauss, Thelonious Monk.

He tapped on a muezzin's call to prayer, which also featured a yellow dot, and a clear, rippling skein of song filled the room from hidden speakers. For all the room's ghastly decor, the acoustics were indeed excellent.

"Nice," said Ángel, when the last echoes had faded.

"I think so too," said Oberon.

"But why do this? Your people are interested in our music?"

"Yes."

"Why? I've heard your music. It's completely different from ours."

"It is the same in many ways. And the differences are interesting, don't you think?"

"So you really like it? You're not just . . . just studying it? Studying us?"

Oberon paused. Ángel kept his eyes on the tablet, afraid to look at him. After a moment, the fae said, "I have studied music my whole life. I would not do so if I didn't like it. We are a musical people."

Ángel scrolled, chewing the inside of his lip. It seemed unlikely that the Otherworld would send one guy in eight years, just to have him listen to and annotate songs. But he only said, "This is a cool idea. How do you decide which to include?"

"I try to pick pieces that are significant. Historically interesting. Illustrative of some factor of human character. Although truly, much of it is personal taste."

"I've never even heard of some of this stuff. I see you're sending lots of Mahler."

"Yes. I admire Mahler." Oberon's voice had gone warm. "Do you like Mahler?"

"I haven't listened to much classical music. I guess I'll have time to do that now. *Ay*, so many show tunes."

"I'm still working my way through those. Chandler recommended them."

"Chandler Evanston? Really?" Ángel smiled at the thought of the cool chief of security listening to *Les Misérables*. "I wouldn't have spotted her for a typical show-tune fan."

"What is a typical show-tune fan like?"

"Oh. A queer like me, I suppose. But that just goes to show you can't make generalizations. I think *Les Mis* is terrible. But probably, if you wanted to understand show tunes, you'd need to see the shows live. So you'd get the context."

"I'd like that."

"Hmm, who recommended all this Pink Floyd?"

"I think he was on a list of great rock and roll," said Oberon. "You can see I have not listened to him yet, either."

"They. It's a band. I had a big Floyd phase when I was a teenager, but it's been ages since I listened to them." Ángel selected "Run Like Hell," hit Play, and David Gilmour's guitar chattered menacingly through the room.

They sat and listened to the song together—driving power chords, ominous lyrics, weird laughter echoing over thumping rhythm guitar. When it was over, Oberon asked, "Do you like that?"

"I love it." Ángel looked up at the envoy for the first time. "Do you?"

"I'm not sure."

Ángel smiled. "No? But you really would have to listen to the whole album. It's a story about a man who is slowly losing his mind; that song is, like, a paranoid fantasy he's having. Their guitarist *es volao*."

"*Volao?*" repeated Oberon, eyes on Ángel's face.

"Crazy good. Listen to this one, I think it's like their most famous song."

Ángel played "Comfortably Numb." When Gilmour launched into the closing guitar solo, Ángel closed his eyes, letting the sound swell and soar through his chest. As the music faded into silence, he opened his eyes, and found that Oberon was still watching him.

He swallowed, looked away. *Come on, Ángel, get it together.* He could manage a polite conversation about music. "What do you make music about in the Otherworld?"

"Haven't you heard any?"

"Yes, but I didn't understand it very much."

"Well." Oberon leaned gracefully back in the swan chair and pulled his feet up, curling his legs beneath him. "It's about love and sex and fear and anger and joy. The same as your music."

Ángel dropped his eyes to the tablet as his face heated, the weirdness of the situation feeling hollow in his chest.

"Also," continued Oberon, "we have many pieces of music about trees. It seems strange to me how few tree songs you have."

"Tree songs?"

"Yes, joy in a tree, grief when a tree dies. You don't ever seem to sing about that."

"No," admitted Ángel. "I can't think of any."

That's when his eye fell on the yellow dot next to "Hopelessly Devoted to You" by Olivia Newton-John. His vision blurred the dot into a smear of yellow.

He bit his lip and tapped the song.

Swoony opening chords. Then the love ballad from *Grease* filled the room. Ángel snickered. By the time the song reached its climactic conclusion he was doubled over laughing, the tablet having fallen from his nerveless fingers to the carpet.

Oberon sat in chilling silence. Ángel tried to get control of himself, but when he thought of the elves of the Otherworld listening to Sandy's lament for Danny, the hysteria bubbled up again. "Oh God," he said, giggling. "I'm sorry."

"Why does that song make you laugh?" asked Oberon.

"It's— I mean—"

"It expresses a universal sentiment," said Oberon gravely. "The pain of rejection. Loss of love. And she has a very attractive voice."

"No, she does." Ángel laughed again. "She absolutely does. It's— There's cultural associations that I'm not sure I can explain."

"Do you refer to the movie? I watched it. I didn't really understand it."

"Oh, no, no, don't watch the movie," he said, wiping his eyes. "*Don't* send *Grease* to the Otherworld. They'll obliterate us with death-magic."

"They wouldn't. We don't obliterate people," said Oberon, possibly not realizing that Ángel was joking. "I've already obtained her permission to send the song, though. We spoke on the phone."

"You talked to Olivia Newton-John on the phone?"

"She seemed quite nice."

Ángel made the mistake of staring at him. Oberon stared back. His eyes shone like citrines, the way a leopard in a tree watches an antelope.

CHAPTER FIVE

Ángel groped for a topic to help them move past the awkward moment. "You don't seem to have any Cuban music."

"I would like some," said Oberon. "My collection of popular music is skewed toward American artists; it would be good to include more from other cultures. Will you make me a list? I'll buy some."

"You could just tell Evanston to give me my phone back," suggested Ángel. "I have a lot."

"You brought a phone?"

Was Oberon's voice cooler? Ángel nodded. Oberon pulled the latest model iPhone out of the pocket of his shirt and leaned back in his chair, crossing his ankles, delicately tapping the touch screen as he made a call. "Good evening, Chandler," he said. "Very well, thank you. Ángel wants the songs from his phone. Will you please upload them to the house computer? Yes, that will be fine." He rang off, glancing down at Ángel. "Will that do?"

Feeling outmaneuvered, Ángel said, "Uh-huh, thanks." He silently watched the music list between his hands expand as his own songs appeared, one by one: Celia Cruz. Pérez Prado. Buena Vista Social Club. The Afro-Cuban All Stars.

The incident was an awkward reminder that he didn't understand his status here. Was he a guest? Employee? Prisoner? Sex slave?

"You seem comfortable with computers," he said.

"We don't have them at home," said Oberon. "I've had to learn."

"How do you send the music home?"

"With spells. I'll show you, if you like."

Ángel wasn't sure he could handle *spells*, after everything else. He stood up. "Actually, I'm kind of tired. I guess I'll turn in for tonight."

"Keep that tablet," said Oberon. "Your room has speakers, like this one, so you can listen to music there."

Ángel nodded. The tablet had a wi-fi connection. "I'd like . . ." he said, hesitantly. "Could I use this to email my friend Marissa? I want to let her know I'm okay."

"Is she on Chandler's approved list?"

"Yes. She got clearance from the DOR."

"Very well. All emails from that tablet go to Chandler; she'll make sure it's safe before forwarding it on. She gets all incoming emails too, of course."

"Of course she does." Ángel glanced at Oberon doubtfully from under his eyebrows. "Is that really necessary?"

"You don't think it is?"

"No, it's not," Ángel said. "The DOR researched me and Marissa both. You know we're not connected to any plot against you."

"No, but you're connected to me," said Oberon. "By asking you to come here, I brought you into considerable peril. If the people who want to hurt me learn that you are here, they could try to get at me by hurting you. They could try to get at you by hurting those you love. Secrecy keeps both you and your friends safe."

It had never actually occurred to Ángel that he might be in danger from anyone except Oberon. He wasn't sure he believed he was, but then he remembered the brick-throwing sign-wavers that Chandler had showed him, and the back of his neck prickled.

"Chandler is very good at what she does. You should trust her," added Oberon.

"Right. Okay. Um, thanks for the . . ." Ángel waved a hand vaguely around his head, to indicate the music.

Oberon copied the gesture with his own long hand. It looked absurd, and Ángel bristled, wondering again if he were being mocked. But Oberon said only, "You are welcome."

"Okay. Good night."

"You may come to my room tonight, if you'd like."

Ángel's throat closed with fear. He managed to say, "Thanks. No. I'll just, um—"

Clutching the tablet, he escaped.

In his peacock room, he closed the door and slid bonelessly down it to collapse on the floor, where he spent several minutes shaking.

He calmed down by looking around the room. Peacocks were painted on the murky green walls in shiny gold and purple paint. The hangings on the four-poster king-size bed were embroidered, in gold thread, with peacock feathers. In the corner slumped a soft purple leather armchair like a cluster of grapes. It was hideous, but soothingly dark and quiet.

After a while he managed to get up. He took off his shirt—he was going to need to do laundry soon, the way he kept fear-sweating through his clothes—and sat cross-legged in the center of the bed. He took up the tablet and found a Django Reinhardt collection in Oberon's music library, and set it to play on low volume. He shot off quick status emails to his brothers, Ned and Michael, and then began to compose a longer one for Marissa.

Knowing that Chandler Evanston would be reading and censoring it—knowing that the envoy would have access to it, if he wanted— made it hard to write. He described his journey without telling her exactly where he was; described the house in terms too vague to convey how funny it was; barely mentioned Oberon at all. He let her know that all emails were going through security, since it seemed rude not to warn her, and ended with a plea to hear from her soon and a fervent *Wish you were here.* And then a postscript:

That reminds me: I introduced the cultural envoy from the Otherworld to Pink Floyd. Not sure how it went over. I think he might be more of a classical kind of guy.

Dissatisfied, he hit Send.

He tossed aside the tablet, turned off the music, and lay back on the bed, exhausted but too wired to sleep, his mind still whirling with questions. Eventually he got up, found his guitar in the closet, took it out of its case, and tuned it. It was an old Martin that he'd bought at a pawnshop in Ocala: not much to look at, a scuffed cutaway six-string with a cracked tortoiseshell guard and a loose pickup. But it played like a dream, warm-toned and vibrant, familiar as a lover under his fingers.

He noodled on the guitar for a while, trying to do Django Rheinhardt, stopping when fatigue made his fingers sloppy.

His eyes wandered over the details of the hideous peacock décor. Were the other bedrooms this bad? Or worse?

"Mine is at the end of the hall, on the left. You are welcome to come there whenever you wish."

He shivered, and his gaze fell across the dark monitor panel on the wall.

Returning the Martin to its case, he went over to the panel and turned it on. After a few minutes' exploration he figured out the interface and scrolled through the feeds.

Kitchen: empty. Gym, foyer, dining room, music room, staircase, all empty. Office: Oberon was there, sitting at his big desk. There was a volume knob on the control panel: so the rooms had mikes, as well as cameras. Ángel switched it on, and from hidden speakers he could hear the music that Oberon was listening to. Perez Prado, probably from Ángel's phone.

Ángel, uncomfortable watching Oberon, rapidly flipped to the next feed, which was his own bedroom. And there he was, live, watching himself on the monitor.

He turned around, trying to see the camera. It must be in the crown molding over the purple armchair.

He looked back at the monitor. It displayed a nice clear picture of the top of his head, his bare back and arms, hair tucked behind an ear and curling over his shoulders. He snapped his fingers, heard the crisp snap on the speakers.

The camera gave a good view of the center of the bed.

Unacceptable. The thought of that camera on him in bed—of the security team, of Oberon, watching him while he slept—made his blood run cold with fear and anger.

There was no way this level of surveillance was required for security. This was just wrong. Was there a camera in the bathroom too? He was afraid to find out.

He was shivering again. He thought about going down to the office and demanding that Oberon disable the surveillance in this room. But honestly, after the day he'd had, he felt too edgy for another conversation with Oberon.

I can't deal with this right now.

He turned off the monitor. Gathering up a pillow and the gleaming peacock comforter, he crawled under the bed. He stripped to his underwear and wrapped himself up in the comforter. Like a rabbit in a dusty hole, he curled up tight against the wall at the head of the bed. But though he closed his eyes and tried to sleep, his mind was whirling with questions.

Why was there so much surveillance in this house?

Oberon said he couldn't read minds. What kind of magic could he do?

Why had he touched Ángel? Why had he invited him to his room? Was he going to watch Ángel all the time?

What did he really want?

It was a long time before Ángel was able to sleep.

CHAPTER SIX

Ángel stumbled downstairs the next morning as rain tapped on the windows, in search of coffee. Lily found him hunting through the cabinets.

"Coffee?" he mumbled.

"We have tea."

"No coffee?" He stared at her blearily.

She put the kettle on. "Tea has caffeine," she said. He blinked at this specious and irrelevant comment, and she added, "I can get some coffee next time I go shopping in town."

"Thank you. That would be nice. When will you go into town?"

"I shop on Friday afternoons. Today's Wednesday." She pulled a notepad out of a drawer and wrote on it. "Is instant coffee okay? Should I get cream to go with it?"

"No," he said. "Espresso beans, and sugar and milk. Whole milk, *por favor, señora*. A grinder for the beans. Or you could buy pre-ground beans, if you have to. Does this place have an espresso maker?"

"Like a machine?"

"Like, a little metal pot?" He gestured. "You put water and coffee in it, and it goes on the stove. Or a French press?"

Lily was not a coffee drinker. She made him buttered toast, and they drank hot tea together while he ate and explained the correct preparation of *café con leche*.

"You like anything else to eat? Did you like dinner last night?"

"It was really good," said Ángel. "Maybe some sriracha?"

She laughed. "If you want to put sriracha on it, it wasn't really good."

"It was almost perfect," he said, smiling, hand to heart. "Just needed some sriracha."

"What other foods do you like?" she asked. "He doesn't eat a lot of meat. I usually make sandwiches for lunch, and stir-fry with rice or noodles for dinner, or soup. He likes it okay, but we could use some variety. He doesn't eat as much as he used to."

"Why not?"

She shrugged. "He's not doing so well. Used to be a better color, his skin? Now he's sort of pale."

"He's *literally* white."

"Yes, but he used to be not so pale. You should go talk to him," she said, with a nudge. "He didn't hire you to sit in the kitchen and talk to me."

Ángel sipped his tea. "Is he up?"

"Oh, yes, he gets up at five. Exercises in the gym for ninety minutes every morning. Then works in his office, sometimes ten, eleven hours. I give him his lunch in there, but some days he forgets to eat it. Go say good morning to him."

"The envoy is lonely."

"You can come to my room."

Ángel couldn't disguise his reluctance. "I—I think I'll explore the house."

Lily frowned. "He's not going to hurt you."

"I know. He's just kind of . . ."

She raised her eyebrows at him.

Cameras. Oberon could be listening to this right now. "I'll take him his lunch at noon. Okay?"

She nodded and smiled.

Temporarily released from an unpleasant duty, he explored.

The house was absurdly huge. Unused rooms included a couple of superfluous sitting rooms, an empty wine cellar, a game room with a pool table, a media room with a wet bar (no alcohol), a library lined with acres of empty shelves. To his surprise, the envoy had chosen reasonably well when he'd picked the peacock room for Ángel: the others were even worse. Ángel tried to decide which one he would give Marissa, if she were to visit: the hot-pink and zebra-stripe one? Or the red-and-orange Navajo-themed one, with lamps made out of antlers and a taxidermied mountain goat head over the bed? Whoever decorated this house had never heard the phrase "too much."

He wondered how Oberon's room was decorated. But he neither went there, nor looked at it on the monitors.

Exploring the house kept him busy until lunchtime, when he dutifully took a tray of sandwiches and fruit salad from Lily and made his way to the music room. He hesitated outside the door to the office for a long minute, before setting his jaw and rapping on the door.

"Come in."

The room, which had been closed all morning, smelled like Oberon—not unpleasant, but not human. A toasty sort of smell. A white rosebud, tightly furled, had been cut from the plant by the window and stood in a vase on the desk. Oberon was at the desk, listening to piano music. Oberon's hair fell over his forehead in silky wisps, pale ash streaked with mint. His gaze, when he looked up, was remote.

The mansion's very tackiness made it easy to forget that he was in the home of a magical being. But here in this room, with the baked-bread smell in the air and the Otherworldly rose on the desk, the strange green eyes of the elf-lord regarding him dispassionately, Ángel felt frightened again. Far from home, at the mercy of something he didn't understand.

"Hi," said Ángel, falling back on casual politeness as he put the tray on the desk. "Lily says you forget to eat lunch."

"I do, sometimes." Though Oberon's face was as aloof and expressionless as Mount Rushmore, his voice was warm. He pressed a button on his desk, and the music's volume lowered. "Thank you for bringing me food. Will you stay to eat with me?"

"I think that's Lily's plan. All these sandwiches can't be just for you." Ángel managed to keep his voice light, though his stomach was in knots from being in the elf's presence. He took a plate and sat on one of the wingback chairs—its tufted leather upholstery was smooth and hard as polished wood, surely deliberately uncomfortable. "Did I get any emails today?" He forced himself to take a bite of his sandwich.

"No. I will send them immediately to your tablet, if you do."

After reading them, presumably.

They ate in silence for a moment, before Ángel nerved himself to ask, "What are we listening to?"

"Dmitri Shostakovich," said Oberon. "Piano concerto number two, in F major."

"I told my friend Marissa that you liked classical music more than pop or rock and roll." Talking about music seemed safe.

"I'm not sure that's true," Oberon replied. "I would say that I am more comfortable with instrumental music, generally, because I often don't understand lyrics."

"Your English is great," protested Ángel. "Better than mine. You could be on NPR."

"You illustrate the problem perfectly, Ángel. My English is fluent, but I have no idea what NPR is."

"Oh, it's public radio. News and information. People with nice voices who tell you what's happening in the world. My dad loves it." Ángel belatedly remembered that his dad had tried to steal Oberon's money, and wondered if he shouldn't have mentioned him.

"Well," said Oberon, either unaware or too polite to mention this gaffe. "Thank you. But I am often puzzled. I know I should listen to more music with lyrics, because it's so popular, and I came here to learn and to understand. But it's uncomfortable when I know that I don't understand something."

It was the most sympathetic—the most human—thing Oberon had said to Ángel. "Well, I guess we have that in common," he said. "I mean, *all* of us."

"Do you think so? That is reassuring, if true, Ángel."

Oberon tapped on the tablet. The Shostakovich fell silent, and was replaced by Mike Doughty's "White Lexus." Lonely guitar; sorrowful lyrics. "I cover this," said Ángel, when it was over. "Covered, I mean."

"You perform this song?"

"Yep. Sometimes I play in bars or restaurants. I like this song."

"What does it mean?" Oberon asked. "A Lexus is a car?"

"It's a metaphor."

"I know what metaphors are, but I often cannot understand them. What does the Lexus represent?"

"I dunno, maybe a terrible relationship? Although it's supposed to be a pretty good car," said Ángel. Oberon gazed at him with blank green eyes, so Ángel tried again. "That's the way I sing it. Like you're trying to stop loving someone. Someone who only hurts you, but you love them, and you know it's wrong to love this person. So you try to stop, and that hurts even worse? Does that make sense? I don't think I'm explaining this very well."

"No. That makes a kind of sense."

"But here's the thing," said Ángel, putting his plate down so he could lean forward, gesturing as he spoke. "I don't know this guy, the songwriter, or what it meant to him. Maybe he's singing about something else. That's just how I react to it. And songwriters do that on purpose, *sí*? He could just openly say, 'This is a song about my relationship with my ex, and the car represents my, whatever, my loneliness.' But instead, he made it a little obscure. So you can tell he's sad and bitter, and you listen to it and put your own sad bitter experiences into it and think, 'This song is about my relationship with my mother,' or 'This song is about, I don't know, my cousin Enrique.' Or my car, or whatever. It's totally okay to not understand every reference—you're not really supposed to. So long as you get the feeling."

When he stopped talking, Oberon didn't reply. But he seemed to be emitting a soft, subsonic vibration, more felt than heard. Ángel flushed; the skin on his arms erupted in goose bumps. "I mean, obviously you know all that."

The almost-sound died away. "What other songs do you play?"

Ángel rubbed his chilled arms. "Um. The place I usually play is pretty laid-back. So nothing too loud, just background noise while people drink chardonnay. I do Cuban stuff. Folky stuff. I like Jason Isbell. Richard Shindell. I mix them with some Spanish guitar, and some songs everyone knows. James Taylor. Paul Simon."

"I enjoyed listening to you play last night," said Oberon.

The words were like a bucket of cold water dashed in Ángel's face. The sandwich turned to cold lead in his stomach.

He was a professional musician. Playing for people was what he did. But he didn't want to be eavesdropped on in his bedroom.

He stood up and began bussing their empty plates to the tray to take them back to the kitchen.

"Ángel," said Oberon. "Why did you sleep under your bed?"

Ángel went still. Like a field mouse when a hawk's shadow passes over.

When he didn't answer, Oberon said, "I talked about it with Chandler. She said she thought it was because you were trying to avoid the camera. Is that right?"

Ángel carefully put the tray down. The cowardly part of him, the part that was afraid of a confrontation, wanted to politely deny that the surveillance bothered him.

Through lips stiff with anxiety, he said, "Yes. That's right."

"She said that you might think that the camera violates your privacy."

"I do. It does."

Oberon gracefully brushed his hair out of his eyes. "I have studied your culture my whole life, and I have been on Earth for eight years. Though I know it is very important, I still do not really understand the concept of privacy. We in the Otherworld have some similar ideas about it—we, too, have specific taboos about what is appropriate in public versus what is appropriate in private."

He paused. Ángel didn't reply.

"But I don't understand why a person would need privacy from the people he lives with. Where I am from, within a house, with people who live together, there are no private spaces. Can you explain this to me?"

The warm, golden timbre had gone out of Oberon's voice. Coupled with his expressionless face, the flat and cool tone made Ángel wonder if he were angry. Or if he was playing some game with Ángel. His angular face looked distant and cruel.

Ángel put his hands in his jeans pockets, unsure how to put words around something that was so obvious. "Just because I came to live here doesn't mean I forfeit the right to privacy," he said. "The camera—and also the microphones—in my bedroom should be deactivated."

"Why?"

"It's just wrong. It . . . it upsets me to think that you watch me when I'm alone. When I sleep."

"Why is that? Everyone sleeps."

Ángel knotted his brows. ". . . Are you kidding now? You really don't get this?"

"No," said Oberon. "I am not kidding. I gave you your own room, because I understand that you need to be alone sometimes for your comfort. For my comfort, I need the cameras. You have access to them too."

"I don't want access to the cameras," said Ángel. "I want to not be under surveillance."

"To sleep?"

"Yes. To sleep."

"Is there a taboo surrounding sleep that I don't understand? To me, there is nothing peculiar or shameful about sleep, that you must hide to do it."

"Some things are private," said Ángel. "Not peculiar or shameful. *Private.*"

They stared at each other. Then Ángel said, "Oberon. Please. Could you—could you just take my word for it? I won't object to any of the other cameras, in the rest of the house, if there were one place—my room—where I knew I had privacy."

"No," said Oberon. "I don't think so. You will get used to it. What other things are private?"

Ángel felt as though he'd been slapped. He worked his jaw, trying to relax the muscles in his face, then picked up the tray again and went to the office door.

"Ángel?" asked Oberon. "Are you going to go, before we're finished talking about this?"

"We are finished talking about this."

"We aren't."

Was he annoyed? Angry? Was Oberon *toying* with him? Ángel couldn't tell. His gut was hot with thwarted fury, but he forced himself to speak rationally. "Sometimes, two people in a conversation have different goals. Right? Your goal is to learn and understand. Like you said, that's why you're here. But my goal, in this conversation, was to get you to turn off the camera and the microphone in my room. You said no. So for me, the conversation is over."

Oberon stared at him with flat eyes. "I refused your request, so you are retaliating by not helping me understand?"

"It's not *retaliation*," snapped Ángel. "You can't make me like it, and I can't make you give a shit. So there's no point in talking about it."

"Isn't there?"

Shaking his head, Ángel turned and walked out.

So much for courtesy. That had lasted for a day.

Ángel burned with frustration. He returned the tray to the kitchen, where he found himself pacing. It sounded like Lily was vacuuming upstairs. He didn't want to see her—or anyone. He needed to get out of the house.

It was raining, a sparse nothing rain, totally different from the warm soaking Florida rain he was used to. He didn't have any rain gear, so he just took off his shoes and socks and went out barefoot.

He could not believe how cold it was outside. His soles were hard from walking barefoot on beaches and boardwalks, but this grass was brittle and sharp, like needles. The rain blew in his face like tiny pinpricks of ice.

It was the end of August. Why was it so cold?

Gritting his teeth, and under no illusion that he was not being watched by outdoor cameras, he picked his way around the estate, letting the rain bead on his hair and soak into his clothes. It was an empty expanse of lawn, no bushes or trees or gardens. There was a detached garage, four bays, locked up tight. He peered through the dusty windows—there was only one car, a white Land Rover, and the walls were tidily hung with a variety of clean, well-cared-for tools.

Behind the house stretched a big swimming pool, long and narrow. White statues of naked goddesses stood at the four corners of the pool. It was probably really nice on hot days, but right now its surface, pocked with rain, reflected a dark-gray sky.

Ángel dove straight into the pool, and the water that closed over his head was so cold he almost screamed. He'd swum in cold water before, but this was six-minutes-and-you're-dead cold. Who kept an unheated outdoor pool in Montana?

He swam down to the bottom of the deep end, where a black scum of fallen pine needles and twigs drifted in the turquoise corners. He hung there, hooking his fingertips into the grille at the bottom of the pool to hold himself below the icy water.

This is only the second day, he told himself. *Day two. You got four years to go.*

Four years, every instant of it on camera.

When he needed to breathe, he swam back up to the surface and, almost numb with cold, hauled himself out. Carefully, he squelched across the slate patio toward the back of the house. The door there opened into a mud room off the kitchen, where Lily was waiting for him. "What are you doing?" she demanded at the sight of his shivering, streaming form. "Oberon just called me to say you were swimming!"

"*Por supuesto*," said Ángel, taking the towel she handed him. "Nice pool."

"It's fifty degrees out!" she yelled. "You'll freeze to death!"

"It's August." He was shivering so hard his teeth were chattering. "Perfect day for a swim."

She lightly slapped his arm. "You shouldn't make him worry like that."

He headed upstairs. "Well, now he can watch me take a shower and see that I'm fine."

CHAPTER
SEVEN

A fter his shower, Ángel spent the afternoon in his bedroom, practicing classical fingerstyle arpeggios. He usually played with a pick, but he admired fingerstyle guitarists, and wanted to be better at the technique.

He wasn't *hiding*. He really did need the practice. And the sound of his fingers stumbling repeatedly over the strings had to be far too boring to listen to.

Dinner was noodles with stir-fry vegetables and stilted, polite conversation. Ángel could think of nothing to say to Oberon, and as far as he could tell, the feeling was mutual. The envoy sat aloofly and ate very little of his food. Flat-voiced, he repeated his invitation to Ángel to come to his room for the night and, when Ángel shook his head, retreated to his office. Ángel was chilled.

Before bed, the tablet pinged. Ángel picked it up and found that Chandler Evanston had forwarded an email from his brother Michael. Michael was fine, his wife was fine, their brother Ned and his wife and children were fine. The weather in Georgia was good.

Michael didn't ask Ángel how he was. Maybe he had in the original email, and Chandler had edited it out. There was an attachment: a Word document that Michael said was a letter from their mother. Ángel wondered again if the Ponzi scheme had been hers, or her husband's. It must have been. Somehow she'd gotten Victor to pay the price for it. Somehow she'd gotten *Ángel* to pay the price for it, and he hadn't even known about it. Ángel shook his head, deleted the letter unread, and replied to his brother: *I know you're not a message boy between me and Mom. But I'm not reading anything from her, okay? Tell her not to send any more. I got the message when she told me to come here.*

There was no email from Marissa. Ángel suppressed the intense desire to send her another one, begging her to reply.

He retreated to his cave under the bed to try to sleep. It was less dusty today; apparently Lily had vacuumed under the bed, and had also pulled the peacock green comforter off the bed and folded it underneath like a sleeping bag, arranging two pillows at one end.

He needed comfort, so in hurried, intense silence, he jerked off. He felt even more alone when he was done.

The security goons were in the house when Ángel came down the next morning. Oberon was talking quietly with Chandler Evanston in the lavender dining room while Ángel prepared his tea and toast. One of the goons, a handsome Asian man, had his arm around Lily. That must be her husband. The young goon who had searched Ángel, Logan—the one who had said that Oberon gave him the willies—was here, too, carrying an overnight bag. He looked nervous.

Oberon came into the kitchen while Ángel was squeezing water out of his teabag. "I'm going to New York," he said. His voice and face were inscrutable. "My foundation gave some money to schools there, and they're having a banquet. Chandler is coming with me, but a small security team is remaining here to protect you. John Va is in command, if you need anything."

"Okay." Ángel tucked his hair behind his ears. "Oberon?"

"Yes, Ángel?"

"Did I get any email?" He was conscious that Chandler and the rest of the team were listening.

"No," said Oberon.

"Okay. Thanks."

Oberon turned to Lily. "Lily, when you go to town tomorrow, will you please pick up some winter clothes for Ángel? A coat, and some boots. He doesn't have any warm things."

"Of course," said Lily.

"Thank you. I will be back tomorrow afternoon."

"Can I go to the store too?" asked Ángel.

Oberon briefly met Ángel's eyes. "No," he said, and walked out, Chandler and the rest of the security team falling in behind him.

When the door closed behind them, Ángel and Lily looked at each other. Chilled and unsettled by the encounter, Ángel hugged himself. Lily put the kettle away and began wiping down the countertops. "The banquet will be on TV," she said. "We can watch it, if you like."

"Why would we do that?"

"It's at the Tiepolo Ballroom. He'll give a speech. He gave a million dollars to keep arts programs open in New York schools."

"He gave ten million to get me to come here," said Ángel.

Lily's chin went up. "He did that? Why?"

"I was hoping you'd know."

"I didn't even know he had ten million dollars."

Ángel sipped his tea. "Four albums. Seven Grammys."

"Oh. Fae music, is it?" She shook her head, rinsing out her sponge. "I don't like it. It sounds like wolves howling."

"I think they teach it in schools. Will you let me come to the store?"

"It's not safe. You need to stay here."

"Please?"

"He said no."

She began to take dishes out of the dishwasher and stack them on the counter. When she pulled a stool out of the pantry, he realized that she was too short to reach the cabinets. "Oh, let me," he said, and began to put the dishes away. "When you buy me clothes, will you take it out of my account?" He was earning a gross salary of about $100,000 per year living here, all of which was going straight into an investment account that the DOR was managing for him.

"No. He didn't tell me to. He's not paying for them, either—I have a DOR expense account."

He sighed. She was the only one he had to talk to in this place. "I like your shirt." Lily often wore wear soft boho cotton shirts in pastel colors.

"I get them at Wal-Mart."

"Can you get me some of those? They're cute."

She said severely, "You aren't here to make friends with *me*."

He raised his eyebrows and gave her his best smile. "But there's nothing preventing it, is there?"

The house was enormously less tense without Oberon in it, but somehow even lonelier. Ángel tried not to think about Marissa. Why hadn't she written him back? He was in the home of the cultural envoy from the Otherworld, and she waited *days* to send him an email? Was she mad at him? Maybe she was sick? Maybe she just had better things to do?

No. But it wasn't like her. He was torn between anger and worry.

Chandler had uploaded his playlists as well as his songs to the house computer, so he had his favorite dance playlist for exercising. He ran on the treadmill in the gym. He walked around the outside of the house, this time keeping his shoes on— It was cold enough to turn his breath to fog, and he was glad that he was getting some warmer clothes.

He practiced his guitar. Without worrying about anyone listening—except John Va and the goons at the gatehouse, who didn't bother him—he was able to relax into the music, and the arpeggio practice resolved itself into a fragile melody. He fingerpicked it out, slow first, then faster, tapping the rhythm on the soundboard as he played. It was a wistful little song, flamenco-inflected but sadder, and he played with it for hours, trying this and that variation, until Lily brought him a bowl of stir-fry and rice and told him to stop and eat.

Finally, he gave in to the temptation that had nagged him since Oberon left, and snuck into the envoy's room.

Long before he'd had any association with Oberon, he and Marissa had wondered why the elf-lord always wore the same clothes: did he have twenty black shirts, twenty pairs of black pants? How many pairs of shiny black leather dress shoes did he have? Did he own anything else? Now Ángel had an opportunity to snoop in Oberon's closet—*his very closet*, as Marissa would say, *in his indubitable bedroom*. He would look, and describe it to her in an email, and then she would write back.

Not sneaking, he told himself, padding down the empty hallway to the last door on the left. It wasn't like he hadn't been invited.

Oberon's room was different from the rest of the house. Clearly it had been redecorated. Whatever fanciful décor had originally adorned this chamber had been stripped away, down to white plaster walls and bare windows overlooking the distant forest. Somewhere Oberon had collected a lot of oriental-style rugs and laid them over every inch of the hardwood floor, several deep, overlapping and at odd angles, some rug corners curled up the wall. As a result the floor was a soft, uneven, lumpy mass of carpeted pattern: red and blue, purple and green. The bed was unmade, piled with an overabundance of duvets and throws: brown, indigo, blue, green. You couldn't lie down on that bed, you'd have to crawl into it, and be surrounded by softness.

Nervously, Ángel peeked into the closet. Sure enough, there were ranks of black shirts, black pants, black shoes. A tidy hanger of black belts. The clothes seemed at odds with the colorful carpets and mounds of soft bedding.

But one item—back behind the shirts—didn't. A turquoise silk kimono, embroidered with green and orange and pink leaves.

Oberon had arrived naked in the world. So he must have bought this since he arrived, or chosen it. Or it had been a gift. No one, as far as Ángel knew, had ever seen him wear it.

In the evening, he and Lily went into the room with the empty wet bar and the flat-screen TV, where John patched through Oberon's speech at the Tiepolo Ballroom. It was a black-tie event; the other people were wearing tuxedoes and evening gowns. Oberon looked like an eccentric human, slim and pale in his crisp black shirt, his green-blond hair shining under the artificial lights, his essential weirdness flattened and disguised by the television. He was talking about the importance of the arts in education.

"He always wears the same thing." Ángel generally had little use for fashion for himself, but he enjoyed it on others. His mind on the turquoise kimono, he asked, "Have you ever seen him wear anything else?"

"When he exercises," she said. "Black sweats."

"Huh."

"I don't think he understands clothes," said Lily. "Lord, the questions he asked when he first came here. Why do people dye their hair? Why do people wear earrings? What is the significance of Chandler's tattoo?"

"Chandler has a tattoo?"

"The Tasmanian Devil, on her ankle."

"No."

Lily smiled. "I think it suits her."

The newscast abruptly cut away from Oberon's speech to a gigantic protest happening outside the Tiepolo Ballroom. The narrow Manhattan street was full of shouting, chanting people. They waved hand-lettered signs:

GO BACK TO HELL DEMON
EARTH FOR HUMANS
GOD HATES THE ELF

"Why do you think he's here?" he asked Lily. "Do you think he really just wants to study our music?"

"What else *could* he study, living all the way out here?"

"I don't know. Maybe living out here wasn't the plan."

"It wasn't," she said. "But he wasn't safe. They needed to hide him."

It certainly didn't look safe in Manhattan right now. A row of police in riot gear, with plexiglass shields, were struggling to keep the surging, screaming crowd away from the building. An amber glass bottle, shining in the lights of the streetlamps, arced over the crowd; it smashed onto the façade of the building and burst into a huge chrysanthemum of red flame.

"Jesus!" said Ángel.

On the screen before them, the angry crowd overwhelmed the line of police. Individual cops were thrust aside, struggling, as the crowd surged toward the elegant doorway of the Tiepolo like a single organism. More Molotov cocktails flew; more blossoms of flame.

"Jesus," breathed Ángel again. "They'll tear him to pieces."

Lily picked up her phone and called the gatehouse. "John," she said, her voice taut with fear.

After a moment she turned to Ángel. "They're evacuating the building. They had a plan. It's going to be all right."

"Holy shit." Ángel's eyes were glued to the screen. Lit by the flames and the whirling lights of police cars, chaos reigned in the street: fire crews, cops, shouting people, flying bottles. Searchlights played over a chaotic riot of hundreds of furious people, all struggling as one to kill Oberon.

The talking heads on the television announced that the cultural envoy from the Otherworld was no longer in the building. Ángel watched as the people broke through the doors of the Tiepolo Ballroom and begin pouring inside. Apparently they were going room to room, trying to find Oberon. He shivered, chilled by the animal violence of the mob.

John Va called later that night to report that seven people had been injured, over two hundred arrested, and Oberon was safe.

Ángel slept poorly that night, his dreams haunted by visions of hatred and fire. The next day he did what he always did when he was unsettled—he turned to music. Specifically, he checked out the music room, which turned out to be home to dozens of instruments. Along with the obvious—piano, electric keyboards, guitar—others were packed into black boxes on the shelves. Banjo, violin, flute, clarinet, trumpet, xylophone, and several hand drums. *You could rig out a high school band in here.* He wondered if the envoy had bought these instruments, or if they'd come with the house. Most of it was acoustic. Did Oberon have a prejudice against electronic amplification? Maybe he would ask him.

The guitar was a Yamaha dreadnought, newer and certainly more expensive than Ángel's beloved Martin, no fancy inlay to obscure the gleaming, perfectly even grain of the pale-yellow spruce soundboard. It was plain and beautiful and Ángel would bet money that it had *not* come with the house. This was Oberon's guitar.

There was a mandolin, cute and round-bellied. He'd never played one. He took it out of its case and touched the pick to its twinned strings, liking the high plaintive sweetness of its tone. It didn't sound right when he strummed it like a guitar, though: he didn't know what he was doing. It was difficult to finger the strings while at the same time supporting the instrument's neck with his left hand. Digging around the case to see if there was a strap, he glanced up to the open door that led to the foyer when Lily came in from her shopping trip to the mecca of civilization called Stahlberg, accompanied by Logan the goon, carrying shopping bags.

"Take those up to Ángel's room," she said to Logan, shedding her coat, "and that one to Oberon's office. Ooh, it's cold out! Ángel, help me with the groceries?"

Ángel hauled bags into the kitchen with her. "Are the stores all empty now? Was there anything there you decided *not* to buy?"

"It's getting late in the year," she said. "When it starts to snow, it's a lot harder to get into town. I like to stock up, just in case we get snowed in."

"Snowed in?" he asked incredulously, unpacking cans from the bags and stacking them on the counter. "Like *Little House on the Prairie*?"

Lily rolled her eyes. "Most places have this thing called *winter*, Ángel. The county snowplows don't come all this way. Unpack that bag next. We sometimes get trapped for a while. Have you ever seen snow?"

"Of course I've seen snow. I don't think I've ever seen a snowplow, though."

He pulled a plastic jar of instant coffee powder out of the bag and dropped it on the counter as though it were hot. "¡Nooo!" he cried theatrically, clutching his hair. "¿*Ai, señora, qué has hecho?*"

"Now, Ángel," she said sternly, "there's nothing wrong with instant coffee—"

"¡*Mierda de perro!*"

"And it's cheaper than these beans," she said, plopping a fat bag of dark-roast espresso beans on the counter, "and you don't need one of *these* to make it!" She tossed a moka pot into the air, and he caught it, laughing.

"And if you were smart you'd stick with tea," she went on, shaking her finger at him. "It's full of antioxidants and flavonoids—"

"You are going to love my coffee." He grabbed her hands and began foxtrotting her around the kitchen. "You'll never touch tea again."

She clearly didn't know the dance, but she was tiny and pliable, and she laughed as he whirled her around. He dipped her extravagantly, and she squeaked.

That's when he spotted Oberon leaning in the kitchen doorway, watching them. Ángel jumped like a scalded cat, almost dropping Lily to the floor and staggering away from them both.

Lily recovered her feet gracefully. "Oberon!" She went to him, gingerly touched his sleeve with her fingertips. "We saw the riot on TV. Are you all right?"

"I am fine, Lily," he said. "Chandler and the others got me out, and then stayed to evacuate the building. No one was seriously hurt."

"Did she know there were going to be protests?"

"There usually are. She didn't know they were going to turn violent, but she was prepared."

"Well, we're glad you're home safe," she said. "Are you hungry? Would you like some tea?" Lily glanced over her shoulder at Ángel, who was hovering awkwardly in the shadow by the mudroom door. "Or Ángel could make you some coffee?"

Oberon's gaze touched Ángel and he swallowed. Would he ever get used to the electric sensation of being looked at by those luminous eyes?

"I don't really like coffee," said Oberon.

Ángel steeled himself. "That's only because you haven't tried mine," he said, stepping forward to pick up the new moka pot. "Did you buy milk?"

CHAPTER EIGHT

Á ngel looked over the clothes Lily had brought him yesterday. It was the first of September, and apparently up here that meant that summer was over. The weather had turned gray and blustery, and the wind whined and cried at the windows. Ángel's Florida wardrobe of shorts, jeans, and T-shirts was already obsolete.

He now owned a forest-green heavy waterproof coat with a hood; lace-up boots with rubbery soles and insulated lining; three extra pairs of jeans and several long-sleeved waffle-knit henley shirts; some sweaters and sweatshirts; and one boho cotton smock shirt, like the ones she wore every day, in a soft sky blue.

Everything fit, even the boots: she must have made notes of his sizes when she unpacked his bag. He suspected she had spent at least a thousand dollars on clothes for him.

Oberon's voice emerged from the security monitor. "Ángel, will you please come down to my office?"

"Okay," Ángel said to the empty air. He padded barefoot down the stairs to Oberon's office, nervous as a schoolboy called before the principal.

Oberon was behind his desk, as usual. Behind him, the white roses almost glowed, stranger and more Otherworldly than ever now that the weather had turned wintery.

"You've had an email from your friend Marissa Sommers," Oberon said.

"I do?" *Finally!* Delighted, Ángel bounced a little on his toes as he approached the desk.

"You do," said Oberon. "Please sit down. Chandler has some concerns."

Ángel looked around and saw, to his surprise, that Chandler was standing in the corner, her face grave. A page of letter-sized paper was in her hand.

"This email seems to be in some sort of code." She brandished the paper. Ángel reached for it, but she pulled it back.

"What?" Angel blinked at her. "Give it to me."

Oberon said, "Ángel. Please sit."

He looked from Oberon to Chandler. The envoy was, as usual, beautiful and strange and entirely unreadable, watching Ángel with the patient impassivity of a cat. Chandler stood as straight as a Marine in her navy pantsuit, dark braid shining, shoulders back. Nothing about her military bearing suggested that she was a woman who liked Broadway melodies or Looney Tunes marsupials.

Cold fright streaked down Ángel's spine. Was he in trouble? What was wrong? He perched on the edge of one of the wingback chairs.

"The email," said Oberon, "contains deliberate gender subversion in the salutation. Chandler thinks that this might be a signal to the reader to look out for a hidden message in the body of the email, which is, even to my eye, written in a very stilted manner. It closes with a signature that is not the sender's name. It is, all in all, a rather strange letter, and I've judged Chandler's concerns to be valid."

Ángel listened to this with growing bewilderment. "I don't understand this. Marissa is my best friend, closer than family. She would never write anything that would put me in danger, or you either. She's not a . . . She's a *drummer*. She tends bar. She's not a secret agent. We don't write to each other in code."

"I told you I don't like lies, Ángel," said Chandler, folding her arms over her chest.

Ángel spread his hands incredulously.

"Why would she address the letter to you as if you were a woman?" asked Chandler.

"I don't know. She doesn't, usually."

"Why would she sign a name other than her own?"

"I don't know." Ángel chewed his lip "Sometimes she calls me Angie or Angela. And I call her Mickey. Is that what she did? It's just to be silly. It doesn't mean anything."

Chandler was clearly more in the mood to ask questions than to answer them. "In your email to Marissa, you alerted her to the fact that security would be reading her reply. How did you expect her to respond to that?"

"Chandler, I *don't know*. We've never been in a situation like this before; we didn't plan to . . ." She looked skeptical. Impatiently, he said, "Just let me read the letter. I can't interpret it if you won't let me read it."

"And if you do interpret it," asked Chandler, "will you explain it? Or will you keep Marissa's secrets?"

Ángel stared at her. "I can't answer that without knowing what the letter says."

Chandler looked him like a doctor examining a specimen, and then turned briskly to Oberon. "I'm not sure we can risk it. I'll send a man to Miami to interview the girl and make sure that she's not being coerced in any way, and in the meantime—"

"No," said Ángel loudly, standing up, his face hot. In an instant all his fear and anxiety had changed to anger. "Leave her alone."

"In the meantime," pressed Chandler, "we should quarantine Ángel from any further communications."

Ángel's temper snapped. "No you *don't*. You give me that letter, or I'm walking out of here." Her mouth tightened, but he overrode her. "No!" he said again, glaring between her and Oberon. "This is the fucking end of enough. You can take back the money and go ahead and prosecute my dad—he can face the consequences of his fuckup. You let me have my letters from Marissa, or I'm going over the wall."

Chandler's face was like stone. "There could be legal consequences for you if you break your contract with the DOR."

"Then I'll go to jail!" cried Ángel. "Where I'll have no privacy, no right to come and go, and I'll *get my letters from Marissa*!"

"Enough," said Oberon, quietly.

Ángel glared at Chandler, nearly vibrating with fury.

"That's enough," said Oberon again. "There is no need for threats or ultimatums. This quandary is easily resolved." He was doing something with his voice, using some soothing tone, like warm maple syrup. "Chandler, please let Ángel read the letter. Ángel will explain to you the letter's import, if it has one, and then we will all understand."

The muscle in Chandler's jaw was working. "And if he doesn't?"

"I think he will. Please, Chandler."

She reluctantly handed Ángel the folded sheet of paper. He unfolded it, and read it.

Oh my sweet Rebecca,

How your sadness claims you, how your loneliness chains you.

I haven't heard you on the telephone, but I know you're all alone. My heart has been broken since the day you said goodbye. My tears flow, but they don't show in the Baltic rain. How can I go on without you?

Feel the spirit of the sky, feel the birds flying by. The angels fly over your head, we'll be friends until the end.

You don't have to face it alone. Look at the stars, remember how the world was all ours. Call my name. Someday I'll see your smile again. My love is strong enough to last until the end of the world.

I love you,

Ricardo

P.S. In a strange place, in a new land, remember he's your brother under that different skin.

He sat down and read it again.

"Well?" said Chandler, impatiently.

He looked up at her, his mouth trembling with the urge to either laugh or cry. "You read this and thought 'secret code conspiracy'? You have got to be out of your fucking mind." She drew an indignant breath. Ángel pointed at Oberon with the letter. "*He* is from Magical Fairy Land. *You* have no goddamn excuse."

"Why does she sign her name Ricardo?" demanded Chandler.

Ángel met her eyes and sang, "'I love you, Ricardo, Ricardo, I love you, Ricardo, do you love me still?'"

Chandler's eyes widened.

"Do you want me to sing them all for you?" Ángel asked. "I can. 'Oh my sweet Rebecca, how your sadness claims you,'" he sang, filling his voice with mocking tenderness, "'my sweet Rebecca, how your loneliness chains you.'"

She held out her hand for the letter. He gave it to her, and she studied it. Then she snarled, "Seriously," dropped the letter on the floor, and stalked out of the room.

"Apology accepted!" yelled Ángel at her disappearing back.

Snorting, he bent and picked up the letter.

"Ángel," said Oberon, and the laugh died in Ángel's throat. He warily eyed the envoy, still sitting impassively at his desk.

"I am from Magical Fairy Land," said the envoy drily. "Will you explain this to me?"

Ángel returned to his perch on the edge of the uncomfortable leather chair, folding the paper nervously between his fingers. "It's all lyrics," he explained, "from MelodEye songs."

"MelodEye?"

"Um, they were a band. From Denmark. The meaning of the letter is exactly what it says—that Marissa misses me and she loves me. And she even tells me to be nice to you, there at the end. There isn't any hidden message; it reads weird because it's just entirely MelodEye lyrics."

"Why is it entirely MelodEye lyrics?"

Ángel sighed, scratching his head. "It's—it's kind of a joke? She knew I would like it."

Oberon kept examining him with those faultless gold-green eyes, so Ángel tried again. "We met in college and we bonded over MelodEye songs. They were really popular in the seventies, so almost everyone knows their songs, but they are definitely not a cool band, and when we found out we both loved them, it was like . . . We went to their reunion concert together a few years ago, and we were the youngest people there, and it was incredibly great. She knew I would remember the times we went out and danced to these songs, or when we played them and sang them together. She knew it would make me happy to think of that." He looked down at the paper. "She's a very cool person. Honestly, you can't blame Chandler for not getting it, because no one else would think to write a letter like this. It probably took Marissa hours to find lyrics that would make even this much sense."

"It is a gift of love that she made for you."

"Yeah," said Ángel, tears pricking his eyes. "That's what it is."

"Thank you for the explanation." Oberon's voice held that warm sweet timbre that it sometimes took on. "I'll tell Chandler not to threaten to cut you off from Marissa again."

Ángel breathed deeply, and the constriction in his chest eased. "That means a lot to me."

"Would I like MelodEye songs?"

Ángel laughed. "I don't know. But you uploaded a bunch of them from my phone, so you can check them out. I should warn you, though," he added, "it ain't no Shostakovich. MelodEye can be kind of awesomely dumb."

Oberon emitted a low subsonic rumble. "I'm not sure what 'awesomely dumb' means."

Ángel smiled at him. "Well, listen to some MelodEye and you'll see."

At dinner they perched, as usual, on stools at the island in the kitchen, and as they ate soup Oberon told Lily that Ángel had introduced him to MelodEye. "Oh my Lord," said Lily, "that's all they played at my sister Tammy's wedding reception. *Everyone* danced. You should have seen all the old Vietnamese men dancing to 'Waterloo.'"

"That was ABBA," said Ángel. "Lots of people get them mixed up. MelodEye was like ABBA's less-cool Danish cousin."

"Did MelodEye do 'Dancing Queen'?"

"ABBA. MelodEye did 'Baltic Rain.'" He sang a few bars, and she nodded.

"Oh. Well, I like it a little," said Lily. "Not too much. After a while it starts to scratch at your nerves. Ángel, I am soaking beans for tomorrow night's soup."

"Great."

"I found a similar recipe with no ham," she said. "Oberon doesn't really like ham. And I might put a little ginger in it."

"Then it won't be just like my *abuelita*'s," said Ángel, smiling, "but that's okay. I'm looking forward to your version."

After she'd wiped down the counters, she put on her coat and headed back to the gatehouse. When the door closed behind her, Oberon said quietly, "She is married."

"I know."

"Her husband is an important member of my security team. I highly value them both."

"Yes. *Oh*," said Ángel, with a puff of laughter. "No, oh my God. Don't worry. I'm not trying to get with Lily."

"Does she know that?"

"I think so. She hasn't slapped me across the kitchen."

"I wouldn't want misunderstandings to make her, or her husband, unhappy." Oberon seemed to be serious. The envoy's eyes were as green as jade and just as hard.

"Neither would I."

"You smile at her," said Oberon. "You are very beautiful when you smile."

Ángel's face heated. "No," he said, averting his eyes.

"And you danced with her."

"And I flirt, yes." God, he was blushing like a little girl at a surprise birthday party. "I know. But she is my mother's age and married, and I am *extremely* gay. So."

"But," said Oberon, "does she know that?"

"That I'm gay? Yes. It's totally obvious."

"How?"

"I don't know. People can tell."

"Explain to me how you communicate that you are gay."

Ángel reminded himself that Oberon's questioning wasn't intended as a challenge, but came from genuine desire to understand. "The way I walk and move, probably," he said. "And also I have gay voice?" He deliberately upspoke. "I don't do it on purpose. Some guys are really kind of swishy all the time, but I usually tone it down, unless I'm out with other gay guys. Or trying to annoy people."

Oberon was silent, and Ángel shrugged. "If it makes you feel better, go ahead and talk to Lily and her husband. Assure them of my innocent intentions."

"You would not be offended if I did that?"

"No." Ángel smiled wryly. "I think they'll be surprised that you're worried about it."

They ate in silence for a moment, and then Oberon said, "Ángel. I know you are not very happy here. Please do not leave."

Then disable the cameras in my room.

But he didn't say it. Because what would he do if Oberon refused his ultimatum? Make good on his threat to walk away from this mansion? Put on his new coat and try to hitch a ride in the dark through the mountains? He wouldn't even know which direction to go. And then what?

He shook his head, refusing to commit either way.

Oberon's voice went very soft, sweet-toned, as he asked, "Then will you come to my room tonight?"

What was Oberon actually asking? Did he want them to sleep together? Or to *sleep together*? For a split second he imagined himself agreeing to join Oberon in that soft pile of blankets and duvets. Imagined what might happen next. He glanced into Oberon's mask-like face, the lustrous but empty green eyes, and felt himself shiver.

"No, Oberon."

In the dream, the cultural envoy from the Otherworld was chasing Ángel across the flat sand at Neptune Beach, not far from where he'd grown up. He fled into the surf, but running in knee-deep water slowed him down, and he couldn't run or escape or scream. Oberon pounced on him like a lion, a full-body tackle that drove Ángel down into the water. Falling, drowning, he awakened with a gasp. It took him a moment to remember where he was, and why he was under the bed.

Even disoriented from the dream, Ángel found that he was fully aroused, his cock hard and throbbing with inappropriate excitement. The slide of the silky bedspread on the heated skin of his thighs and belly was wickedly delicious; his dick strained against the cotton of his underwear and quested up under the elastic waistband. He breathed deeply, pulling the bedspread away and his underwear down, hoping that in the cool air his erection would subside on its own.

It didn't happen. This was both ridiculous and horrifying. He'd nearly had a heart attack at the slightest contact with Oberon's hand. An autonomous fight-or-flight reaction, an instinctive recoil from the touch of something genuinely inhuman, like the touch of a snake's scales or an octopus's tentacle.

Ángel's dick wasn't listening.

He covered his face with his left arm and wrapped his right hand around his shaft, stroking up and down the entire rigid length, biting his lip against a groan of pleasure.

Quiet.

He remembered feeling a similar mix of shame and sexual agitation when he was thirteen or fourteen years old. For some time he'd been secretly fascinated by the faces and bodies of men, but his feelings had never found a specific objective until a visiting priest had come to Assumption Catholic Church from another diocese. Father Joseph had been young, clean-shaven and doe-eyed, androgynous in a way that Ángel would always dig. All Ángel's inchoate desires had focused on him like a laser. Ángel had stared at him, rapt, throughout Mass, his heart beating with admiration, his penis quiveringly rigid beneath the missal clutched in his lap. He'd known it was wrong to have those feelings—toward a man, toward a *man of God*—but that knowledge had done nothing whatever to mitigate them.

This was wronger than that. Oberon was not a person, not human. Still, Ángel spread his legs, brought his left hand down to palm his balls, to stroke behind them, while with his right hand he worked his wretchedly excited cock. He squeezed his eyes shut as his pleasure climbed and climbed, and the fantasy of Oberon being here with him invaded his mind. He grabbed his discarded shirt, pressed it to his body, and came into it—silently, silently, his hips spearing the shirt, soaking it with spunk.

God, I am so gross, he thought, even while his body luxuriated in the aftermath of release. *What the hell is wrong with me?*

CHAPTER NINE

Logan the goon rousted him early the next morning. "Get up," he said, kneeling beside the bed and reaching under it to tug on Ángel's blanket.

"*¿Qué bolá?*" Never a morning person, Ángel bumped his forehead on the bottom of the bed. "Ow." He crawled out of his cave and pushed his snarled hair out of his eyes.

"Put some clothes on," said the goon. "You need to go to the basement for a while."

"I do?"

Logan seemed nervous, glancing around the room. He was the one who'd said that Oberon gave him the willies. Ángel washed his face, brushed his teeth and, clad in jeans, socks, and his new blue embroidered shirt, headed downstairs.

He paused on the stairs when he saw the whole security team was there. Oberon was just emerging from the gym, wearing nothing but black track pants, one of his black button-down shirts in his hands. Ángel got a long look at the expanse of the fae's bare torso.

His body was fatless, pale as milk, shimmering with sweat. All covered in that weird hairless inhuman skin, gleaming across his pecs and shoulders and hipbones, darker and rougher in texture toward his waistband. His biceps and shoulders, slender but curved with muscle, vanished beneath the shirt as he shrugged it on. Collarbones arched like wings above a lean chest that tapered to narrow hips and sinuously rippled abdomen; a flat mark, like a scar, shone where a navel should be. He looked both graceful and powerful, his body somehow eloquent as a dancer's.

And then Oberon closed his shirt.

Oh shit, that was way, way *too hot.* He hadn't been that moved by a glimpse of a shirtless chest in years. He would have turned around and gone right back up the stairs, but Logan the goon gave him a nudge. Ángel cleared his dry throat and continued down.

"A grounds crew is here to do some work," said Chandler, crisp in her usual navy suit. "They got here early; I apologize for interrupting your morning routine." She spoke to Oberon, who was now buttoning his cuffs, but Ángel decided to assume it included waking him up as well. "We haven't had time to check them all out, so we'd like you to go down to the wine cellar until they're gone."

"All right." Oberon glanced around, found Ángel with his eyes, then turned back to Chandler. "What are they doing?"

"General maintenance to get ready for winter," she said. "Fertilizing the lawn, clearing the gutters, that sort of thing. Draining the pool." She, too, glanced at Ángel as she said this, and he smiled at her.

"*Qué vergüenza,*" he said. "I was looking forward to my daily swim."

Chandler clearly did not find him amusing. "They should be done by this afternoon. Someone will bring you some food."

They headed for the stairs down to the wine cellar. In passing, Ángel said to Chandler, "I'll have bacon and scrambleds, whole wheat toast, and keep the coffee coming. Thanks."

She visibly restrained herself from shoving him down the stairs.

The wine cellar was a picturesquely arched room, dimly lit and rather chilly, its whitewashed stone walls sporting a mural of Pan and his satyrs frolicking among grape vines. Dusty racks were empty of wine. There wasn't any furniture, either.

Ángel and Oberon sat on the floor, leaning against opposite walls. Ángel hugged his knees and closed his eyes.

He could smell Oberon.

The fae was still warm from exercise, patches of sweat soaking through his black shirt, and his scent filled the enclosed space. Ángel had noticed a toasted-bread smell around him before. This odor was headier, more pungent, and somehow spicy. Musky, like a man, but also . . . cinnamony, a little. Or nutmeg or something. It was a really good smell—only not like food. It was kind of sexy.

This was bad.

Ángel had embraced his gayness in the face of implacable family resistance, and he had long ago stopped trying to deny the direction his dick pointed him in. But lusting after Oberon? That was just *creepy*.

Trying to shake off discomfort and find a neutral topic, Ángel asked, "What is your real name?"

Oberon sang a rapid series of syllables, almost too quickly for Ángel to track, his singing voice low and pure and lovely.

"Again? Slower."

Oberon sang it again, slower, and the notes echoed off the curved walls of the wine cellar. Ángel tried to imitate him: "Ke pa lo ro—"

"Ro," sang Oberon, correcting.

"Ro— Wait, pitch matters?"

"Oh, yes."

The man's name was a song. Ángel groped in his pockets, found a ball-point pen but no paper. He wrote on his palm: the five parallel lines of a staff. He dotted in the notes: b4, a4, d5.

"Let me." Oberon held out his hand, and Ángel passed him the pen. Oberon began to write on the white inside of his own forearm. Ángel got up and sat beside him, watching, as Oberon drew a staff on his arm, a tidy treble clef with an A-major key signature, and nine notes: alternating 16th and 32nd notes, with a 32nd rest after the seventh note and a slur connecting the third, fourth, and fifth. "This is imperfect, but recognizable," he said, writing the syllables beneath each note, then tilting his arm so that Ángel could see it better.

Ángel studied it, brows drawing together. The rhythm was confounding, the sequence of pitches tricky. No wonder the Otherworld had made no effort to teach humans their language, if it was all like this.

Experimentally, he sang, "Daa da daa-a-aa da dah da daa."

"You are charming," said Oberon.

"I— What?" The momentary ease between them vanished; Ángel looked up at Oberon, his face flushing. Good God, he was singing the envoy's name like a child learning a nursery rhyme. "I'm not. I wasn't trying to—"

"I know you weren't trying."

Alarmed, Ángel scootched away, putting a few feet between them.

They sat in silence for a while, Ángel trying not to squirm with embarrassment, and then Oberon said, "You deliberately antagonize Chandler."

Ángel snorted. Maybe Oberon, like himself, wanted something neutral to talk about. "What, you're not worried that Chandler's going to fall in love with my smiles?"

"Somehow, no," said the envoy, and Ángel grinned.

"No, she finds me resistible," he agreed. "Even though she strip-searched me."

"She strip-searched you?"

"Uh," said Ángel, wishing he hadn't mentioned nakedness. "Yeah, when I first came. Not on your orders?"

Oberon gave a soft snort. "No. I am hardly so blind to my advantage."

Did that mean what Ángel thought it meant? "I don't really get the distinction," he said. "With the cameras in my room, you can watch me undress any time."

"The distinction is obvious," said Oberon. "The distinction between *watching* and *searching* is as clear in your language as in mine. The first implies enjoyment and appreciation, the second something hidden, and therefore suspicion of wrongdoing."

"There is no distinction if I'm not a willing participant in either the watching or the searching. It's disturbing to know I have cameras on me when I should be alone."

"Why should you be alone?"

"I can't believe you don't understand this," Ángel grumbled.

Giving up, he crossed his arms on his knees, rested his forehead on his arms. Beside him, Oberon stretched his legs, leaned his head back against the wall, and sighed.

Ángel discovered something, in the quiet minutes that followed.

If he didn't look at Oberon—if he just breathed his air, his warm smell, and listened to his rich voice—Oberon was attractive. He was always beautiful, in an achingly uncomfortable way. But if Ángel didn't confront that terrible face, those expressionless eyes, the mouth that always seemed to be judging, mocking—Oberon was . . .

After a moment, Ángel cleared his throat. "Do they make you do this often? Come down to the cellar?"

"A few times a year, when there are people about."

"Alone, usually?"

"Yes."

"I asked the DOR agent who brought me if you liked living out here all by yourself. He didn't really answer me."

"I hate it." Oberon's face was blank, but his voice was sad. Resigned. "When I first came I lived in a condo near Candler Park, in Atlanta, and I liked that much better. I lived alone, with security of course, but I could look out the windows and see people on the street. Going about their lives. And there were trees. But the protests in the street grew and grew, and the DOR agents hated being so close to me. And then I got shot. So when this place became available they moved me here, where I never see anyone."

"And there aren't any trees," Ángel realized. "You're in the middle of miles of forests, but they cut down all the trees."

"Security." Oberon rubbed his thigh absently, perhaps touching the scar from his bullet wound; the loose fabric of his pants rustled softly against his skin. "There is a small Japanese maple on the terrace. It is a very good tree." His face was still, aloof, but his voice was sorrowful. "We underestimated the degree of resistance to my being here," admitted Oberon. "When I first came, I read about elves, and watched movies, trying to understand what humans think of us. All the movies about beings from other worlds. *Something Wicked This Way Comes. Nightmare on Elm Street. The Thing.*"

"One of my favorites," murmured Ángel into his folded arms.

"Yes?" said Oberon. "Brave little humans menaced by a horrible monster. Somehow it took me a long time to realize that The Thing is *me.*" His voice resonated bafflement. "And in the legends, we lie and steal children and lure men to their deaths. Still, I thought it would be obvious, as time went on, that I am not a violent predator masquerading as a man. And the nickname Oberon seemed encouraging. Until I read the play."

"Not a *Midsummer Night's Dream* fan?"

"He drugs his wife to humiliate her, because she doesn't obey him."

JENYA KEEFE

Good point. "Uh," said Ángel. "I guess we think your morality is different from ours."

Oberon only sighed.

Maybe Oberon was just lonely. Maybe he wasn't angry, demanding, or critical. He was just desperately alone.

Ángel . . . sort of wanted to touch him.

It was crazy—Oberon was *not human*, for God's sake, not a man. But why should that matter so much? Had he been brainwashed by all those monster movies? Is that what Oberon was trying to tell him?

"Brave little humans menaced by a horrible monster."

Was it so wrong, to want to comfort a fellow creature?

Stop kidding yourself. Oberon had the body of an Olympic gymnast and smelled like an unholy combination of freshly baked gingerbread and sweat, and if he wasn't also terrifying, if he wasn't also *not human*, he'd be fuckable as hell. Was comfort really what Ángel wanted to give him?

Maybe comfort was what Oberon wanted, though. Not sex at all. Maybe that was just Ángel's deviance.

God, Oberon smelled good. He closed his eyes and took in the spicy odor that rose from Oberon's body. He felt light-headed and sensual, and he wondered if Oberon's scent was acting on him like a drug. That would explain why he was tempted to reach out, right now, and touch Oberon's arm. Oberon was fully clothed. Ángel wouldn't have to touch his skin at all; he could wrap a hand around the powerful bicep, damp with sweat.

And then he remembered the way it had felt, the one time Oberon's skin had touched his—different, *different*—and he shivered, and his cock throbbed.

"I don't think most humans think of you that way," he said. But Oberon didn't reply, and Ángel knew it was inadequate, given how he had reacted when Oberon had touched him.

At noon someone sent down a tray of banh mi sandwiches and bottled water. "I have seen a video of you on YouTube," said Oberon, picking up a sandwich.

"Oh? The one with the gull?"

"Yes."

The gull video was Ángel's one viral social media moment. It was a low-quality iPhone recording, and there was a lot of ambient noise: wind and the surf, people chattering. Ángel had been performing on the patio of the Blowhole Beachside Brewpub on Captiva Island. He'd played Paul Simon's "Homeward Bound," and some of the audience had sung along.

It wasn't his greatest moment of solo fame because of the quality of the recording or the brilliance of his performance, but because of the big white gull that had sailed through the air and alighted on the railing beside him in the middle of the song. He hadn't missed a beat—he was, after all, a professional—though he'd given the gull a startled glance. He'd finished the song with a flourish of guitar strings. The bar patrons had applauded, and he'd smiled his thanks. And then he'd gestured to the gull, indicating that they should applaud his fellow-performer as well, and, as if on cue, the bird had opened its beak and emitted a cry. The audience had erupted into cheers and laughter. The video ended with Ángel laughing too.

"Your voice is pleasing," said Oberon. "Untrained, but your breath control is very good, and so is your pitch."

Ángel smirked. "Thank you." He wasn't the world's most gifted musician, but he worked hard and was sober and reliable—valuable traits in a session man.

"That video got over ten thousand views."

"It was a nice-looking bird."

"It was," said Oberon. "If one didn't know better, one might think it was your familiar."

"Huh." That was one of the legends of the fae, of course: the animal companions, with whom they shared some mystic bond. "No familiars, then?"

"No."

"Too bad, that would be cool." He brushed crumbs off his fingers, stealing a glance at Oberon. "You *do* do magic though," he ventured. "You came through the veil. They say you can read people's minds, and charm people into doing what you want." Oberon said nothing. After a moment, Ángel shook his head at himself. "No, huh?"

"Not noticeably."

No. Oberon had tried to charm Ángel, tried to touch him, tried to get him to come to his room. But no matter how much he liked Oberon's smell, Ángel wasn't seriously considering taking him up on it. Ever.

"I wonder, sometimes, if it would be worth the risk," continued Oberon, thankfully unaware of Ángel's thoughts. "If I moved back into a town or a city, where more people were exposed to me, if they could grow to know me . . . Even if I were killed, it might make it easier for the next envoy. And I would like it better if I weren't so isolated."

"Until you got killed," Ángel noted.

"I am starving to death anyway." There was resignation and sorrow in Oberon's voice now. "No one expected me to last this long."

Ángel opened his eyes. "What?"

Oberon waved a hand. "Nothing. Sometimes I feel melancholy. Don't you?"

"Yes," said Ángel, and then, "No. That isn't what you meant at all. Don't lie."

"Ah, Ángel," said Oberon, his face expressionless but his voice smiling, "I am very new to lying, you know. I need the practice."

Since Oberon refused to elaborate on that disturbing comment, they passed the rest of the time talking about the one thing they had in common—music. Ángel was a professional player and performer; he was a competent singer and a good guitarist, he was reliable, and he knew the magic that sometimes stirred to life between fellow musicians, between musicians and audience. But as Oberon talked about his favorite—Mahler—it became clear that the fae's knowledge of music history and theory far outstripped his.

Oberon seemed to have no conception of what was cool or uncool, high- or lowbrow, popular or elite. He knew that musical styles went in and out of fashion, but he either found this difficult to understand, or he just didn't care. He gave the same grave attention to the latest K-pop single as to a Wagner aria.

Eventually Chandler let them out of the wine cellar. Ángel was longing for caffeine and went straight to the kitchen to make coffee. "Do you want some?" he asked, glancing over his shoulder at Oberon.

"No, thank you. I should try to get some work done today," said Oberon.

"What are you working on?"

Oberon, evidently in no hurry to retreat behind his office door, leaned on the kitchen counter and watched Ángel putter with coffee beans and water. "I decided to send an ABBA song home."

"*Really*?" Ángel turned to stare at him.

"They've obviously achieved a high level of cultural significance. I called the DOR and talked to several people, and every one of them knows ABBA and has an opinion. And I like 'Waterloo.'"

"Well, good," said Ángel, grinning as he filled the moka pot with water. "That will make a nice change from Mahler."

"I have listened to both, and I find I prefer ABBA to MelodEye. I hope that does not bother you."

"You and everyone else," Ángel assured him. "We MelodEye stans are a rare breed."

"But translating 'Waterloo' has become a problem. I had to look up the battle, and then the Napoleonic Wars, and then the French Revolution. I think it might require too much annotation to be a good choice."

Ángel put the pot on a burner and opening a cabinet for the sugar. "I love that song, but the lyrics are a little, um. I guess it was a pretty horrible battle. I wouldn't want to try to explain how that spells 'romance.'"

"So I'm not the only one who finds that confusing? I'm not very good with metaphors."

"No," laughed Ángel, rummaging in the refrigerator for milk. "I'm not sure anyone has a handle on that metaphor."

"Do you have a favorite ABBA song?"

Ángel paused thoughtfully. "I like 'Angeleyes' a lot," he said at last. "It's simple but kind of sad. Really fun to sing. You might have to explain what angels are, but at least you won't need to write a master's thesis on European history."

"Thank you for the suggestion," said Oberon. "I will listen to it."

The air thrummed between them with a low pulsing note, just below hearing. It did something strange to Ángel, made his blood rush, the hair on his arms stand up.

"What *is* that?" demanded Ángel, his face hot. "Are you *humming*? I can almost hear it."

The subsonic vibration briefly intensified, then died away. "It only means that I'm pleased, Ángel."

CHAPTER TEN

After Oberon went into his office, Ángel took his coffee into the living room and leaned against the big picture window, taking in the view. The clouds were low and gray, blustery. He thought it was threatening rain, and as he sipped his coffee he was surprised to see a few feathery white flakes whirl past. A moment later the sky was full of snow.

Ángel nearly jumped up and down with excitement. He was not a complete stranger to snow—he'd seen dirty piles of it on the sidewalks and street corners on recording trips to Nashville, and even a few flakes now and then in Florida—but he'd never been outside in an actual snowstorm before. He went to the kitchen to leave his cup in the sink, then dashed up the stairs to his room to put on his new boots and coat. Then he went outside, tramping around the outside of the house, enjoying the cold wind on his face.

Who knew that falling snow made a noise? It was a hushed, whispery sound, the snow falling straight down from a low gray sky, landing on the crisp brown lawn. He leaned his head back and caught a flake on his tongue.

He came around the side of the house to the garage, and saw that the morning's workers had forgotten to close the side door. *They must have gone in there for tools*, he thought, walking toward the building to close the door for them.

Tools. In the garage there were tools.

Heart beating in his throat, he went into the dark garage through the side door. He didn't dare turn on a light—if the security force wasn't already tracking his movements, that would alert them to his presence here. A red tool box shone in the dim light coming through the rectangular garage door windows. Inside he found a tidy array of clean, well-cared-for hand tools.

He stared at the tools for a moment, hugging himself, his hands tucked into his armpits for warmth. ¿De verdad, Ángel?

Yeah.

He selected the tools that seemed most likely to be useful—a small pry bar, two screwdrivers with different heads, two sizes of pliers, a hammer, some electrician's tape—and closed the box. Stowing his treasurers in the capacious pockets of his coat—*thank you, Lily Va*—he walked back to the house and ran straight up to his room.

They would be watching this, of course.

Oberon. Would be watching.

Ángel shucked off his coat and laid out the tools tidily in a row on the bed. He removed his boots and climbed up onto the purple leather chair in the corner of his room. The crown molding was ornate, its whorls painted peacock-green. Concealed in the center of a stylized rose was a small hole. He examined it and spotted the shine of a camera lens. Anyone who might be watching was getting an excellent close-up of his face.

He used the pry bar to lever the molding off the wall, careful not to damage either it or the drywall. The camera had an attached microphone and was hardwired into the house's electrical system. With a screwdriver, he unhoused the camera from its bracket, and then he used the wire cutter on the pliers to snip it free, his hands protected from shock by the rubberized grip.

The camera fell to the rug like a dead cockroach.

He took a moment to tape the ends of the wires. His father, along with being a Ponzi schemer, was an electrician, after all.

No one came in to stop him or shoot him or yell at him.

Encouraged, he pulled down all the crown molding, stowing it neatly against the wall behind the bed's headboard. He found and disabled a second camera. Then he attacked the pink crown molding in his bathroom and found a third. This one was pointed at the shower. "*Vete pa la pinga,*" he gritted. His outrage probably showed on his face in the moments before he clipped its wires.

He put all three cameras on the bathroom counter and vengefully crushed them with the hammer, brushing the broken glass and plastic into the bathroom wastebasket.

Then he went to the security monitor and turned the feed to his own room. Blue screen of nothing. He turned up the volume and whistled, snapped his fingers. Nothing. He'd gotten the mikes too.

The alarm clock on the bedside table said it was seven thirty: dinnertime. He had to go down and face Oberon now.

They'd had a nice day, he and Oberon. Down in the wine cellar, eating sandwiches and chatting about the gull video. They'd talked about Mahler and Ella Fitzgerald. Vocal improvisation. "Angeleyes." And Oberon had purred at him.

Now Oberon would be angry.

Ángel wasn't sorry about what he'd done, but he was suddenly worried about Oberon's anger. What his punishment would be for disobeying Oberon and destroying DOR property.

He washed his hands, dried them, and went slowly down to the kitchen, his stomach heavy with dread.

He wasn't as afraid of Oberon as he'd been at first. The envoy's calm demeanor, his palpable air of restraint, and even his knowledge of music had reassured him. The adrenaline-fueled terror of the first day had largely dissipated, replaced by caution. Illogical attraction, maybe.

But he'd never openly challenged Oberon before. He'd never seen Oberon really angry. What would he do?

Stop being such a fucking coward, he told himself, bracingly. The cameras were just *wrong*, an intolerable violation. There was one in the *bathroom*, for God's sake. Ángel had a right to take a shower without being spied upon; the fact that Oberon genuinely didn't seem to understand why didn't change that.

Ángel went into the kitchen. Oberon was there at the island counter. Lily, who seemed to know something was up, was dishing up black bean soup. She cast him a huge-eyed glance that seemed full of worry. After putting a bowl of soup at his place, she retreated, putting on her coat and slipping out, back to the gatehouse.

Ángel stood waiting, braced for battle.

"Ángel."

Oberon's face was as expressionless as usual. His voice vibrated hotly, but Ángel didn't know what that meant. Was he angry? Upset?

Maybe even kind of . . . ill? His gleaming pale skin had faded to a dull beige.

"Hi," said Ángel, and sat beside him.

"You disabled the cameras in your room."

Taking his courage in his hands, he said, "I destroyed them. Yes. And the bathroom too."

Oberon stirred his soup, not eating. Ángel brought a spoonful to his mouth, but he could barely swallow, his stomach was so knotted.

"And if you put them back, I'll leave," he added. "I can climb the wall if you shut the gates. I can walk to town." *In the snow?* he thought, but didn't say it. "You would have to hold me here by force if you put the cameras back."

Oberon said, "Forgive me. I find that I'm not very hungry," put down his spoon, and got up to walk away.

As he was leaving the room, Ángel nerved himself. "Oberon."

The envoy turned his head.

Ángel said, quietly, "Please try to understand." Had he hurt Oberon's feelings? *Sorry* seemed like a stupid thing to say. "I couldn't bear it, Oberon."

After a pause, Oberon said, "Very well, Ángel." The blankness of his voice, coupled with the unreadability of his expression, was unnerving. "Do you think you will be happier now?"

"I don't know," said Ángel. "Did I get them all?"

"You got them all," said Oberon, and left the room.

CHAPTER ELEVEN

T he week that followed was extremely strained.

Ángel got up at around seven every morning and ran on the treadmill. Then he would shower, play his guitar, email Marissa, or otherwise mark time until lunch. In the afternoons he would walk around the estate—the weather had warmed, melting the snow—listen to and play music, or surf the internet and watch movies on the tablet. No porn. Chandler was undoubtedly monitoring his online activities.

The isolation was getting to him. He almost never saw Oberon. The fae would be gone from the gym by the time Ángel got there each morning, though it sometimes still smelled like him. He always took him a lunch tray. Oberon would be listening to music—Kate Bush, or B.B. King, or Handel—but he would not look at Ángel or speak to him, so Ángel would drop off the tray and leave. And Oberon never emerged from his office for dinner anymore, so Ángel ate alone.

He'd never thought that he would crave Oberon's company before, but he'd never felt so lonely before, either. He suspected it was wearing on Oberon as well—the rich cream of his skin had washed out to a kind of fish-white. Ángel wasn't certain what that meant, but it couldn't be good.

He wasn't sorry the cameras were gone. He slept on top of the bed now, rather than underneath it, but when he masturbated—which he did every night, feverishly, unable to satisfy his longing for human touch—he still did so in complete silence, buried under the covers, not trusting that no one could hear him.

Oberon didn't invite him to his bedroom again.

"This has to stop," said Lily in the first week of October.

"What?" said Ángel, as if he didn't know.

She scowled at him, tiny and fierce, dumping the remains of Oberon's lunch in the garbage with a flourish. "He's not eating right. He's not coming out of his office. He's all gray and he smells weird."

Ángel had noticed that too: Oberon didn't smell like cinnamon anymore. Instead, there was a slightly bitter tang in the air around him. "He's mad at me because I got rid of the cameras in my room."

She stamped her foot. "Well, make him not mad at you anymore!"

"How?" demanded Ángel, defensively. "I'm not sorry!"

"I don't care if you're sorry! You're supposed to be helping him, not making him worse!"

Ángel glared at her. But after a moment he sat dejectedly at the counter. "I know," he admitted. "I didn't mean to *hurt* him."

"I know, but maybe you did."

"I'm scared of him." He ran a hand through his hair. "One time he told me he was starving to death. Is he really not eating?"

"He's not eating very well." She sighed, hands on hips. "He doesn't have anyone but us, Ángel."

"Okay. You're right."

"He likes sweet things. I made zucchini bread. Take him some, and make him eat it."

Ángel took the tray with zucchini bread, butter, and tea, and went into Oberon's office without knocking. He was surprised to hear issuing from the speakers a song he knew all too well: "Sunrise Love" by an indie country artist named Conner Marr.

The cups on the tray rattled a little—his hands were shaking. He set the tray down on Oberon's desk to stop the clatter.

"Please tell me you're not sending this song back to the Otherworld," he said lightly, hiding his nervousness with a smile. He picked up a plate and sat down in one of the uncomfortable leather chairs.

"Don't you like it?" asked Oberon.

"Not really." Ángel nibbled a corner of zucchini bread, letting the familiar sound of Con's voice warble through the excellent speakers. "Do you?"

The bread was sweet and moist, studded with walnuts. It was good, but it was hard to eat while he waited for Oberon to answer. He forced himself to swallow.

After a moment, Oberon said, "I like listening to you sing."

"Hah, you read the liner notes," guessed Ángel.

"No liner notes," said Oberon. "This is one of the songs uploaded from your phone. I recognized your voice."

"Are you serious?" Ángel, incredulous, glanced up from his plate to Oberon's impassive expression. "You're telling me you recognized my voice from *this*?"

"Of course I did."

Ángel licked crumbs off his thumb and cocked his head, listening closely to the song's final chorus. Not only was Ángel's backing harmony layered under Con's rich, flexible baritone melody, but his part was distorted by the production, and he was singing in a breathy falsetto completely unlike his usual voice.

The song faded to silence and Ángel said, "That is fucking amazing, Oberon. Did you isolate the backing track?"

"I did, but I wouldn't have bothered if I hadn't known it was you," said Oberon. "Why is it surprising? I hear your voice every day. You often sing while you're doing other things."

"This song buries me, though." Ángel shook his head. "I doubt most people would even realize that there are backing vocals, much less recognize my voice."

"You're playing the guitar too."

"Yep, that's me on lead guitar. Con's playing rhythm. Are you going to eat that?"

Oberon looked down at the zucchini bread on his plate. "All right." Without noticeable enthusiasm, he began to eat.

Around another bite of bread, Ángel said, "That's really impressive. I mean, guitar's pretty individual, but I don't think any human ears could have picked my voice out. *I* wouldn't know that was me, and we must have sung it fifty-seven times to get this take. I was singing this song in my dreams for weeks."

With gentle politeness, Oberon said, "He sometimes tends to be a little flat."

Ángel snorted. "Ya think? He wanted a live set for every song on the album, and he's ethically opposed to auto-tune. All of which is fine if you can stay on key, but Con has trouble. Never go see him live. It can be tough."

"I'll cross his concerts off my schedule," said Oberon gravely. "You are conspicuously the better singer, more controlled and on-pitch even though you're singing above your modal voice. The only interesting thing about this song is that he's singing the melody and not you."

Ángel smiled. "Thank you, but it was his album, Oberon. I'm just a session man."

"Why don't you have an album?"

"Never really wanted to be a star. I like session work, and I like to write and play and perform in small venues. It's fun, and I make a living. But I don't want fame. Fame sucks. As you know."

"And why did you have this song on your phone?"

That was a perceptive question. Ángel had been playing and singing other people's music for years; he didn't carry around many examples in his pocket. "We dated for a while," he admitted. "Con and me. We broke up not long after we recorded this. I guess it's nostalgia or something."

"Do you love him still?"

"No," said Ángel, surprised. They ate in silence until "Sunrise Love" automatically started up again, Ángel's guitar ringing through the room. Then Conner started to sing, and Ángel winced. "I don't even miss him much, not anymore. It's just, I don't really know what happened. Why we didn't work out. He wanted me to tour with him, but I had my business, my clients, in Miami. It wasn't personal. But he got mad." He listened regretfully. "It's too bad I don't have a better song to remember him by, but the rest of his stuff isn't any better. He has a pretty voice, but he's not a very interesting songwriter."

He stood up to collect their plates, and frowned to see that Oberon had barely eaten half his slice of bread. "Eat that."

"I'm not hungry."

"I don't care," said Ángel, brusquely. "You work out for ninety minutes every morning. You can't support that on no food. Eat."

Oberon's green-gold eyes glinted at him. "Will you stay with me for a few minutes, while I eat?"

Did he really just want company? Somehow it was easy to forget how alone Oberon was.

He sat in the chair. Oberon took another bite of his zucchini bread. "Happy?"

Ángel gestured in the air, indicating "Sunrise Love," which was winding down again. "Kill this?"

Oberon brushed the crumbs off his fingertips, and tapped the surface of his tablet. Con Marr's voice, blended with Ángel's, cut off abruptly. "Magpie to the Morning" by Neko Case came on.

"Now I'm happy," said Ángel.

They listened to the song, then discussed its cryptic lyrics. Ángel found himself enjoying the conversation—he could relax and enjoy talking to Oberon so long as he kept his eyes on the gray sky outside the window. The tension and fear only came back when he looked at him.

After a while Oberon said, "What made you decide to seek me out today?"

Ángel continued staring out the window. "Well," he said, reluctantly. "This is why I'm here, isn't it? To keep you company. I wasn't holding up my end of the bargain."

"Because you are afraid that I'll hurt you?"

"No— I mean— I'm not really sure what I'm afraid of."

Oberon sipped his tea. "I am bad at communicating with humans. I am only now realizing how very bad at it I am. I thought that learning a language would be enough, but there seems to be so much that I am incapable of either conveying or understanding. No wonder people want to kill me."

Ángel dared a glance at him. "Your English is great."

"It isn't enough. And you—well. You are confusing. Do you want to know what I think?"

"Okay."

"We of the fae—we speak a language, just like you. And like you, we have another way of speaking, which helps us understand when language is not precise. Your second way of speaking is visual. You move your faces, you send signals with your expressions. And your clothes, and ornaments. You constantly speak without sound. It is part of what makes you such a beautiful species," he added. "You are so colorful, so visually varied. So constantly in motion."

We are? Ángel bit his lip. *I guess we are.*

"But my species does not speak that way," continued Oberon. "Our faces are always the same. While I think humans are lovely and

I enjoy watching you, I can easily misinterpret the signals you are sending."

Ángel thought about this, with the sensation of puzzle pieces falling into place.

Oberon said, "The fae's second way of speaking— We *feel* each other. You've asked me if we read minds. We do not. But we feel each other's feelings, we experience feelings together, in our skin, and in our hearts. Do you understand?"

Creepy. "Neat," Ángel said, a little hoarsely, looking out the window so that he wouldn't be confronted by Oberon's eyes. "Do you have to, um, touch, skin to skin, to pick up each other's emotions?"

"Not at all," said Oberon. "Nearness is enough. But when we do touch, it is especially beautiful. Sometimes, when we touch, the emotions of two will combine and blend in our hearts; we will feel each other, in our skin, and the feelings will change. Like voices in harmony, in a song. It is a language to which you have no access at all. And since I came here," he added, "neither do I."

And did that grieve him? How could it not? But the sight of that still, angular face told Ángel nothing.

"So you can't feel humans' emotions?"

"I can," Oberon said, "but it's like when you hear another language. I don't understand them. I have come to understand Lily, a little, and Chandler. But you, you are baffling to me. The first day you were here, your heart was beating fast. You were almost dancing. Your skin seemed warm, and I thought you were excited to be here. I thought you were happy. I didn't understand that you were terrified. I could hardly have made a worse mistake."

"I wish I knew this sooner. Am I still baffling?"

"Yes," said Oberon. "Constantly. I can tell you are having feelings, but I have no idea what they are. It is very disconcerting, Ángel."

The way Oberon's lack of expression was disconcerting to Ángel, presumably. They both spoke English, but there was a communication gap that they couldn't seem to bridge. But Oberon wanted to bridge it. Oberon was reaching out to him for help.

"For me too," he offered. "You know, you have another way, as well. Your voice changes when you talk. And sometimes I can sort of smell you, and your smell changes. I suppose that over the next four years, I'll learn how to interpret the way your voice changes. And you'll learn to interpret, uh, me."

"I hope so," said Oberon. "But until that happens, I have a request, Ángel."

Ángel forced himself to meet Oberon's green-gold eyes again.

"My species' sensitivity to magic makes it almost impossible for us to lie to each other. But I could easily lie to you, because you can't interpret my magic. And you can easily lie to me, because I don't reliably understand your expressions and movements. So I ask that, since we must rely upon spoken language, we do so without lies. Or do not speak at all, if we cannot speak honestly."

"Okay. I'll try."

"Shall we try now?"

"Oh, you want to . . . Okay. Sure. Ask me anything."

"You'll answer truthfully?" Oberon was watching him fixedly.

Ángel squirmed. "Or I won't answer."

"I will do the same. Do you miss your home?"

"Yes," said Ángel. "So much."

"I miss mine too." They were quiet for a moment, and then Oberon gently said, "Now you."

Ángel imagined asking Oberon if he'd been brought here for sex, and quailed. Instead he ventured, "Are you angry with me?"

"No. Did you think I was?"

"Yes." Ángel could no longer look at him; he focused on his own knees. "Because I destroyed the cameras in my room."

"Where I am from . . . we live, many, in one home. And we all sense one another all the time. There is no privacy, because we can feel one another, from anywhere in the house. For us, that is . . . comfortable, to know our friends can tell how we feel, or if anything is wrong. It's a feeling of safety, of *home*, to know that the people I live with can feel me, and I can feel them." He paused. "I often cannot feel you, and when I do I cannot understand. So I use the cameras, so I can see you. It is comfort. Or it was."

"It comforted you to watch me on the cameras when I slept?"

"Yes. Does it comfort you, to watch me?"

"On the cameras? No. I would never."

"Even if I said I didn't mind?"

Ángel shook his head.

"I thought I was offering you contentment." Oberon's voice was soft, and his scent had taken on a wintery note, like snow. "Easing your loneliness. But I think I only made it worse. Are you angry with me?"

Ángel bit his lip. "Sort of. Sometimes. But I agreed to come. And I know you're doing what feels normal to you. It's not your fault that it isn't normal to me. I'm trying my best."

"I will try harder. I should have listened to you, when you said you hated the cameras. Thank you for not lying to me, Ángel."

"You're welcome, I guess."

"I have another question."

"Okay."

"Do you really like this house?"

Ángel laughed. "Oberon," he said, "this is the ugliest house I have ever seen."

CHAPTER TWELVE

D ays passed, and Ángel and Oberon eased into a sort of careful friendship. They had lunch together. Oberon ate, and Ángel was pleased that his color returned to what seemed to be its normal golden cream. They talked about music. The jazz influences and unreliable narrators of Steely Dan; the function of the movie score, and if it could stand alone without its movie; whether punk music had any aesthetic value or redeeming social importance at all. (Oberon was *not* a fan of punk.) Sometimes Oberon would consult Ángel about a song's cultural significance, or meanings of lyrics. More often he would share his greater technical knowledge with Ángel. One afternoon, they had a discussion of harmony and counterpoint that so vastly expanded Ángel's largely instinctive understanding of the topic it made his head spin. Ángel ruefully thought that his four years in Oberon's company could easily be the equivalent of a graduate degree in music theory, if he paid attention.

"How do you send stuff back to the Otherworld?" asked Ángel one day. "Music, and your notes and things? I thought the veil was one-way only."

"That is a simplification," said Oberon. "There are libraries of books on the veil, universities of scholars who study it. I am not a scholar, but I understand that it takes a huge amount of energy for something to pass through the veil. Exponentially more energy to pass from this side to the Otherworld, than from the Otherworld to this side. But either way, it is very difficult. So I am alone here." He gestured toward the rose bush by the window. "Except for that plant, which is an Otherworld plant. It is full of magic—its magic ceaselessly draws it toward home, through the veil. So I use a spell to put music and my notes and my ideas into the flowers, and it passes them through."

Ángel hesitantly examined the rose bush. In its large ceramic pot, it was not a particularly graceful plant: sturdy stems bristling with hooked thorns, shiny dark-green leaves. It bore flowers in all stages of development—tight buds, flowers that were just opened, perfectly formed flowers that were blown wide, all silver-white, almost sparkling. "It's magic?" he asked. "If I touch it, will it suck me through?"

"No. Neither you nor I can go through."

Ángel touched a flower with a fingertip, and the whole rose bush seemed to tremble. "And they can, like, read the roses, there?"

"That flower holds Bach's Suite number 1 in G Major, played by Johannes Moser," said Oberon. "Perhaps they will feel your touch too." Ángel snatched his hand away. "The entire experience is there. I put my notes in this one—" Oberon indicated a different flower "—so that they can listen to the music without my interpretation."

"Is that something that you are born knowing how to do?"

"Oh, no, I studied. I am not a naturally gifted spell-caster—I had to learn. And also, one person doing magic alone can do very little. Great spell-casters work together; they dance together, and their magic combines, and becomes stronger than anything any one spell-caster could ever do. Because I am alone, I am weak in magic." He touched the rose. "But the plant helps."

Ángel pictured groups of dancing fae, creating magics. He had read about things like that, in folktales: faerie rings, spells.

To help Ángel pass the time, Lily began to bring him library books with her weekly shopping: biographies, mysteries, poetry, romance novels, whatever was new. Ángel read them all and begged for more. He asked for fewer romances—not because he didn't like them, necessarily, but because he got through them too quickly. Plus some of them were pretty sexy, and his libido didn't need the encouragement. Dense and slow was better. Nonfiction. Classics. Tolstoy.

Craving stimulation, he began to teach himself to play the mandolin. He watched technique and tuning videos on YouTube, and got Lily to bring him books and sheet music from the library. He practiced at tedious length, getting used to the small neck under his left fingers, keeping his right wrist loose as he picked the paired strings. It was probably agonizing to listen to, but Ángel wanted to sound like a mandolin player, not like a guitarist messing around on a mandolin, and for him that meant learning the instrument deep, through repetition. He needed to embed the instrument into his hands' muscle memory.

And he tried to understand Oberon. To not be distracted by that predatory face, but to pay attention to his words, and the fluid gestures of his slim hands, of the tones and timbre of his voice, and to correlate them to the scent of his body and the color of his skin.

One day they were eating cucumber hummus sandwiches and tomato soup, listening to the throbbing strains of a piano concerto.

"What is this?" asked Ángel. "It's so sad."

"Rachmaninov." Oberon was leaning back in his chair, his head resting on its cushion, his eyes closed.

Hesitantly, Ángel asked, "Are you sad?"

Oberon didn't answer the question directly. "Each thinning of the veil, I expect a message from Otherworld. I thought it would happen this summer, but it hasn't. That makes me very anxious."

"The veil thins? Is another envoy coming?"

"No, I am afraid not," he said, regret washing through his voice like a drop of blue ink in a glass of water. "No. When the veil thins, I hope for messages. I am longing for news of home."

Ángel considered his own loneliness and desperation for contact with the outside world. He had only been here for two months. "How often does the veil thin?"

"Every few months. But I have had no messages."

Ángel wrinkled his brow. "When was the last time you had news from home?"

"Almost three years."

He grimaced with horror. "Oh shit. I'm so sorry. That would be driving me crazy. I can barely go three days without an email from Marissa. I don't know how you can concentrate on this crap." He gestured in the air.

"What else can I do?" asked Oberon. "Do you really think it's crap?"

"No—"

But the Rachmaninov was wildly emotive, a tumult of agitated sorrow. Somehow it made Ángel think of the protests—the Molotov cocktails, the hateful signs. The assassination attempts.

What would those people think if they knew how homesick Oberon was? That he sat around listening to Rachmaninov and pining, because he'd had no news of home?

"Oh my God," said Ángel. "I just had an idea."

He sprang to his feet and began pacing, running his fingers through his hair to pull it back off his face, tugging it by the roots as if to stimulate his brain. Oberon leaned forward and turned off the music.

"The problem is that people want to kill you," Ángel said.

"That *is* one of my problems, yes," agreed Oberon. If Ángel didn't look at him, he thought he could hear warmth in his voice. Amusement?

"They want to kill you because they're afraid of you," said Ángel. "But you're really only scary when people can see you. I mean, your face is scary."

"It is?"

"Even on TV, it's not so bad, but still. A little. In person . . . But your *voice*. If people could just hear you talking—if they could get to know you, without having to see you—"

"Are you suggesting I do radio interviews?"

"Easier," said Ángel. "A podcast. It's low tech, it's so damn simple to do. You wouldn't have to go to New York to get shot at. We could do it here. People could learn who you are."

"What would I talk about?"

"*We* could talk. Like we already do. We could talk about music, and the lyrics you don't understand, and, oh my God. We could talk about the project you're working on. How you're sending our music back to your people. How you decide which pieces you're going to send home to the Otherworld. Maybe we could talk about one piece of music per week." He paced. "Not the Ramones. The entire city of New York will unite against you like a hive of bees if you dis the Ramones."

"The Ramones are simplistic to the point of idiocy," said Oberon, "but I can't imagine that they would have been troubled by controversy."

"Yeah, nope, let's not go there. But . . . anything else. Really. Marissa's brother has a podcast about motorcycles, which could not *be* more boring, and he has hundreds of listeners. But everyone is interested in you."

Oberon was silent, but Ángel's mind continued to whir with possibilities. "I could get some books from the library about how to do it," he said. "We could listen to some podcasts, decide how we want it to sound. I think the best ones are short, like twenty minutes or a half hour per episode, max, and sort of off-the-cuff and casual. The DOR could make a nice website, do promotions. And get permissions from the artists so we could play the music and then talk about it."

"Do you truly believe people would listen to what I have to say about Rachmaninov?" Oberon sounded doubtful.

"Yes!"

"You've had Rachmaninov for a hundred years."

"Maybe you have fresh perspective on Rachmaninov that we never thought of," said Ángel. "I mean, *obviously*. How could you not? And how will people know, unless they listen to what you have to say?"

"I suppose."

"But the music, the music wouldn't really be the point. People would listen because it's *you*."

Oberon was watching him intently. "You are enthusiastic about this idea."

"It could work. What could go wrong? If it doesn't, we'll stop doing it." Ángel smiled at him, bouncing on his toes. "Want to try?"

Slowly, Oberon said, "You think if people learned who I am, they would be less afraid of me? Not more?"

"No, of course not more. Absolutely. They'd get to know you. They'd get to know *you*, not the elf-lord, not the monster from another world, not the scary face. Then they'd learn that you're just a—a person. Who loves music. Not a threat. And then maybe you could go places and not be stuck here all the time."

"That would be welcome." Oberon's voice had gone soft. "I'll talk to the DOR. What we're doing now isn't working."

Ángel grinned and headed for the door.

"Will you come back?"

"I'm just gonna go to the kitchen. I left the tablet there."

"Yes. When you're done, come back?"

Ángel hesitated. The fae must be really craving company. "Okay," he said. "Let me go get it."

So he fetched the tablet and came back to the office and curled up on the couch. First he went to the library's website and reserved some books on podcasting. Then he began surfing how-to blogs.

Oberon started the Rachmaninov again. This time maybe a different performance, with a different orchestra and pianist, though Ángel wasn't sure.

When the concerto finished, Oberon broke the silence. "What sorts of books does Lily bring you?"

"Um, novels," said Ángel. "Stories."

"Like what?"

"I'm reading *One Hundred Years of Solitude* by Gabriel García Márquez." He sensed the expectation in the air, and went on, "It's about a family. How generation after generation they keep making the same kinds of mistakes. It's good, but it's also super-sad." He looked up at Oberon. "Do you like to read? You could send books back to the Otherworld too."

"I am, but without the annotations. I find reading English rather tiring."

"Really?"

"I can read," clarified Oberon. "But your alphabet starts to blur after a while. I prefer to listen."

"I know a guy who can barely read at all, although he's very smart. He has dyslexia. His brain has a hard time interpreting written language. He can read music, though, which seems weird. Does our musical notation blur for you too?"

"Not at all. But I find it quite incomplete. There are qualities of sound it cannot capture."

"Is that because we can't hear as much as you hear?"

"Only partly."

Oberon switched the music to something atonal and chilly. They fell into companionable silence.

Ángel was unable to focus on podcasting best practices, but it wasn't because of the Schoenberg. It was because of Oberon, of course, sitting there all scholarly at his desk, black shirt sleeves rolled up to expose pale sinewy forearms, typing on his weird keyboard and smelling, faintly, of toast and black pepper and butterscotch.

Ángel shouldn't have told Oberon about Conner Marr. Too many memories, memories he didn't want to associate with Oberon. The relationship had ended in a confusing series of arguments and accusations and hurt, neither of them seeming to understand each other. But Con was great in bed. So good that Ángel had kept going back for more sex even after they broke up. Even after Con hadn't liked him anymore. He was sort of ashamed of that, but also aware that if Con were here he'd totally have sex with him.

If Con were here, he'd pin Ángel down on this couch. Tickle him, pinch his nipples, grab his ass. Con knew Ángel liked it just a little rough, knew to pull Ángel's hair, to use his teeth, to dig his fingers into Ángel's flesh a little too hard. Con would perspire when he was excited, which was hot. He would talk dirty and laugh at himself doing it, would kiss him like he wanted to eat him, until Ángel was moaning and desperate to come.

Ángel wasn't really thinking about Con.

He shifted the tablet in his lap, glad that the long tail of his shirt concealed the ridge of his cock, solid against the placket of his jeans.

What would sex with Oberon be like? How did he do it? His species reproduced itself *somehow*. Exchanged genetic material. But. Maybe . . . Surely they wouldn't laugh or tease or savor. Oberon didn't *play*, and his sweat was—his skin was—

Ángel shivered. He didn't think he'd made a sound, but Oberon immediately glanced at him.

Was Oberon feeling him? Feeling what he was feeling? Did he understand?

The idea of Oberon sensing Ángel's arousal sent a zing down his spine—not fear, but excitement. Horrified, Ángel blurted, "Sorry. I think I need to go for a walk. I'll see you at dinner," and escaped.

CHAPTER
THIRTEEN

"Welcome to the first episode of *The Oberon Podcast*," said Ángel. "I'm Ángel, and I'm joined by the cultural envoy from the Otherworld, Oberon."

"Hello," said Oberon.

The okay from the DOR had come in so quickly, Ángel suspected that someone there was a podcast fan. They'd sent the equipment right away, and now, only a few days after having had the original idea, Ángel and Oberon were speaking into brand-new microphones on Oberon's desk.

"Oberon, please tell us your real name," he said.

Oberon sang his name. It really was beautiful.

"Does your whole language sound like that?"

"Yes, very much like it," said Oberon. "The words, the syllables, carry meaning, and so does the pitch of each syllable. I understand it is a little different from tonal languages here on Earth, because the absolute pitch, rather than the relative pitch, is what's important. But I have not studied any tonal human languages, so I'm not sure."

"You have perfect pitch?"

"I do, of course. In the Otherworld, not to have absolute pitch would be quite a serious disability, like, perhaps, a severe hearing impairment. A person would have great trouble communicating without accurate pitch."

Ángel encouraged Oberon to describe his project. They talked about the criteria he used to choose which music he'd send back to the Otherworld, and Oberon admitted that, while he took artistic and cultural significance into account, his final arbiter was simply what he liked.

Throughout their conversation Ángel kept his eyes focused on the window, away from Oberon, just listening to the smooth, deep voice. It was fluent, easy, warming sometimes with humor. A *charming* voice.

This is going to work.

"So why do this?" asked Ángel. "Why do the people of the Otherworld want to know about our music?"

"The Otherworld is . . . We love to study. We love to learn new things. When I was a child I began to devote myself to learning music, to learning about other people. And so when the opportunity arose to travel here, naturally I was excited to come."

"If that's true, why are you the only envoy who's ever come? Wouldn't others like to come and learn?"

"Oh, yes," said Oberon. "The Otherworld would like to send other envoys, to learn more about this planet's life forms and chemistry and history, but it takes an enormous amount of energy to send someone across the veil. I am not a master spell-caster, so I cannot explain this—there was only enough energy to send one."

"How did you get the job?"

"I was selected from among many candidates. It was a competitive process."

"And they chose you—a musician, rather than, like, a scientist—because the Otherworld wants to know about our music that much?"

"Among other things, yes. Very much."

"Why? Why go to all this expense to send you here, so that you could send back music? It seems kind of frivolous."

"Do you think so?"

"Maybe," said Ángel. "I mean, I love music. I make my living playing music. But for most people, it's just entertainment. There are people who think you're actually here to find out everything you can about our military defenses, so that the Otherworld can invade us and steal our resources and—I don't know—eat us. You say you're really here for the music?"

"Well, yes. We don't want to eat you or invade you, and if we did, they wouldn't have sent someone like me. I am not a soldier. I don't know anything about military defenses—I would not know how to assess those if I saw them. We want to learn about you."

"About our music?" prodded Ángel.

Oberon paused long enough to make Ángel wonder if he needed to pause the recording. Finally Oberon said, "Think of it this way. We have many species of large and lovely trees, but we don't have redwood trees. No redwoods live in the Otherworld. Perhaps someday we will find a way to bring redwoods back to the Otherworld, and to plant them there and make them thrive. But until that time, I am the only living fae who has ever seen one in person. The Otherworld has beautiful birds that wade in the water and hunt, but I am the only fae who has ever seen a great blue heron. Which I think is a very beautiful and very strange bird. Strange, because no such thing ever lived in the Otherworld, and never will."

Ángel waved a hand, encouraging him to keep going.

"So in the same way," said Oberon, "the Otherworld has many varieties of music, but we do not have jazz. John Coltrane's music could never have existed on the Otherworld. But I sent recordings home, so now the Otherworld, the people of the Otherworld, have John Coltrane's music. Now we can listen to jazz, and learn from it. We can play it in our own way, and make a new kind of music that we could never have had without John Coltrane. And that is wonderful to us, as wonderful as redwoods and herons."

Perfect.

It wasn't going to get better than that, so he began to wrap up the interview. "We'd like to thank the Department of Otherworld Relations for making this podcast possible. On future episodes, we're going to discuss specific pieces of music that Oberon has chosen to send home, and why. If you have suggestions for future episodes, or questions for us, please send an email to OberonPodcast-at-DOR-dot-gov. I'm Ángel."

"And I am Oberon, the cultural envoy from the Otherworld."

"Thanks for listening," said Ángel, and killed the recording.

The first episode of *The Oberon Podcast* went live on October second, edited and hosted and with professional artwork provided by the DOR. It was just over eighteen minutes long, and it ended with a resonant clip of Oberon singing his fae name. That day it got over nine thousand downloads.

The next day the download count was up to nine hundred thousand.

Ángel, bleary-eyed from obsessively refreshing the tablet and watching the numbers climb, said, "I guess we can do episode two."

They went ahead and recorded three episodes the next afternoon. In the first, Oberon disassembled a Chopin étude like a carburetor, discussed its constituent parts, and put it back together again. Occasionally he illustrated his point by singing the melody, clear and true. Ángel asked questions and made no effort to disguise that Oberon's understanding and musicality took his breath away.

The second podcast they recorded that day centered around the Otherworld's storytelling musical tradition, and they played and talked about "On My Own" from *Les Misérables*. Oberon said that he had never actually seen *Les Mis* live, and confessed that he would like to do that. Ángel admitted his resistance to show tunes, which he found melodramatic and emotionally manipulative. He could concede, when questioned by Oberon, that "On My Own" had good qualities, but he still found little pleasure in it.

The topic of the third podcast was "Magpie to the Morning," which gave Ángel the opportunity to pull out his guitar and demonstrate Neko Case's chord progression. They discussed the lyrics and Oberon's difficulty understanding figurative language. This conversation led (naturally) to the *Star Trek: The Next Generation* episode "Darmok," and to Ángel laughing breathlessly as he described the plot.

"See, the guy is from a culture that can only communicate in references to old stories, basically, so he keeps saying 'Darmok and Jalad at Tanagra.' But because Picard has never heard that story, he has no idea what the guy is talking about."

"That is exactly how I often feel," said Oberon, his voice warm with amusement. "They call me the elf-lord, but they should call me Picard at Tanagra."

The DOR put the podcast up every Tuesday, ending each one with Oberon's song-name. By the end of October they had over seven million downloads per week. The DOR was barely able to cope with the floods of emails it was getting—everything from lavish praise, listener requests, artists' campaigns to get their songs included in the Otherworld Project, and, of course, hate mail and death threats. It was difficult to tell if the podcast was having its intended effect of making Oberon more popular.

But the *Oberon Podcast* definitely did have one unintended effect: it made Ángel a star.

"Oh my God," said Ángel, clutching his hair. Chandler Evanston had brought some laptops from the gatehouse, and, along with Lily and Oberon, they were clicking link after link on the internet. "Oh my fucking God."

"Who is Ángel From the Oberon Podcast? We Found Out" screamed the headline at *The AV Club*. Their writer had done her homework, finding his full name and the professional website where he advertised his services as a session musician. Also featured was his long-inactive Facebook page, photos from high school and college, and the gull video.

"*How* did they find out?" he asked Chandler. At the DOR's insistence, for security, Ángel had never mentioned his last name on the podcast, and Ángel wasn't a terribly unusual name, at least among Latino men.

"I don't know," she said. "We didn't tell anyone; it makes our jobs twenty times harder."

"Maybe someone just recognized your voice," said Lily.

Ángel clicked another link. "Quiz: How Well Do You Really Know Ángel Cruz?" was on *TigerBeat*, along with the cutest of the old college pictures.

"Father of Elf-Friend Ángel Cruz Convicted of Fraud." *The Huffington Post* had Victor's Ponzi scheme plea bargain. Thankfully, they didn't seem to know that the plea had resulted in Ángel working for the DOR and living with Oberon, but the fact that Ángel was the son of a crook was now generally known across the globe. Ángel bit his lip, looking at a blurry photograph of his father leaving the Duval County Courthouse.

How humiliated Victor must feel, having his dirty laundry splashed around like that. It wasn't Ángel's fault, but guilt still clotted around his heart.

Artists he'd collaborated with over the years had been quick to advertise which songs featured Ángel Cruz on guitar, perhaps hoping for a jump in sales. Including Conner Marr.

"The DOR has been getting a lot of phone calls from the media," said Chandler. "I mean, they've always gotten a lot of press questions, but ever since you came along they've tripled."

"What do they want?"

"Confirmation of your identity. Who you are, how you met, what your relationship is."

Ángel looked up at Chandler. "Are your people protecting my friends and family from the, um, the paparazzi?" It seemed bizarre to use the word *paparazzi* in the context to his own life, but here they were. "And my brothers?"

"As much as we can," said Chandler. "Some people will eventually talk, of course. It's good that no one knows where you are."

"Ángel Cruz: Oberon's Companion Is Fiery as a Chilli Pepper." Ángel grimaced. That was a British gossip site; the chili pepper metaphor purportedly referred to his guitar-playing, but the sexual innuendo was not subtle.

Another site cut right to the heart of the matter that all the others were dancing around: "Is Ángel Cruz Gay?" They didn't know, but they managed to whip up an eight hundred-word think piece anyway, based on the available evidence: on the one hand, Ángel didn't like show tunes, but on the other hand, Ángel laughed like a girl.

"Oh, and this," said Ángel, hitting Play on a blurry online video, now a white-hot trend on Twitter. "*This* should answer that question. This is the gayest gig I ever played. I've had actual sex with men that was less gay than this gig."

The video showed Ángel on electric guitar, with Tonio Ortiz on bass and Marissa on drums, performing a raucous, gender-bending version of "Good Girls" by Elle King. Tonio and Ángel leaned into each other, their lips nearly touching the mike as they sang.

"You look so tall," said Lily.

"I look taller when I perform."

Oberon asked, "What makes this performance particularly gay? Aside from the fact that you're singing about being a bad girl."

"This was at a wedding reception down in Miami Beach right after same-sex marriage became legal," explained Ángel. "These guys had been a couple for thirty years. And they never thought they'd ever get to get married, you know? So they, and all their friends— they *really* came to party. Holy fuck, did those old gay dudes know how to party. Jesus Christ. We could barely keep up, and we were the band." The camera panned unsteadily around the reception hall, showing a sweaty swirl of dancers in their most flamboyant celebratory outfits.

"That's—" said Lily, clapping a hand over her mouth. "Oh my."

Ángel watched the video to the end. Marissa kept a rock-solid beat on the drums, her biceps flexing beneath her butterfly tattoos, and Tonio danced and flirted with Ángel as they played. Tonio was straight but an inveterate performer, and he responded to the energy in the room, strutting and leering at Ángel as he worked his bass. Ángel sighed at the loud, imperfect music, the noise, the sheer fun of it. He missed performing.

He asked Chandler, "Is the DOR going to, like, address this? Issue a press release about it?"

"No," she said.

"Do you think we should say something in the podcast?"

"No."

"If no one mentions it at all, people will keep wondering," objected Lily.

"Address what?" asked Oberon.

"I mean, we can just deny it," said Ángel. "One sentence, and then on with the show."

"If you deny it, people will take that as confirmation," said Chandler, exasperated. "Damn it, Ángel. We can't afford to have this kind of speculation."

"I'm sorry. I *do* laugh like a girl."

"Speculation about what?" asked Oberon.

"People want to know if we're fucking," said Ángel.

"Oh." Oberon paused. "No. I don't intend to address that."

"Why?" asked Ángel, curiously.

"Am I misunderstanding?" asked Oberon. "It would be a violation of your privacy to discuss that with people, wouldn't it?"

"Uh, yeah," said Ángel, clicking on a Tumblr blog called Oberangler. It was full of manga-style fan drawings of himself and Oberon. Not too X-rated, mostly just kissing. "*Carajo*. I mean. I'm not Katy Perry or anything. I can't imagine that anyone will care about this for more than five minutes. But now the God Hates Fags people and the God Hates Elves people will team up."

"They were already on the same team," said Lily.

"Probably true," sighed Chandler.

"The privacy being violated is yours." Oberon regarded Ángel gravely. "You have avoided celebrity until now. Is it too much for you? Do you want to stop doing the podcast?"

"Hell no." Ángel glared at the tablet, the headlines laden with coded homophobia and racism. "Screw these people. Let's record more today. What do you think about John Lennon?"

CHAPTER
FOURTEEN

A message from the Otherworld arrived that week.

The rose bush in Oberon's office began to softly glow at around nine in the morning. By evening it was brilliant, radiating golden light and an intoxicating floral scent, so powerful and heady that it filled the house and made Ángel dizzy. When the moon rose, the plant produced a small, oval wooden box filled with what looked like seeds. Oberon told Lily that he wasn't to be interrupted, and locked himself in his office. Ángel brought him lunch on a tray but didn't stay to eat with him, not wanting to interrupt his rapt concentration.

At dinnertime, he brought him another tray. Oberon ignored him. His lunch hadn't been touched.

The next morning, Lily said that she hadn't seen Oberon; he must have skipped his usual exercise routine and gone straight to his office.

He didn't come out for lunch. He didn't come out for dinner. Ángel's anxiety grew.

Something was wrong. He was sure of it.

Eventually, chewing his thumbnail, he went to the kitchen bank of monitors and queued up the feed for Oberon's office.

He was in there, at his desk. His head was down on his folded arms, his thick pale hair falling forward to conceal his face. The posture of his shoulders, his bowed head, spoke of dejection and defeat.

"Lily, you can call John, right?"

"Yes," she said. "I can call John. I can't call out, though."

"Will you ask John to check the video feed of Oberon's office? I want to know if Oberon has come out of there at all since the message arrived."

She called and spoke to her husband while Ángel stood and watched the monitor. After a few minutes, Lily hung up and said, "John says he's been there all night. He hasn't moved in hours."

"This is bad," said Ángel. "He could be sick or dead or something."

"Yes."

"Someone should go see."

Lily nodded. She looked pale. She had known Oberon for years, but she was clearly afraid to go into that office. "Should I—should I ask Chandler to come?"

"No. I'll go. I'll do it."

He went through the foyer into the music room, and then stood uncertainly outside the door of the office. His heart was beating fearfully. Why? Oberon needed help. Ángel was, bizarrely, Oberon's closest friend, the only person who would do this for him.

He pushed open the door.

The stereo system was playing a fae song, pure, lovely, incomprehensible, and loud enough to reverberate through Ángel's chest. Oberon was still slumped across his desk, arms folded, face buried, hair mussed.

Seeds—the messages from the oval box—were scattered across the surface of the desk and on the floor. There was a sharp chemical smell in the air, like vinegar. *Emotion*, thought Ángel, *magically expressing itself from his skin, with no one able to understand.*

Ángel approached the desk, reached for the tablet, and turned off the music. Oberon was breathing. Asleep?

"Oberon?"

He didn't move.

"Oberon." Ángel pulled a leather armchair close to the desk and sat in it, then leaned over the desk, noting that the acrid smell was rising from the fae's body.

God, what if he was really ill? Was there a doctor on the planet who would have the faintest idea how to treat him?

"Oberon!" he said loudly.

He didn't stir.

Ángel drew a breath and, in full voice, sang the nine notes of Oberon's name. Oberon's head lifted with a jerk that made Ángel jump. His eyes, flat and dull, found Ángel's.

His face was as lacking expression as the head of a coin, but his skin was gray and shiny like wet cement, and the smell rolling off him was overpowering. Not vinegar—closer to ammonia. He stared at Ángel for a blank moment, and then closed his stony eyes and dropped his head back onto the desk.

"Oberon," whispered Ángel, shocked. "What's wrong?"

He bit his lip, and grasped Oberon's hand. Oberon's whole body lurched at his touch.

Ángel sucked in a breath.

God, somehow he'd forgotten.

Electric tingles shot up Ángel's arm. The hairs lifted on Ángel's arms, on the back of his neck.

He'd gotten used to Oberon, gotten comfortable enough around him to find him attractive: his body and scent, the graceful way he moved his hands. But oh, Christ. The appalling *weirdness* of Oberon's touch, the jolt of wrongness that contact with Oberon's skin brought. Ángel closed his eyes, bit down on his cheek in the effort to not flinch away.

Oberon's palm felt cold and almost greasy. Ángel squeezed it.

"Ángel," whispered Oberon. His voice made Ángel shiver.

"Please," he said, tightening his grip. "*Oberon.* Tell me what's happened. Are you sick?"

"Sick," Oberon repeated.

Could the messages from the Otherworld have done this to him? "Tell me," he said, pressing Oberon's hand harder, ignoring the way the nerve endings in his hand prickled, the way it made his legs judder with tension. "I want to help you. Please. What can I do?"

"My friend . . . my cousin . . . is dead. She was killed. An accident. I loved her." His head was still down on the desk, concealed by the soft fall of his hair, and his voice vibrated with grief. "I knew I would never see her again, of course. I can never go home, and she could never come here. But I thought of her often. When I imagined home, I imagined her. I imagined that she was happy. But she's been dead for years, and I didn't know."

Ángel's eyes filled with tears. "I'm so sorry." He clasped Oberon's hand between both of his. Oberon didn't lift his head, but squeezed his hand back.

"You— We— When we grieve, we cry," Ángel said. "I'm sorry, I have to ask you. Is this how you grieve? Because you look *terrible*. You look like you're dying."

"I . . . might be."

"No," said Ángel. "Do you need medicine? What do you need?"

Oberon lifted his head, looked at Ángel. "I cannot," he said dully.

"Oberon, I don't know anything," insisted Ángel. "You have to tell me what to do." Oberon made no move though, and Ángel begged, "Please, baby. Please tell me."

Oberon leaned back in his chair, breaking contact with Ángel's hands; he folded his arms tightly over his chest. The rotting-turnip color of his complexion was frightening; his eyes looked glassy.

He said, "We grieve . . . When we grieve, we send our grief out for others to feel. And then those who love us come to give us comfort." He sighed. "How can I explain? If a friend were here, he would share my grief. He would touch my skin, and we would grieve together; he would feel my grief and I would feel his love, and the feelings would combine to create a new feeling, and that would, that would be . . . comforting. But there is no one, and so the feelings just build and build. There's no one to feel or to share the feeling, so it just builds. And I can't . . . I can't . . . Do you understand? What's the name for a system that reinforces itself?"

"I don't know," said Ángel, slowly. "A feedback loop, maybe?" He hesitated. "A vicious cycle."

"Yes." Oberon's voice was strained and tired. "A cycle. I don't know if I can break out of it this time."

"This time? This can kill you?"

"We aren't well adapted to living alone." Oberon's eyes closed. "We poison ourselves with our emotions when we're alone. I wasn't expected to make it this long, really."

Oh my sweet Rebecca, how your sadness claims you. Ridiculously, the MelodEye lyrics sang in Ángel's head. *How your loneliness chains you.*

He knew what he had to do, of course.

"I can't believe they sent you here by yourself," he said angrily, getting to his feet. "Fae are assholes."

He stood up and crossed around the desk to Oberon. "Put your arms down at your sides," he said, brusque with nerves. Oberon unfolded his arms and rested them on the arms of his chair, his head back, throat open and vulnerable.

"Keep your eyes closed." Ángel couldn't control the tremor in his voice. "Don't look."

He unbuttoned Oberon's black shirt and pushed it open, exposing his lean chest. "Don't look at me," he repeated, reaching over his own head to grab his shirt, pulling it off and dropping it to the floor. He climbed into Oberon's lap, legs over the arm of the chair, wrapped his arms around Oberon's shoulders, and pressed his naked torso flush against Oberon's, chest to belly.

Oberon shuddered violently.

Oh-God-oh-God-oh-God. It was like hugging an electric fence. Ángel squeezed his eyes shut against all that frightening skin touching his. His throat tightened as alien sensations flooded into him through the contact. The emotions were Oberon's—he could tell they were not his own—but he still felt them: a sharp knife-point of grief in his heart, pain that made him gasp; and a bigger, yawning emptiness, like a cold and vast sea. He bit his lip, swallowing a throat suddenly aching with sorrow. Tears of discomfort leaked out of his clenched eyelids.

After a second's hesitation, Oberon's arms wrapped tightly around Ángel's body; he pushed his face into the crook of Ángel's neck and shoulder, hugged him so hard that he forced the breath out of Ángel's lungs. He shivered and shivered in uncontrollable spasmodic bursts. His breath heaved. Ángel gritted his own teeth, concentrating on Oberon's distress. The sour smell of his body filled Ángel's nostrils; his grief continued to flood into him.

"Shh, baby," whispered Ángel, running a hand inside Oberon's shirt collar and rubbing the bare skin of his shoulders, ignoring the tears that were streaming down his own face. "It's okay. It'll be okay." His other hand stroked Oberon's hair.

Oh, Oberon's hair was so soft. Straight, cool, silky threads that slipped between his fingers. He'd always wanted to touch it. He turned his face and wept silently into that corn silk hair.

How long they sat entwined like that, Ángel didn't know. It seemed to take a long time—hours, maybe—before Oberon's convulsive shivering quieted, his gulping breaths calmed. The nature of the emotions filling Ángel's chest seemed to change, became something softer and sweeter, something he didn't have words for. Still strange, and uncomfortable, but different.

"What was her name?" asked Ángel.

Oberon sang the name. Seven syllables, lovely. He rocked slightly, cradling Ángel, and sang the name, again and again.

After a while, he stopped rocking and fell quiet, relaxing against Ángel.

"Is it helping?" Ángel managed to ask. "I know I'm not— I don't know how to . . . whatever." *How do you make an emotion-song that would comfort a fae? How long do I have to do this?*

"It's helping," Oberon said softly.

He stroked a broad palm up and down Ángel's bare spine, and it was all Ángel could do not to physically squirm.

"I almost think I could sleep," said Oberon.

"That sounds good. Sleep, and tomorrow eat something." He started to move.

"Will you stay?" Oberon's arms tightened. "I am selfish, Ángel. I know it is hard for you. But I am afraid to be alone. Afraid of falling. Will you stay while I sleep?"

"It's like medicine, right?" Ángel said shakily. "Yes, okay."

Oberon stood up, lifting Ángel in his arms. Ángel was shocked by how strong the fae was; Ángel was skinny but had never, until now, felt particularly dainty. Oberon carried him effortlessly to the couch and collapsed onto it, lying on his side and tucking Ángel against his chest, belly to belly, wrapping his arms around him. A big hand went into Ángel's hair, cupping his head. Ángel repressed a whimper.

"All right?"

"Yes," Ángel whispered.

Oberon sighed deeply and fell heavily asleep, his body pinning Ángel's to the couch.

Somehow, eventually, Ángel slept too.

He woke up in the morning, after a night of wild and discordant dreams, deeply relaxed and drowning in sensual pleasure.

He was warm. He was being cuddled. His cock was hard and was cradled against something toasty, and his body tingled everywhere in an entirely pleasant way. A smell like gingersnaps and sex filled his nostrils.

Oberon was better.

The envoy had rolled over onto his back, and Ángel was sprawled on his chest, his hair spread on Oberon's smooth pecs and his dick and balls pressed against the slim thigh that lodged firmly between his legs. Apparently still asleep, Oberon was vibrating—not shivering anymore, but purring. The rolling pulse went through Ángel's body. It was the noise Oberon sometimes made when he was happy: sustained, barely audible.

Ángel had done it. He'd comforted Oberon, he'd helped keep the grief from building up in his skin and killing him. What his skin was doing to Ángel now was the shivery agony of fae magic that he had felt before yesterday. It was thrilling through Ángel's belly and chest, which were pressed against Oberon's bare skin.

Agony was maybe not the right word. Because it was weird and uncomfortable, but shudderingly pleasurable too.

Gently, so as not to awaken him, Ángel lifted his head. Oberon wasn't gray anymore—his face was restored to an even white color, like sweet cream, flushed a little darker across his lips and under his eyes. Ángel looked blearily through the tendrils of his hair, down at the sinewy chest under his cheek and saw that the strange pale skin there was now dappled with shadowy golden-pink rosettes.

Those had definitely not been there last night. Did he have measles or something? Worried, Ángel jostled Oberon to waken him.

"Oberon?" he said. "You've broken out in spots, baby. Are you okay?"

"Yes," said Oberon, without opening his eyes. "I'm much better. Don't worry about the spots."

Okay. Ángel tried to disentangle himself from Oberon's grasp, so that he could crawl back to the privacy of his room. It was hopeless to imagine that Oberon hadn't noticed his erection digging into his thigh, but at least he could take it away.

But Oberon did not let him go. He tightened his hold and rolled over onto his side. Ángel found himself sandwiched between the back of the couch and Oberon's warm body, spooned, Oberon's chest against his back, sending tingles through his skin. Ángel could protest. He could struggle. He could scramble over the back of the couch and escape. Instead, he remained still, frozen with equal parts excitement and fear, allowing Oberon to press a thigh between his legs, nuzzle his face in Ángel's hair. Oberon put his palm over Ángel's hammering heart, stroked his chest. Ángel closed his eyes, pressed his hot cheek against the cool leather of the couch, and breathed deeply. His erect dick was trapped in his jeans.

"You restored me," Oberon said softly. "You probably saved my life. I never expected you would do this."

"Is . . . that why I'm here?" asked Ángel, his voice throaty. "To do this?"

Oberon sighed, cheek against Ángel's nape. "Watching people helps," he said. "I expected little more than the comfort of watching you. Listening to you. Though I did hope we would be friends, of course." He continued petting Ángel's chest for a moment. "I hoped that you might turn to me, as you were already partially estranged from your family, and must be lonely. I told you before, I am enormously selfish."

"You could have just grabbed me. Taken what you need."

"And absorb your fear and horror through my skin into my brain? Like a thirsty man drinking poison? No, never."

"I was scared. Did you feel that?"

"Yes. It interrupted my own feelings, changed them . . . I could tell you did not find it pleasant. But that you were not unwilling."

Currently Ángel was, more or less, willing. Though Oberon's powerful body pinned him fast to the couch, it was an embrace, not a wrestling hold. He could get free, if he truly wanted to. But the horrible truth was that he had never been so turned on in his life, so he continued to lie still, feeling Oberon purring against his back.

Oberon's hand caressed his chest and throat, making Ángel shiver. "You called me baby," he said, his voice a velvety whisper. "Like a lover."

Ángel drew a breath to deny it but Oberon said, "Don't lie. Ángel. I've learned so much about you this night." His hand stroked Ángel, throat down to navel and then back up, sending jolts of terrified desire through Ángel's body. Ángel shifted anxiously, fingers seeking purchase on the shiny leather of the couch. His butt was pressed tight into Oberon's groin, but he felt no hard bulge there. Once again, he wondered if Oberon was actually not male, or if male fae were different from male humans.

But then Oberon blew all rational thought out of Ángel's mind.

"You're very sensual," said Oberon. "Very sensitive. I think you are easily aroused. Quick to climax and quick to revive for more. You are made for pleasure." His purring voice and stroking hands were creating electric shocks in Ángel's skin. Ángel was breathing hard; he squeezed his eyes shut, feeling his body approach the verge of orgasm just from Oberon's words, his voice.

"How you fight it, though, beloved. How you've transformed delight into shame. Your love of sex makes you feel out of control and demeaned, but it's a joyous thing." His lips against Ángel's ear, his fingers playing with Ángel's nipples, Oberon breathed, "I can feel it in your skin."

"Oh, don't say that," protested Ángel, shuddering.

"Ángel." Oberon's hand slid straight down into the front of Ángel's jeans and firmly grasped Ángel's cock through the cotton of his underwear.

"Oh *God*," gasped Ángel.

He knew he should say *Don't*, but couldn't. He should stop this, but he didn't want it to stop. The cotton protected his most sensitive skin from the shock of direct contact, but not from the controlled and commanding friction of Oberon's palm as it stroked up and down in the tightly confined space of Ángel's jeans. So hot, and so slow, giving intense pleasure while denying him the rhythm he needed to get off. Ángel whimpered, writhed, wanting both to escape and to thrust wildly into that burning hand, able somehow to do neither.

"It's all right to love it," whispered Oberon.

"I—"

"I am only a man."

"You *aren't*!"

Oberon began to pull his hand out of Ángel's pants, but Ángel grabbed his wrist. He pressed Oberon's palm hard against his erection. Oberon wrapped his fingers around him tightly again, stroking. Need overwhelmed fear, and Ángel avidly fucked his hand, unable to help himself. The motion dragged his underwear down. Oberon's bare palm found the corona of his cock, and that was all it took: Ángel's body arched like a bow, taut with ecstasy, his head back on Oberon's shoulder. He made no sound as delight smashed through him, but Oberon grunted, hand continuing to work the head of Ángel's cock as come shot from it in thick spurts. Then Oberon's mouth and tongue were on his neck, as if he were tasting Ángel's orgasm on his skin, and Ángel shuddered, bringing his hands to his face.

A few minutes passed. Oberon held him while his breathing and heartbeat gradually returned to something resembling normal.

As the white-hot haze of sex slowly cleared from Ángel's mind, the intimacy of what had just happened hit him. *Oh shit.*

"That was so beautiful," murmured Oberon. "Oh, I definitely did not expect this, beloved."

Aaand, that meant it was Oberon's turn now, right? The thought was unbearable. Suddenly Ángel needed to get away. Leaving a man unsatisfied was pure selfishness. He was inconsiderate, terrible in bed—it didn't matter. *Gotta go.* He tried to sit, and when Oberon's arms tightened on him he said, a little sharply, "Let me up."

Oberon's embrace fell away, and Ángel scrambled over him off the couch and staggered. Weak-legged with shock, he found his shirt on the floor and pulled it on, mopping the spunk off his abdomen as he did so. Most of it had gone onto the couch and Oberon's hand.

"You require privacy now?" asked Oberon politely.

He was reclining on the couch, propped up on his elbows. His face was as remote as ever, like the surface of the moon, but his skin was practically glowing. His shirt was open to expose his lovely white chest, now strongly marked with rosettes the deep red-brown of balsamic vinegar. Ángel expected to see an erection tenting the front of his black pants, but there was none.

Was Oberon not excited? Had what happened been totally one-sided? Or maybe he didn't have a penis at all?

And what could Ángel say now? Thanks? *Thanks for the really effective handjob—thanks for calling me beautiful? Thanks, sorry, but please don't ever touch me again?*

They were all the wrong thing to say, flippant or hurtful or true. "Yes," he managed. "Privacy."

Oberon gazed at him silently for a moment. "Then I will see you later."

CHAPTER FIFTEEN

Ángel shivered in the shower, hands braced on the tiles. Hot water pounded on his head and poured down his body, washing away come, sweat, and whatever emotion-magic Oberon had infused into his skin, but failing to warm him.

It wasn't just that the fae had gotten him off in about seven seconds, although that was bad enough. It wasn't just that the experience had—if fae physiognomy were anything like human—apparently left Oberon unmoved.

But the way Oberon could read Ángel's skin. Feel his feelings.

"Quick to climax and quick to revive for more. . . . Your love of sex makes you feel out of control and demeaned."

True, true. Goddamn it, damningly true. And not something he'd never heard before.

"You fuck like an alley cat," Con had said.

Before that: *"Yeah, that's the way you spics like it, isn't it?"* laughed the anonymous guy in the Orlando parking garage. A mean laugh, after he held him by the hair and came in his face.

And before that: the priest, the confessional. Seventeen-year-old Ángel, gay as a daffodil, who didn't exactly feel a deep connection to God, but who loved belonging to the Church. Even though he knew perfectly well that the Church's stance on homosexuality wasn't terribly welcoming, he'd somehow trusted in the Church's welcome. Perhaps because Father Dennis was a good friend of his father's, a kind of benevolent, distant uncle to Ángel. He hadn't expected . . . Well. He certainly hadn't expected Father Dennis's weary cynicism:

"I'll tell you what you're going to do, because you're all the same. You'll care about sex above the righteousness or the love of God.

You'll be promiscuous. You'll spend your life seeking pleasure, trying to find meaning in more and more and more sex, and with every orgasm you're going to get farther and farther away from Christ. And in your soul you'll know this is true, but you'll do it anyway, and you'll die sick and alone and unloved, a million miles away from God."

He ducked his head under the spray for one final rinse, then turned off the shower and stood, feeling the water turn cold as it streamed from his hair down his back. He groped for a towel and scrubbed his skin harshly.

He believed that there was nothing wrong with being gay. He believed that there was nothing wrong with having a healthy sex drive, or even with having a taste for sex that was a little rough and raunchy. He believed that being Latino had nothing to do with how much he liked sex, though he'd encountered plenty of people who did. He believed that the priest had been a bad priest, who was not supposed to talk to people that way, and who was also not supposed to out gay teenagers to their parents—*Thanks a lot, Father Dennis.*

But the priest's words had bruised him, and sometimes he could still feel the ache. There had been times he'd felt unbalanced and uncontrolled, because he wanted sex so much. Times he'd sought sex at the expense of his self-respect. A recurring, high-risk compulsion that he couldn't seem to leave behind. A secret frenzy under the skin: *"fiery chili pepper."*

This afternoon on the couch had to be a new low.

And Oberon had felt Ángel's shameful weakness. Knew all about it.

Ángel had never felt so exposed before. Just by touching him, Oberon had learned more about Ángel than any lover ever had. It was an alarmingly helpless sensation. What else had he learned? Could he feel Ángel's physical sensations, as well as his emotions? He'd *licked* Ángel when he came—had he somehow tasted it? Felt Ángel's climax? Did Ángel's come, slick on his hand, give him accurate information about Ángel's hormonal balance, general health, fertility, history?

Ugh. Ángel shuddered.

He wanted to go back under the bed.

He pulled on warm clothes and went outside. It was clear and cold, the wind sharp as glass even through his new coat, freezing his wet hair; the grass was crunchy under his feet.

He walked the perimeter of the wall. There was nowhere else to go.

Eventually he had to go back in. He was, on top of everything else, light-headed with hunger; he hadn't eaten since yesterday, and he had the kind of rabbitlike metabolism that wouldn't let him skip too many meals.

He went in, hung up his coat, toed off his boots, and padded into the kitchen, hoping to raid the refrigerator without attracting notice.

But luck was not with him. As he went through the music room toward the kitchen, Oberon came out of his office. He approached Ángel, a hand extended to touch his shoulder.

Ángel shied violently, dodging the hand and stepping away from Oberon until his hip hit the piano.

Oberon froze. "Are you angry, Ángel?"

"No, of course not." Ángel carefully avoided Oberon and went into the kitchen.

Oberon followed him. "You're frightened?" he guessed. Like he was tasting the air, trying to figure out what emotional signal Ángel was sending.

"Just hungry." Ángel found some bread and peanut butter and began assembling a sandwich, aware that Oberon was watching. "Are you all better? That was quick."

"You are lying. You are upset. But I can't tell what's wrong from your expression. Won't you tell me? Or let me—" He extended a hand again, as if to cup Ángel's cheek.

"Stop!" snapped Ángel, leaning away from him.

"Ángel—"

"No!" His hand was tight around the knife he was using to spread peanut butter. A pathetic, blunt weapon, but he was clutching it. "I get to say *no*, right?" he snarled.

Oberon faltered backward, as from a hot stove or a vicious dog. "Of course you get to say no," he said, his voice low.

"You won't get sick, will you? You're not telling me you'll die if I don't let you touch me?" Ángel knew he had gone nasty, and couldn't seem to help it.

After a moment, Oberon replied, "Not touching you hardly causes the same degree of pain as learning of the death of one of my oldest friends," he said. "I expect I will survive it."

Ángel's face went hot, as though he'd been slapped. It *stung*; not just the words, but something in Oberon's tone scorched the tips of Ángel's nerve endings.

He drew in a shuddering breath. "What was *that*?" he whispered.

Oberon didn't say anything.

Ángel carefully braced his hands on the counter.

Oberon copied the gesture, his fingers splayed on the granite countertop.

Okay, Ángel told himself. *Okay*. Oberon didn't understand. He was trying to understand. He had requested that they not lie to each other. He had asked for information. They needed to get clear. Ángel could do this.

"You have magic…" Ángel's words came out slowly, not sure what he was trying to say. "You have magic in your voice, and you can use it."

"That was wrong of me," Oberon said. "I am confused and angry. I hurt you and I am sorry. I apologize."

"Okay." He nodded. "And I'm sorry for lying to you. I *am* upset."

Oberon nodded as well—an unnatural thing for him to do; he must be copying Ángel's gesture. "Will you tell me why you are upset?"

"I—" Ángel took a steadying breath. "Okay. I'll try. But sometimes when I'm upset, it's hard to talk about why."

"Oh. I did not know that."

"I'll try," he repeated. "So. You can't go home again, even if you get sick?"

"*When* I get sick. No. I cannot go back, and I know of no plans to send another. I am alone here, until I die."

"Which is why you need me."

Oberon's voice had gone soothing. "This was my life before you came. This will be my life when you leave. It's not something I expect you to fix."

The muscles in Ángel's jaw and shoulder felt tight. He forced himself to relax. "You can read my mind when you touch me."

"Certainly not."

"Don't lie. You can," he said. "This is . . . this is about privacy. Which I know you don't understand. But when you touched me you read me like a book, and learned things that I don't actually reveal to people. And it scared me."

"No. It's no different than seeing the expressions on your face."

"It's totally different. It's— You told me there was a difference between watching and searching. You *searched* me. I didn't let you. I can't do the same to you."

After a pause, Oberon said, "I see. It is natural for me to touch my friends, to understand how they feel. I learned immediately that humans find my touch uncomfortable. But you and I are friends. Isn't that right?"

Misery choked Ángel, replacing his anger. "I know I'm not being fair," he said. "I touched you first. I didn't *not* want what happened. And now I'm being a jerk about it. I just . . . I didn't expect you were going to . . . It was really intimate, and I—I don't—I don't."

Oberon's voice, when he spoke, was soothing and warm. "Intimacy, like privacy, is a concept that I struggle to understand."

"It's when you're with someone . . . in private? When you choose to share your privacy with someone? I don't know how to explain it." Ángel backed away from the counter, leaned on the refrigerator. "They say women are better at talking about stuff like this, but the girls I know don't talk about it with me. My mom would cut off her hand before she sat down to talk about intimacy."

"Then how do you know what it is?" asked Oberon reasonably.

"You ask hard questions," complained Ángel.

He had no better answer than that, and after a moment Oberon said, "Ángel, I cannot read your thoughts. I am learning to read emotions on your skin, and these are always truthful, but I don't always understand what they mean." He paused. "Right now, I can tell that you are upset, but I don't truly understand why. But I have made you feel unhappy, and I am sorry for that."

Ángel nodded. "Same here."

"Thank you. I cannot turn off my perception of your emotions, any more than you can strike yourself deaf. I would not if I could. But I will not touch you again, unless you invite me to."

"Thank you," repeated Ángel, through a dry throat.

"I did not learn anything about you that was not beautiful."

Ángel laughed bitterly. "Oh, right. Okay." Surely nothing about Ángel's weak, confused nature was *beautiful*.

He grabbed an apple and fled up the stairs to his room.

CHAPTER SIXTEEN

Over the next few days, Ángel spent as much time as he could in his room. Oberon kept to his regular schedule of workouts, meals, and work, so it was possible to avoid him. When, over dinner one evening, Oberon broached the topic of recording another podcast, Ángel pleaded a headache: "We have some in the can, don't we?" he said, knowing he was being cowardly. "Maybe tomorrow we could do it?"

"All right," said Oberon peacefully, and they finished eating without any further conversation.

"What is the *matter* with you?" demanded Lily after Oberon went back to his office.

"Don't start," he said.

"But what happened?" Her smooth brow was furrowed with bewilderment.

Which surely meant that John Va and Chandler Evanston and the rest of the security team hadn't watched the tape and seen what had happened in Oberon's office. That was good. But if his behavior became too much of a mystery they would watch it. And that would be bad.

Ángel said, "He was upset because he found out his friend died. And I, uh, hugged him. And that helped, that made him feel better. But it was difficult. Have you ever touched him?"

Lily shook her head, eyes wide.

"It's, um. It's difficult. He— It feels, it feels really—"

She was still shaking her head. "I don't think I could have done it," she whispered. "I don't think I could touch him."

It feels incredible. How could he explain—to anyone—that the problem wasn't how much he hated it, but how much he didn't?

"I'm sorry. I'm trying to get over it. I know it's not good. It's immature and whatever. But today—I'm going outside."

"The sun's starting to go down early. Come in before it gets dark." She smiled at him. "Don't make him worry!"

"Okay. Thanks." And he escaped outside.

He came back in the autumn twilight, in time for dinner. As he was hanging up his coat, he could hear Lily laughing in the kitchen. He followed the sound and found her stirring soup and chatting with Oberon.

"Oberon was asking about Halloween in Vietnam," Lily said, her dark eyes shining. "But I don't know. I'm from Los Angeles. I don't think they do Halloween over there."

Oberon turned his eyes to Ángel. "Do they do Halloween in Cuba?"

"Never been there." Ángel made a stab at relaxing in the kitchen doorway, an arm's-length away from Oberon. "It's the eve of All Saints' Day if you're Catholic. When we remember all the saints and martyrs, and those who have died."

"For most Americans," said Lily, "it's really about children and candy."

"You'd like it," said Ángel. "The neighborhood kids come and ring the doorbell, dressed up in different costumes."

"I would love to see that," Oberon agreed, gravely. "I've only seen it in movies. I understand that it's customary for the children to threaten me with property damage unless I provide them with candy?"

"That's right," said Ángel. "Do we get a lot of trick-or-treaters up here, Lily?"

"Not so many."

"Of course we don't," said Oberon, not picking up on the joke. "We are miles from anywhere. And my security team has always kept children away from me, unfortunately. I think children are very interesting."

Something clicked. "Wait, today is Halloween?"

"October thirty-first," she said.

"Oh." Ángel's mood fell straight down into sadness.

He hadn't gotten any email in several days.

Lily didn't seem to notice. She was saying to Oberon, "There's no special dinner, like other holidays—no Halloween foods, except candy. You give out candy all evening, and then you eat what's left over until you feel sick."

And then you dress up and go out with Marissa and Jason and Trina and Tonio and Lindsey. And you drink weird Halloween-themed shots, and check out the hotties but you don't ditch your friends for them, and you dance and dance and dance.

"Do you like Halloween, Ángel?" asked Oberon.

"I do," Ángel said. "It's my favorite."

Ángel couldn't sleep that night. The clock said 11:15, and he was as awake as if it were noon.

His brothers and their families were probably in bed, since it was a weeknight.

His friends were probably out celebrating. Because it was Halloween, not because it was Ángel's birthday. Which they'd all forgotten.

Stupid that it bothered him so much. Oberon had gone without news from his home for three years—hadn't been in the presence of another member of his own people for over eight years, and his people communicated by touch. How painful would *that* be? Ángel had only been away from home for two months, and was so lonely and so angry about it he wanted to punch a wall.

Hell with this. He put on a pair of shorts, tied his hair back in an elastic, and headed down to the gym. Starting his "Dancy Dance" playlist, he turned up the volume, dimmed the lights, and began to run on the treadmill.

The gym, with its mirrored walls and ceilings, had the worst acoustics in the house, a loud cube of contentious echoes. It reminded him nicely of some of the dance clubs he'd been to.

He ran hard on the treadmill through the first few songs on the playlist—Duran Duran, Shakira, the Black Eyed Peas. After a minute and a half of Elvis Crespo's "Suavamente" he rolled off the back of the treadmill and started dancing.

He danced for over two hours straight, bouncing to Daft Punk, voguing to Madonna, swirling gothily to Siouxsie and the Banshees, breaking out his rudimentary hip-hop moves for Kendrick. "Dancy Dance" was heavy on gay club songs—Pet Shop Boys, New Order, Scissor Sisters—but he'd been steadily adding anything he liked to it. He danced to "Animals" by Maroon 5, remembering the way Marissa would flip her hair and roll her hips to this song, yelling over the noise, *We really shouldn't like this! It's totally problematic!* He jumped around to House of Pain, spun around to Dead or Alive, and lost the elastic in his hair during an exhilarating three-song Lady Gaga streak. When he got to the end of "Ray of Light" by Madonna, he was swaying with exhaustion.

Sweat dripped off the loose tips of his hair. He groped for the tablet and, panting, switched to his "Interesting Acoustic Guitar" playlist. "Cover Me Up" by Jason Isbell began to play; he stood still, letting the soft, sad, undanceable song help cool him down.

"Ángel."

He startled. Oberon was leaning in the doorway to the gym, hands in his pockets, watching him.

Ángel grabbed the tablet and turned off the music. "God, I'm sorry," he said, wondering for the first time whether the gym's soundproofing was proof against Oberon's excellent sense of hearing. "It's the middle of the night. I'm not keeping you awake, am I?"

Oberon didn't answer this. Instead he said, "When I saw you on the monitors I thought you were dancing for joy. But now that I'm here . . ."

"I'm— No, I'm okay," said Ángel automatically.

And then he thought, *God, enough*; it's not like he could pretend. This whole room probably reeked of his emotions, pouring out of his body. He amended, "No, I'm not really okay. Just feeling sorry for myself, I guess. But I feel better now."

"It's because no one emailed you on your birthday?" asked Oberon.

Surprised, Ángel said, "Yeah. You knew?"

"I should have said something."

Ángel shrugged, uncomfortable. "I haven't been talking to you. My own fault."

"But I misjudged the importance of the day." Oberon shoved off the doorway and came into the room. "It's your custom to go dancing on your birthday?"

Ángel mopped sweat off his face with his shirt, avoiding Oberon's eyes. "Do you, uh, do your people dance?"

"We do," said Oberon, approaching slowly. "We dance for celebration. We dance to perform magic. And we dance meditatively, to help process our emotions, as I think perhaps you do. But when we do it, we are not so radiant as you."

Whatever response Ángel might have made to this dried up in his throat when Oberon stepped up to him and lowered his face, as if to kiss him. "I wish you were not so sad, Ángel," he said gently, his lips a breath away from Ángel's.

Ángel's entire body went rigid.

Oberon did not move, just stood close to Ángel. His breath was cool on Ángel's hot face. It might have been nonsexual and unthreatening from anyone else, but from Oberon it was awfully, shockingly erotic. Ángel was hard, motionless, paralyzed on the knife-edge between *Please touch me* and *Please don't*.

"I'm not helping, am I?" Oberon backed away.

"'S'okay," Ángel said, his voice a little rough. Heart hammering, he walked around him, out of the gym, toward the stairs. "Night."

Not running away, not fleeing, he climbed the stairs and went to his bedroom. He closed the door behind him, but didn't turn on the light. In the darkness his shaking hands pulled down his pants.

Couldn't even wait to get to the bed.

He hissed with relief as his palm found his rigid cock, let his head fall back against the door. He pumped himself hard. Harder. He needed to come so desperately. His mind was full of the memory of Oberon's scent, his body, his skin, his hands.

There was no sound in the room except Ángel's breathing and the slap of his hand, fast and urgent. He was deliberately ungentle, his left hand chafing the weeping slit in the end of his cock as his right hand yanked. Almost painfully. If these were Oberon's hands on him—if Oberon were here—

He came so hard he stopped breathing, saw sparks of light behind his closed eyelids.

Cupping himself now protectively, Ángel slid down the door and sat on the floor. He rested his forehead against his knees, his body quivering with ecstasy and satisfaction and shame.

I'm okay. He talked himself through his tangled emotions. His life was fine. It was not so bad. He was safe, he had enough to eat, he had music to listen to, music to play. A friend in Lily. Oberon, who would not touch him unless he requested it.

But he had to stop wanting Oberon. He had to find a way to stop.

CHAPTER SEVENTEEN

He got up late, and when he went down close to lunchtime Chandler was there. She and Oberon were in the dining room under the gigantic chandelier, discussing some matter of security. Ángel quietly prepared a pot of coffee in the kitchen.

His mind was a little clearer this morning, and he was trying to think rationally about last night. He obviously could not go on like this for four years—wanting Oberon and hating himself for wanting him. It was cruelly unfair to Oberon, for one thing.

What would it be like to know that your very touch revolted people? To come from a culture where touch was a basic form of communication, and to find yourself surrounded by people who found touching you repellant? Like being struck blind— Or, no. Like being surrounded by people who *preferred to be blind* rather than to look at you?

How lonely that would be.

Not that Ángel could honestly claim to be *repelled*. Once he had seen a picture of the president of the United States shaking Oberon's hand—hadn't he? He wasn't sure. It seemed unlikely that Oberon's touch affected anyone else quite the way it affected him. Unless the president, after shaking Oberon's hand, had been compelled to beat off too.

Ángel snorted with laughter, pouring coffee into hot sweetened milk.

At that moment the sound of his own name caught his attention.

"—messages for Ángel?" Oberon was asking. Ángel eavesdropped while he sipped his coffee.

"Oh, yes, I forgot," said Chandler. "The DOR forwarded a package a few days ago from his friend. I'll have someone bring it up today."

"Chandler," said Oberon, and the change in his voice was electric—all the grave courtesy had gone out of it, and it was glacier-cold.

Ángel's head whipped around. He saw Chandler's response: her back straightened, her chin went up. Military attention, shoulders back. Perhaps an ingrained reaction to authority.

Oberon, in that quiet but brutal, arctic tone, asked, "Is there a reason you disobeyed my orders?"

"I—"

Ángel put down his coffee and went into the dining room.

"I told you not to interfere with communications between Ángel and Marissa Sommers." Oberon's face was as blank as always, but he had weaponized his voice—activated some musical tone that went straight to the fear center of the brain and flipped a switch there. It was aimed like a pistol at Chandler. "You chose to do so, delaying his package several days, and in doing you caused Ángel pain. *Tell me why.*"

Chandler was pale, her wide eyes fixed on the wall, knees locked to keep from swaying. She looked like she were being screamed at by a drill sergeant. Ángel felt ill with shock, and he was only getting backsplash from the voice. "I'm sorry, sir," Chandler managed to say. "I didn't realize it was important."

"That is a lie," said Oberon, voice bloodcurdling. "I told you it was important. I believe that you prefer annoying Ángel to following my instructions."

"No, sir."

"John Va will take over the security team from now on. You will return to the DOR—"

"No," said Ángel. "No. Please don't do that."

Oberon turned his leopard eyes on Ángel, and Ángel shrank back. But the envoy's voice was slightly gentler when he said, "The position of chief of security is one of trust."

Ángel's mouth and throat were dry as he said, "And you can trust her. To keep you alive. That's her real job. Not forwarding my mail."

"Her malingering made you think that your friends forgot your birthday, and as a result you felt abandoned and estranged. Do you deny this?"

"No. I just— Don't fire her, Oberon. It's not that big a deal."

The air smelled dry and hot, like burning salt. Chandler audibly swallowed. Oberon said softly, "You and I both know that isolation is a big deal. I would minimize yours as much as possible. I can't do that if Chandler is *deliberately undermining my wishes.*" The last sentence came out like the crack of a whip, snapping across Chandler's face, and she flinched.

Ángel clenched his teeth. He forced himself to reach out and brushed his fingertips to the back of Oberon's hand. "That's too much," he said. "Oberon. Let it go."

Oberon went perfectly still at Ángel's touch. Ángel ran his fingers down over Oberon's knuckles, squeezed Oberon's fingers, very gently, and then let go. "Bring it down. Please. Chandler's sorry. She won't do it again."

"I require that she do as she's told," Oberon said, but much of the power of his voice was now leashed.

"Remember the riot at the Tiepolo Ballroom?" asked Ángel. "She had a plan. She kept calm. She kept you safe, evacuated the building, kept the place from burning down. Only seven injuries, right? She's really good. The thing with the package is not as important. Let it go, Oberon."

Oberon stared at him for a long moment. The only sound was Chandler's trembling breathing; she sounded like she was trying not to cry. Ángel kept his eyes averted from her, not wanting to witness her humiliation.

"You are the one injured by her actions, Ángel," said Oberon at last, "so in this instance I will let you decide. But if anything like this happens again—"

"It won't," said Chandler softly.

"No." He gave her one last glare, infused his voice with glinting steel. "Go back to the gatehouse, then. The package from Marissa will be here soon?"

"Immediately, sir."

"All right," growled Oberon.

Chandler threw a fast, wild-eyed glance at Ángel and escaped.

Oberon and Ángel stood there in the dining room for a while after the front door slammed behind her. The air around Oberon hummed with tension, smelled like chalk dust and ozone. Weirdly, Ángel was worried about him, rather than afraid of him. *Bring it down, Oberon.*

In a light tone, Ángel said, "Well, holy shit. That was scary as fuck."

He went to the kitchen, fluttering his hands at the ends of his wrists, rotating his shoulders, trying to shake off the tension. He poured a cup of black espresso for Oberon—he didn't really like coffee, but he liked it better without milk and sugar—and brought it along with his own cup back into the dining room. He dropped into a chair, and after a moment, Oberon sat across the ivory-and-gilt table from him, touching his cup but not drinking.

"Scary?" said Oberon, in an absolutely neutral tone. "I am unarmed. She has no need to actually fear me."

"If you talked to me like that I'd piss my pants."

"Is that a metaphor?"

"No. Literally. That thing you did with your voice was . . . You were blazing at her like the sun; I could see scorch marks on her forehead." Oberon stared at him, and Ángel added, "That was a metaphor. Not really. But I don't think you understand how you affect people, Oberon. Couldn't you . . . couldn't you smell it? How you were frightening her? Or feel it, or whatever you do?"

Oberon lifted the espresso cup to his nose, inhaling the aroma. "I could, actually, but . . . I was annoyed."

"Yeah, that came across," said Ángel. "I was about to start singing 'Let It Go' to distract you."

Oberon took a deliberate sip of his coffee. "I hardly think that would have made me less annoyed."

Ángel laughed, some of the tension in his chest loosening. "I used to like that song, but then I played a *Frozen*-themed birthday party and we sang it over and over again. Imagine three dozen six-year-olds all singing along, all missing that high e-flat at the same time."

"Why did you do that to yourself?"

"A favor for a friend."

They sat companionably for a few minutes, drinking coffee. Ángel's fingertips still tingled slightly from where he had—voluntarily, of his own free will—touched Oberon's skin. Oberon seemed relaxed, willing to sit companionably with Ángel. Above them, the mirrored chandelier cast motes of light around the room.

They were almost finished with their coffee when the front door opened and John appeared with a USPS priority mail box in his hand. "Good morning, sir," he said pleasantly to Oberon, coming into the dining room and handing the box to Ángel. "Here we go."

"Thanks."

"Is Lily in the kitchen?"

"I think she's upstairs cleaning the bedrooms."

"All right if I run up to see her before I head back?"

"Of course, John," said Oberon.

John disappeared up the stairs. Ángel glanced nervously at Oberon, then applied his attention to his present. The tape holding the box closed had, naturally, already been slit, the contents searched by Chandler and her goons. Good thing Marissa hadn't bothered with pretty wrapping paper.

Inside was a card, signed by the whole gang; a handmade braided leather bracelet embellished with one of Ángel's favorite picks—a Gravity Gold—and a used thrift-store T-shirt from the first professional venue Ángel had ever played, the long-extinct Manatee Bar, which featured a peeling pink aquatic mammal and the cursive word *Chillin'*.

It was a totally Marissa gift—not expensive, but highly personal. It was clear that she'd searched for something that he—and only he— would like.

"I really do wish I'd gotten this yesterday," he admitted, holding the bracelet to his wrist, deciding that the black leather of the band and the cream-colored vinyl of the guitar pick looked nice against his brown skin.

"An ornament?" said Oberon.

"Yeah. Not much call for it here, but I want to see how it looks." Ángel fumbled one-handed to secure the bracelet onto his wrist.

Oberon extended a hand. Ángel hesitated, then held out his arm, and Oberon, emitting his rumbling subsonic vibration, fastened the clasp. Ángel's nerves jumped when Oberon's fingers gently brushed the inside of his wrist like nettles, but he bit his lip, hard, and forced himself not to recoil.

He had the strangest feeling—as though the fastening of the bracelet were a ritual. As if, by allowing it, he had given Oberon permission to pay him court.

CHAPTER
EIGHTEEN

Angel awakened the next morning feeling as though everything had changed.

He blinked. The washed-new feeling came from the quality of the light coming through the window: it had a pearly sheen, unlike anything he'd ever seen before. He got up and peered out.

The ground was covered with a thick blanket of snow, and more was falling, heavily, silently, in fat clumps rather than individual flakes. It was like the cover of a Christmas card, all sparkling and soft. Except in Christmas cards the sky was usually blue, not that low menacing gray.

He washed and dressed and ran downstairs, singing "Sweet Baby James." He caught Lily in the kitchen and, since "Sweet Baby James" was in three-four, waltzed her around the island, singing.

"Did you look outside?" He swung her in a circle.

"Yes, it started around midnight, and we have four inches! We're going to be stuck until the snowplows come."

He stopped dancing. "We'll be forced to cannibalism. We should start with the security team. They're beefy. I'm stringy and tough."

"Hah," she said. "You're the youngest, and they have guns."

"That is a good point. I think I'll go outside. Should I make a snowman? Is that an appropriate snow activity?"

"They never look as good as in the cartoons," she warned him. "You want breakfast?"

He pulled on his boots. "Yes, when I come back in. You don't have to make it."

"That's what I do," she said. "Put on a hat, or you'll catch a cold."

He put on a hat and crunched out into the snow. The world was strangely silent, the mountains surrounding the estate invisible behind low clouds, the air full of downy flakes.

Ángel didn't make a snowman, but he did make and throw several snowballs. Then he discovered the satisfaction of creating a line of lone footprints across an unblemished blanket of snow. He walked for an hour, crisscrossing his footprints, the snow getting deeper and deeper around his legs.

As he rounded the house he saw, in the distance, a slim figure waiting for him. He walked toward it, his mood was so light that he considered starting a snowball fight.

The cold did wonderful things for Chandler Evanston's Snow White coloring: her pale cheeks were flushed with red, like poppies; her black-lashed eyes were ice blue and sparkling. She was not smiling. As usual.

"This place is dead to security. The cameras at the house and the cameras on the walls—none of them give a view of this spot."

This was weird. "Oh?" he said, abandoning any idea of playing in the snow with her.

"I wanted to thank you for intervening for me with Oberon, Ángel." Her voice was stiff and awkward.

"Oberon overreacted."

"He did. He was right, though," she said. "I lied about your package. I was being passive-aggressive, and I apologize."

"Well, that was kind of bitchy."

"I know." She pressed her lips together. "This job ties me in knots. But it's not an excuse for dishonesty. I'm sorry."

She was probably not a person who apologized very often. Too lighthearted to hold a grudge, he said, "It wasn't a firing offense. Not bad enough for . . . what he was doing."

"Does he ever talk to you like that? The way he talked to me?"

"No," said Ángel. "Well, maybe once, a little. But I was definitely pissing him off."

He looked around, newly aware of how isolated they were out here on the lawn, in the falling snow. Chandler had come out here deliberately, to talk to him where no cameras, no microphones could find them. He made a note of the location.

Chandler said, "I want you to know something, Ángel. We never watch the cameras inside the house. We installed them, because those were our instructions, and we have access to the feeds, but we're security, not voyeurs. When we heard you'd destroyed the cameras in your room, we cheered."

"Uh, thanks. That's good to know."

She shifted her feet in the snow. "If you need to get away, Ángel, please speak to me. I'll see what I can do."

"What are you saying?" he demanded.

She looked torn, as if what she was doing was a crime against her own loyalty. "Just that. You're in a strange situation—none of us realized how strange until you got here."

"So you did watch that video," said Ángel. "The one from the office. The morning after he was sick."

Chandler dropped her eyes. "Only me," she said. "The others haven't seen it."

"Okay." He wondered how hard it was for her to keep that video from her team. She seemed to hate dishonesty.

"I've been in contact with your friend Marissa," she added.

He raised his eyebrows at her. "Oh, you have, have you? And what do you think? Gorgeous, right?"

It was a complete shot in the dark, intended mostly to annoy, but the way her entire face went as red as cherries told him that he'd hit a bull's-eye.

He laughed. "She's brilliant too. She just got out of a relationship, you know. She might need a shoulder to cry on."

"Be serious!" Chandler snapped, her voice going up. "I got complacent. I forgot he was a monster."

"He's not a monster," scoffed Ángel.

"He *is*." Her face was white and passionate. "I was on his security team when he first arrived. I lived with him in his little condo in Atlanta. I remember how hard it was to be close to him all the time; constantly afraid that he'd try to touch me." He could see a muscle jump in her jaw. "You and Lily both, you're in total denial. I understand that. The only way you can bear to be around him every day—the only way you can bear what he does—is to pretend that he's a man. But he's not a man, any more than a python is a man."

"He's not a python!"

"You have no idea what motivates him or what his agenda is. Marissa asked me to look out for you. But you have to be smart, Ángel. Look out for yourself too."

"You're wrong."

She just shook her head, pityingly. "I'm not wrong. But the point is—you're the only one in the house who has to be alone with him, who has no one to turn to. Lily has John, but you don't have anyone. Except now you have me. If you need to get away from here, you come to me."

"I really don't think—" stammered Ángel. "But thanks. Thank you. It's good to know I've got a—" *friend* didn't seem like the appropriate word "—an out. If I need one. But I really do think you're wrong."

She nodded shortly. "Right or wrong, remember this. I'm keeping constant watch on the camera that overlooks the pool," she said. "It's out of sight from both Oberon's office and his bedroom, and I've looped his feeds of that camera so he won't see anything there. If there's an emergency, go there. Or put a message in front of that camera. I'll see it, and he won't. Got it?"

"Yeah."

"Then you'd better get back," she said, turning to go. "We're in a blind spot here," she called over her shoulder, "but he'll notice if we stay too long."

He stood in the snow and watched her stride away.

He should have been relieved, or even delighted, to know he had an ally on the security team. What he felt was confused.

He's not a python, he thought, stubbornly. *He's not a monster. Is he?*

By the time he got back to the mansion his happy mood had dissipated, and he mostly felt wet and cold. He ate the breakfast Lily had made him—rice with bean sprouts and a soft egg, good with sriracha—then went up to his room and found the tablet. There was an email waiting for him.

Glad you like it, mi vida, it said. *Feliz cumpleaños. Wish we could have gone out to celebrate.*

In the real world, he and Marissa usually communicated via text, which was not allowed here in Oberonville. So their emails tended to be text-like—terse, to the point, full of shorthand and in-jokes.

He typed, *Me too. I miss you. Hope the paps aren't bothering you too much.* Hitting Send, he ran downstairs to fetch the mandolin. Then he sat cross-legged on his bed, tuning the instrument.

The tablet pinged, and he set down the mandolin to read it. *They're assholes. They yell at you just to get a reaction. I still can't wrap my head around you and the cultural envoy of the Otherworld doing something so hipster as a podcast.*

Maybe he is a hipster, typed Ángel. *No one would know. Hence the podcast.*

I think it's working, she wrote. *The podcast is huge. People just call it O-Pod. There are podcasts about the podcast. There are blogs and social media networks and it's like a social movement.*

I stopped reading about it when they started talking about what a hot tamale I am, he admitted. *So tell me about you? Have you run into Trina lately?* Trina was Marissa's ex-girlfriend; the last he'd heard, she'd been determined to woo her back.

The tablet pinged. *Operation Trina is off*, said the email. *Met someone different.*

Intriguing. All emails went through security; both Chandler and Oberon had access to this. Would Chandler get in trouble if the envoy knew she was talking to Marissa? Would Marissa get hurt? Did she know where Chandler's loyalties lay? Because Ángel didn't.

Carefully, he typed, *I dreamed that love would never die, I dreamed that God would be forgiving. But there are dreams that cannot be and there are storms we cannot weather.*

Send.

Five minutes later: *I'll keep that in mind. You take care, Angela. You too, Mickey.*

He went restlessly to the window. It had stopped snowing; the lawn was a sheet of blinding white, blemished only by his own footprints. Then movement caught his eye: dark shapes against the snow.

He gasped, then ran downstairs to the living room, where he could see out the big picture window.

"Oberon," he said aloud, to the air. "Are you listening? You should come out here."

A moment later, Oberon came out of his office. "What is it? Is everything all right?"

"Look."

Oberon came and stood beside him at the window. After a moment, he asked, "Are they deer?"

"Elk," said Ángel. "They're elk. I've never seen one before."

A single file of the animals, pale fawn with chestnut necks, trailed across the snow-covered lawn. "*Mira*, they're so big. So much bigger than deer. Maybe the snow's too deep for them higher up in the mountains so they came down here."

"They are so beautiful," said Oberon. "Look, that one has antlers."

"I think that's the boy," said Ángel. "The male. The others must be his ladies. I've seen videos of the males fighting. The one who wins—the strongest one—gets to mate with all the females."

"How interesting," said Oberon. "I admit I haven't studied the fauna of your world at all. I believe the next envoy—if the Otherworld decides to send one—will be a biologist. Are they rare?"

"Elk? I don't think so." Ángel laughed at his own ignorance. "I'm pretty sure they don't live in Florida, but maybe there are lots of them here. People hunt them for food."

"Are they good to eat?"

"I have no idea," said Ángel, smiling at him.

"They're delicious." Lily came up behind him and threaded an arm through Ángel's. "Elk stew, with red wine and potatoes."

"No!" he teased. "They're too pretty to be stew."

"You wouldn't say that if you had a bowl of stew in front of you," said Lily.

"Well, true," he admitted. "I'm weak."

CHAPTER NINETEEN

A week later, Ángel sat in the swan-shaped chair in the instrument room, fiddling with the music system.

It was about nine thirty, too dark to see outside. He could occasionally hear snow blowing against the window. It had been snowing, on and off, for a week, and the drifts outside were nearly four feet deep. Lily had been serving a lot of rice, noodles, and frozen or tinned vegetables, since she hadn't been able to go into town.

The house was empty except for him and Oberon. And a hundred-thousand-dollar security system that no one was watching. Maybe.

He and Oberon had fallen back into their usual routine. They saw each other every day, ate lunch and dinner together, chatted about music and planned podcast topics. Several more podcast episodes were done, and they were doling them out every week.

Ángel tuned the mandolin, thinking about the podcast. He'd done some online digging and Marissa was right: the podcast was a huge cultural event. *O-Pod*, as it was now known, was the most popular podcast on iTunes by a wide margin, and people all over the world were writing and talking about Oberon, his place in the world, and the world's reception of him. There were scholarly articles that traced the evolution of his public appearances and the global effect of the way he'd been sequestered away by the United States. Vicious Twitter battles raged about his hidden agenda, his dangerous motivations.

Ángel shrugged away these unpleasant thoughts and put on headphones. He set the computer to record, started the track of himself playing the sad fingerpicked song he'd written on the guitar, and then began to play the mandolin. He was attempting to record the mandolin accompaniment, so that he could layer the two tracks together. After a few bars, his plectrum hit the wrong string, and he stopped with a snort.

Marissa's birthday was coming up, and he'd decided to give the song to her. He was proud of it—it was a gentle, complex melody, different from anything else he'd ever composed. Better. In his mind, the mandolin came in on the second verse, in harmony, its high sweet strings chiming beautifully with the mellower notes from the guitar.

But in practice, he wasn't good enough on the mandolin to get the sound he wanted. Hell, he wasn't even good enough to get through the piece without hitting the wrong strings.

He reset the recording and began again. Messed up again, this time on the key change at the bridge. Sighed.

He'd discussed with Oberon the global conversation their podcast had sparked, but neither of them had mentioned the strong tinge of sexual puritanism in some of the conversations: the speculation that the elf-lord wanted sexual relationships with humans, which would inevitably lead to moral degeneration and societal collapse. That would hurt Oberon's feelings.

The fae was doing so much better—Lily had commented on it—but he seemed restless, unable to settle to his work for long stretches of time. Before the snow got too deep, he'd sometimes accompanied Ángel on his tramps around the estate. One day he'd admitted that he did not like the cold weather very much—he was from a warmer climate.

"Me too," Ángel had said.

"You lived near the ocean."

"Yeah. I miss it. I used to swim almost every morning if the weather was nice."

Oberon had shivered a little in his heavy coat, snow blowing across his face. "I don't swim. It's always so cold, and I'm afraid to drown."

"Oh, I know where we could go," said Ángel. "There's an island on the gulf side. The water's calm and smooth, and the bottom's just clean white sand and shells. If you go swimming after the sun goes down, the water's warmer than the air. It's really relaxing. You'd like it."

Stupid thing to have said—he wasn't even allowed to go to the grocery store, and Oberon couldn't show his face without inciting a riot. But cold, stressed, snowed-in people everywhere probably talked longingly about islands and beaches. Sunlit, green, with pearly sands and aqua water, far away, out of reach.

Now he started the recording again, touched the plectrum to the mandolin strings, played, fumbled, stopped.

The door to the office opened and Oberon emerged. He stood in the doorway and gazed at Ángel for a minute. Ángel, recalling his evening of repeatedly failing to play the mandolin, winced. Hopefully Oberon hadn't been listening.

Oberon came into the room and sat on the carpet, his back braced against the turquoise leather armchair, across from Ángel. He stretched out his long legs, crossed his ankles, and extended his hand.

"You play the guitar," he said, "and I'll play the mandolin part."

Apparently Oberon *had been* listening, and Ángel's incompetence was driving him crazy. Ángel blushed, stifled the urge to apologize. "Sounds good." He removed the strap from his neck and passed over the little instrument, then picked up his guitar. Running a thumb over the strings to check the tuning, he glanced at Oberon.

"You should record this," said Oberon. "From the top."

So Ángel set the computer to record, put his fingers on the strings, took a breath to center himself, and began to play.

It was a bittersweet minor-key melody that had evolved from arpeggio practice and his own homesickness. The first verse was the melody on the guitar, accompanied only by the timekeeping thump of his thumb on the soundboard. On the second verse Oberon's mandolin came in impeccably, the notes silvery and sweet, precisely timed to Ángel's guitar. Oberon played with the delicacy that Ángel had utterly failed to achieve.

Ángel closed his eyes and fell into the song.

They flowed together, flawlessly, into the key modulation at the bridge. It sounded good. It sounded *great*. With Oberon playing, it sounded even better than he had imagined it would.

On the final verse, Oberon diverged from the accompaniment as Ángel had written it. He improvised an original harmony that was so perfect, so poignant, that Ángel's eyes watered behind their closed lids. The essence of the song was transformed by Oberon's harmony from loneliness and sorrow to something resembling hope—fearful, longing, hopeless hope.

They brought the song to its trembling close, notes converging, ringing together, then falling silent.

Ángel turned off the recording with shaking fingers.

Magic happened when musicians played together, when their different personalities and talents and skills merged in one piece, and they made each other unexpectedly better, more, than they could be alone. He had never experienced it so strongly before—never before reached such a perfect musical communion, never been elevated so high by another player.

There was really only one thing to do with this feeling in his heart. One place for it to go.

He opened his eyes and faced Oberon, knowing that Oberon could feel how moved he was.

But Oberon was still. Perhaps he wasn't able to interpret Ángel's expression, his signals. Perhaps Ángel needed to be more clear.

He put his guitar aside. He left the swan chair and knelt on the carpet next to Oberon, close enough to feel the warmth of his body without touching him. He kept his eyes on the cushions of the turquoise chair, but breathed Oberon's air, smelled his butterscotch-pepper-rain smell.

It was good, then. Oberon liked it too.

"Thank you," Ángel said. "That was amazing."

Oberon touched Ángel's hair, wrapped a tress around one finger. He didn't say anything, but Ángel could feel the vibration in the air between them.

"I've never heard you play before," said Ángel. "All these instruments. Can you play them all?"

"Yes," Oberon said. "I used to play them all, before you came. I like the piano best. Another of the projects I've wanted to complete is to transcribe some of the Otherworld music to piano. There's a musicologist at Columbia who wants to teach a class in it."

"Why did you stop?" asked Ángel, keeping his eyes on the blue cushions, enjoying the smell of Oberon and the sound of his voice.

"I thought it might irritate you to listen to me trying to adapt Otherworld music to Earth instruments," Oberon said. "I think it sounds a little strange to human ears."

"You've been listening to me torture the mandolin for weeks."

The vibration coming from Oberon intensified: probably amusement. "I have sometimes muted your mandolin practice," he admitted, gently tugging Ángel's hair.

Ángel smiled. "I wouldn't mind it, Oberon. You shouldn't stop playing for me. Shouldn't stop doing anything you like, because you're worried about me."

He closed his eyes and crossed his arms on the chair by Oberon's side, resting his cheek on his arm. Oberon's smell was shifting, the scent of spice emerging, the musky undertones. Ángel suspected those smells meant sex, associated them with the touch of Oberon's hand. His heartbeat picked up. But he didn't move.

"You're still fighting with yourself, Ángel." Oberon tugged Ángel's hair again.

Yeah, but I'm losing.

"It's because I'm a monster," murmured Oberon regretfully. He gave Ángel's hair a last quick pull and released him.

Ángel's eyes flew open. "You're not a monster!"

"I am. You can't bear to look at me."

"That's not why!" protested Ángel. "God, you must think I'm such an asshole." He met Oberon's transparent-jade eyes steadily, though his cheeks heated with a blush. "No. That's not why. It's just that your face doesn't ever move. So it seems—if you were one of us, I'd think you were hiding something. Like a mask. And it's a little— it's a little spooky. That's all, Oberon. I know that's normal for your face, but it's distracting. But if I don't look at you, I can concentrate on your voice and I can smell you, and I think I understand you better." He paused. "It's not—you know—that I think you're ugly."

"Oh," said Oberon softly. "I didn't understand that. Thank you for explaining it to me." He added, "You can look back at the chair now, if you like."

Ángel smiled, dropping his forehead back onto the cushion.

They sat together in companionable silence for a few moments, then Ángel added, "I really don't think you're a Thing. My monkey-brain thinks you're a pride of lions, but it's starting to get used to you."

"Monkey-brain is a metaphor for your primitive instincts?" said Oberon, his voice amused again.

"We evolved from . . . well, from something like monkeys. Very nervous about lions."

"We . . ." Oberon's voice was uncharacteristically hesitant. "We live in trees. We love leaves and flowers. We love to sing and to learn. We aren't predators."

"I wonder why you're so much braver than we are. There's one of you and billions of us, and we're all freaked out, and you're, like, a songbird."

They sat side by side, close enough to kiss. Ángel ran through the mandolin harmony Oberon had played—so beautiful, so unique but so exactly right—which gave him the courage to ask, "Do you have sex the same way we do?"

A resinous smell, like pine, mixed with cinnamon, mixed with musk. A purr. Oberon said, "No one has ever done an adequate study of the question, but judging from the videos and pictures I've researched, yes, it's essentially the same."

Ángel opened his eyes and looked at him sidelong. "Did you just make a joke about watching porn?"

"I did. Was it funny?"

"Not bad." Ángel laughed. "You should wiggle your eyebrows a little, so I don't have to ask."

"I don't have any muscular control over my eyebrows," Oberon said, thumbing his brows. "Or I would."

"I'm sorry I'm such a coward, Oberon. I'm still sort of—"

"It's all right, beloved. Anything you like."

"Touch me."

Oberon's palm was warm and broad on Ángel's neck, fingertips sliding around to his nape, under his hair.

He wasn't getting used to that magic touch—never. He'd never get used to it.

But it was time to stop pretending that he didn't love it.

Nerve endings fired throughout his body, as he had known they would. He closed his eyes in ecstasy, feeling the goose bumps tingle all over his skin. The hair on his arms stood up. His nipples tightened to aching points. Breath stuttered in his lungs, his heart pounded, and blood rushed to his groin. His cock stretched and stiffened in his jeans, pushing of its own will up under the waistband of his underwear.

Just that, one fae hand on his neck, and his whole body was prepared for sex, his skin on fire for more of that touch, his dick and balls and taint and ass all alive and ready and wanting it.

Oberon had to be able to feel Ángel's excitement. Ángel's sense of smell told him that Oberon shared it.

He lifted his face and leaned into Oberon for a kiss. The instant before their lips touched, Oberon's hand on Ángel's neck tightened, pushing him away.

Ángel blinked open his eyes to see that Oberon had averted his face from Ángel's kiss. No answers to be found in Oberon's face.

"Tonight. Will you come to my room, Ángel?" Oberon's hand was still on his neck.

"Tonight?" *Not right now?*

"Take some privacy first," said Oberon. "And then come to my room."

"No."

Oberon dropped his hand.

Then Ángel added, "You should come to mine. Mine doesn't have cameras."

CHAPTER TWENTY

Ángel took some privacy—a very hot, very thorough shower. He brushed his teeth and hair, shaved his face smooth, nervously considered manscaping his scant body hair. Oberon had beautiful hair, but none (as far as Ángel had ever seen) on his body.

Oh, who was he kidding? He could never hope to reach Oberon's state of physical perfection, not if he groomed himself for an hour. He just wouldn't worry about it.

Then he settled himself cross-legged on his bed in the dark, barefoot and shirtless and in flannel pajama pants, his hair curling with damp.

He thought about the passage of time. Oberon hadn't told him how much privacy to take: fifteen minutes? An hour? Two?

And also: *eight years.*

Oberon had been on Earth for eight years.

How would it feel to be Oberon right now, to be thinking, *Tonight I am having sex for the first time in eight years*? With Ángel, of all people. Ángel was excited and nervous, on edge with a mix of hunger and fear; how much more nervous would Oberon be?

But while Ángel's moods and needs and emotions pushed him around from hour to hour and day to day, Oberon rarely seemed out of control. Why was that? Because he was older? How old was he?

His lover didn't keep him waiting for long. Ten minutes later Oberon came in without knocking, fully dressed but barefoot. Even his feet were beautiful, slender and white. He stood beside the bed, leaning on one of the spiral wooden bedposts, graceful as a wisteria vine, eyes like sun-struck water. Ángel, sitting on the bed, stared back at him, half-erection shamelessly filling the front of his sweats. When Oberon didn't move, he raised his eyebrows at him.

"I'm trying not to act like a pride of lions," Oberon explained.

"So don't kill and eat me," suggested Ángel.

"Or stalk you, encircle you, or pounce on you."

Ángel smiled involuntarily—being stalked, encircled, and pounced upon by him sounded pretty good—and rose up on his knees on the edge of the mattress, opening his arms. Oberon stepped into them.

He smelled like happiness and sex, combined with a sharper rainforest scent that might be nervousness. He pressed Ángel to his body, cheek to his hair, and purred. Ángel closed his eyes and forced himself to relax against Oberon's chest, shuddering, inhaling his scent. Though his skin was protected from Oberon's by a shirt, it was still like being embraced by something electric and strange—a rush of magic that shorted out his defenses, overpowered his senses.

Just what he wanted.

Ángel gave in to the temptation to bury his fingers in Oberon's thick green-streaked wheaten hair. Oberon slowly ran his hands over Ángel's bare back, a sure and confident exploration of the planes and angles, making Ángel writhe with discomfort and pleasure. Ángel breathed against his throat and hesitantly put his own hand under Oberon's shirt collar, touching the warm, dense skin at the nape of Oberon's neck with his fingertips. His nerves quivered.

One of Oberon's hands was on his collarbone and throat, cupping his jaw. As natural as breathing, Ángel closed his eyes and lifted his mouth for Oberon's kiss. Instead, Oberon nuzzled the crook of Ángel's neck and shoulder. He brushed his cheek against Ángel's, rubbed their faces and throats together like a big cat, vibrating softly. Disappointed, Ángel tugged his hair.

Oberon pulled back and, crossing his arms, pulled his black shirt off over his head. The distraction worked: Ángel caught his shoulders in his hands and held him at arm's length so he could stare at him.

"God, you are pretty." He tried to keep his tone light, but Oberon's beauty almost daunted him. He hesitantly ran his hands over Oberon's winglike collarbone down to his biceps, his palms tingling. His fingers were irresistibly drawn down to the strong cords of Oberon's forearms, which were sheathed in buttery skin. The rosettes began to appear on Oberon's chest and belly, flushing up pink from under his skin. Ángel traced one on Oberon's pec with his fingertips, and his hand thrilled and burned.

Oberon snagged his hands and pushed him backward onto the bed; Ángel, not quite ready for full-torso contact, twisted, pulling, flipping Oberon over so that he lay on his back, Ángel on top of him. Ángel straddled his hips and, a little hesitantly, put his hands on Oberon's abs, exploring the flat white scar of his navel, the sweet groove beneath his obliques. He was shaking constantly now with a combination of excitement and alarm; Oberon's hands on his back were whisper-gentle, ticklish.

He stretched out full-length on Oberon's body, running his palms up Oberon's chest to his shoulders, shuddering as he allowed his body to lie against Oberon's. His cock, sandwiched between them, was protected from the electric touch of Oberon's skin only by layers of stretchy cotton.

Oberon turned his face so that Ángel's kiss landed on his cheekbone.

Ángel went still, on top of Oberon, feeling the heat of his body rise up through him. He was quaking like a leaf, aroused and scared both, his body's reaction to Oberon as plain as day. Oberon was unmoving beneath his hands though.

Ángel felt no swelling in the fae groin beneath him.

Controlled? Not turned on? But what were those rosettes on his skin, if not arousal?

The touch of Oberon's hands on his back suddenly felt uncomfortable. Ángel squirmed, grabbing Oberon's wrists, pushing his hands down onto the bed beside his head. Oberon put up a token resistance—just enough to remind Ángel that he could easily break free—and then allowed himself to be pinned. They breathed each other's air for a moment.

"Question," Ángel said huskily. "And I don't mind if the answer is no. Do you have a penis?"

One good thing about Oberon: whatever he might think, he never laughed. "Yes."

Ángel slid his body against Oberon's, belly to belly, groin and hips and thighs, his hands still trapping Oberon's wrists. "*Where?*"

"Exactly where you think it is. I'm keeping it small for now."

Ángel nuzzled Oberon's chest, inhaling. He smelled like browned butter, brown sugar, cloves, and underneath that, a heady musky smell that could only be sex. Ángel reminded himself that Oberon was not a bullshitter. "You what?"

"I am controlling the size."

"You can control the size?"

"To an extent. Can't you?"

"Uh, no," he said, with a suggestive roll of his hips. "What you see is what you get." That was intended to be illustrative, but it felt so good that he did it again. "Oberon?"

"Yes, Ángel?" Oberon broke the wrist-hold and wrapped his arms around him, a hand cupping Ángel's ass—not demanding, just feeling him.

"Why are you keeping it small for now?"

"I suppose I am being careful with you." Oberon's eyes were closed. His only signs of excitement were the flushed rosettes on his skin, the hot animal smell, his slightly unsteady breathing.

"Am I going to run away screaming?" asked Ángel. "Or, wait, does it have prongs? I read that cat penises have prongs." He ducked his head and touched the tip of his tongue to one of the purplish mottles that marked Oberon's shoulder, tasting him for the first time. They both shivered. "You like that?"

"No."

Ángel hesitated.

Oberon's hand tightened on Ángel's butt. "Yes, I like that. No, no prongs."

Ángel laughed. "Oh. Good."

He kissed the center of Oberon's chest, rubbing his tingling lips against the suede-like skin, letting the taste fill his mouth. Oberon's heart was throbbing steadily beneath his lips. Oberon's hand was still on his ass, warm and possessive, holding Ángel snugly against him. Apparently Oberon had eased up on whatever he was doing to control the size of his cock, because Ángel felt it now, hard and slender, a warm inflexible stalk against his thigh. Not very big, but that was okay. Ángel wasn't judgy.

He could kiss down or up.

He went up, kissing Oberon's collarbones, sucking on his throat, and Oberon arched his neck, purring. So *beautiful*, the way he moved, powerful and liquid. Ángel's lips followed the strong tendons of his throat up to his jaw. He shifted his hips and their cocks aligned, bumped. Ángel, on top, ground against Oberon through their clothes, squeezing Oberon's hips with his thighs. He caught Oberon's jaw in one hand, tilted his face for a kiss. Oberon turned his head.

Ángel breathed unsteadily for a moment into Oberon's spearmint hair.

"You're definitely avoiding kissing me, right?" he whispered. "It's not just my imagination?"

Big hands clasped his head. Oberon turned to look straight up into Ángel's eyes, his nose brushing Ángel's, lips an inch away. Ángel stared down at him.

Oberon gently massaged the back of Ángel's head with his fingers. "My people don't kiss."

"You kissed my neck before," he objected.

"Yes. I did." Oberon's thumb traced over the freshly shaven, slightly raw skin under Ángel's throat. "I mean, we don't kiss mouth to mouth, the way you do."

"No?"

Ángel's imagination went, grimly, to his dentist. Bacterial growth, plaque. Gingivitis. Oberon was more sensitive than a man. Could he taste . . . that? "Is it, um, is it gross? My mouth?"

"No," said Oberon immediately. His gaze dropped from Ángel's eyes to his lips, a gesture that looked so much like a prelude to a kiss that Ángel's heart kicked. But Oberon held him still, just examining him, still stroking his jaw.

"No," he said again, quietly. "But you . . . In your culture, a kiss is tremendously significant. You have stories and songs of transformative kisses that are thousands of years old. Jesus was betrayed with a kiss. Animals transmuted into men by kisses. The dead awakened. The sick cured. Kisses that symbolize every kind of love. Kissing is of great consequence to you. I . . ." he hesitated, his eyes coming back to Ángel's. "I've never done it."

The room was dim; Oberon's eyes were the color of moss, dark, his pupils wide.

Ángel pressed his lips together against the smile that threatened to stretch across his face. "I guess . . . if you don't get it right, there'll be a really scathing paragraph about it on your Wikipedia page." He bumped Oberon's nose with his. "Which would reflect badly on the Otherworld forever. Or I might leave a negative review on Yelp. One star. Would not kiss again."

They gazed at each other for a moment, and then Oberon, still cupping Ángel's skull, leaned up and kissed him on the mouth. A sweet kiss, a meeting of tingling lips, a little pull. A little caress.

Ángel opened his eyes. Oberon was watching.

"That was nice," he whispered, a smile curling one side of his mouth.

"It was?"

"Yeah. Very." He inched farther up Oberon's body, elbows on either side of his head. "Close your eyes this time."

He tilted his head and slanted his mouth over Oberon's.

Teaching the cultural envoy from the Otherworld to French kiss was possibly the greatest idea he'd ever had. His tongue asked for permission to enter, and when he got it, the thrill that ran through his body almost made him groan aloud. If Oberon's smell was an intoxicant and his touch a stimulant, the taste of his mouth was like a shot of white rum—shocking and toe-curlingly good. Oberon allowed Ángel to explore him, tease him, lips and breath, a nip of teeth. The hot slide of their tongues.

Oberon had no bad habits to unlearn, and if he didn't know how to kiss, he sure as hell knew something about foreplay. He perfectly gauged Ángel's responses, and when he began to kiss Ángel back, there was nothing tentative or awkward about it. He clasped Ángel's face and pressed Ángel's mouth open, the penetration of his tongue slow and deep, blood-hot and hungry.

Then he rolled Ángel over onto his back, covered his body with his own, and Ángel went from playfully teaching him what he liked to swimming in sensation, drowning in the hot velvet friction of

Oberon's mouth. He made a sound like a whimper as Oberon took possession of his mouth; his arms, around Oberon's shoulders, went lax, his whole body loose and welcoming. Oberon kissed him, and kissed him, and all Ángel's pathetic defenses crumbled into nothing.

He was such a total bottom.

Oberon's hands roamed over Ángel's body, stripping his pants off his hips. Ángel squirmed to kick them away, broke the kiss long enough to gasp, "You too. Naked," then pulled Oberon down for another kiss.

Oberon did not seem to be one for rushed fumbling with clothes while swapping spit, however. He pushed Ángel firmly into the mattress, stood up, and undressed, revealing in the dim room a magnificent nakedness. He was graceful and strong, mottled like a jaguar; Ángel's eyes traveled to his smooth, pale, perfectly recognizable cock and balls. Then Oberon crawled over Ángel on the bed, entirely lionlike. He pinned him snugly with his body, their dicks jostling together.

Ángel shuddered. "God!" Oberon lowered his face to Ángel's, his breath on Ángel's lips, and used one big long-fingered hand to grasp their cocks together. "Oh my *God*," moaned Ángel, helplessly clutching Oberon. It was the most intense sensation he'd ever experienced. The magical tingle of Oberon's hand and cock on his, transformed into something so acutely pleasurable it was all Ángel could do to hang on.

"Such a hurry, Ángel," murmured Oberon, his hand tight and hips rolling, his cock grinding against Ángel's with a steady rhythm that sent high-voltage shocks through Ángel's nervous system. "So impatient." He tipped his head to one side and kissed Ángel, open-mouthed, a demanding, encompassing kiss, while Ángel's body worked against him.

So impatient. It was embarrassing to be needier than the man who hadn't had it in eight years, but Ángel could no more control himself than he could sing an aria. He spread his legs, braced his feet on the mattress, and writhed, gasping, his hips bucking.

"I— Oberon— I—I'm sorry, I—"

"Do it now."

He came, crying out into Oberon's mouth, creaming over Oberon's hand, adding a slippery wetness to the friction, and it shook him so intensely he nearly passed out.

"Perfect." Oberon's voice was a groan. He flattened himself onto Ángel like a carpet, grinding their entire bodies together, his slender cock sandwiched between them. There was a hand on Ángel's ass, lifting him, urging him to wrap his legs around Oberon's hips. Ángel was still gulping for air, throbbing with his own orgasm, as Oberon's pelvis revolved, rubbing his cock through the slickness that coated Ángel's belly. Slow and hard. "Hold on to me, beloved," Oberon whispered. "*Oh*, hold on."

Then he stopped breathing, arched his body, went rigid. He was motionless for a long moment while heated, fragrant semen spurted out of him onto Ángel's chest and belly.

Then Oberon gasped with a sob, tightened his grip around Ángel's body, and, to Ángel's astonishment, *kept coming*. For another endless breathless moment, fluid kept pulsing onto Ángel's skin. Then he gasped and cried out again, and Ángel kept holding him tight, because he was somehow still coming.

Finally, *finally*, Oberon's body relaxed from its agonized bow. He collapsed onto Ángel, limp, heavy, wrung out.

That was *unbelievable*.

The room smelled powerfully of sex hormones, sweat, and Oberon's semen, which had a slightly sweet aroma, like fruit. Emotion-magic pulsed through the air. Ángel watched the rosettes fade from Oberon's body, the dead weight of his lover still bearing him down into the mattress.

He liked the heaviness, but he didn't like the stickiness. So after a while he nudged Oberon, who managed to disentangle himself and roll over onto his back. Ángel crawled off the bed, staggered to his feet, and padded to the bathroom, where he toweled a truly amazing amount of greenish jism off himself, then came back to the room with a towel.

Oberon, awake but limp, was still sprawled flat on his back across the bed, his face motionless and calm.

Ángel tenderly mopped their semen off his body. "I think you came for, like, seven minutes."

Without opening his eyes, Oberon said, "Probably not much more than one."

"One minute?" Ángel tossed the towel into the corner and flopped down beside Oberon, who linked a hand around his wrist and began to purr. "A *minute*. I'm not sure if I'm jealous or horrified, baby. I'd have a heart attack if I came for a minute."

"I think I did."

"Is that usual, or was it because it's been eight years?"

Oberon stirred. "Nine years."

"Nine?" repeated Ángel, incredulously. "¡*Ño!*"

"Eight years here, about one in meditation and training." He smelled like ripe honeydew melon and musk. "Does *ño* mean no?"

"No. *No* is no. *Ño* is, like, fucking goddamn whore."

"I shall never achieve fluency," sighed Oberon drowsily. "A minute is . . . not unusual. You're quicker?"

"You were there."

"I mean . . . all of you?"

"Not just me?" Ángel combed his fingers through Oberon's downy hair, and the purring intensified. "That was *way* fast. Sex can definitely last longer than that. I was amped up. But the actual orgasm part, yeah. Ten seconds maybe, bam, we're done."

"Hmm. Quick," Oberon murmured. His voice was slow and heavy with sleep. "I was also amped up."

"I've heard that women can make it last longer, but I don't really know."

Oberon rolled over on his side and pulled Ángel tight against his body, wrapped himself around Ángel like a strangler vine. "You're beautiful," he said. "I like the kissing, except I can't watch you and kiss at the same time. And you're so beautiful."

Ángel bit his lip. "Not like you're beautiful."

"Me, no," denied Oberon. "We fae all look the same."

"That doesn't even make sense." Ángel had never seen anyone more beautiful than Oberon. "Are you going to sleep?"

But Oberon was already out, arms heavy around Ángel's waist.

CHAPTER
TWENTY-ONE

Ángel drowsed restlessly.

He wasn't really used to sleeping with another person, much less a full-body octopus-cuddler with electric-eel skin like Oberon.

Not that he didn't like it—he did—but every breath or shift brought him up against the fae's body and woke him.

So he wasn't asleep when the tablet *ping*ed softly. He recognized the sound. Incoming email from Marissa.

He opened his eyes. The room was dim, but moonlight was streaming in through the window, and he could see the tablet on the bedside table. He reached for it, careful not to jostle the deeply asleep Oberon.

You should check this out when you have a chance. Be sure you're sitting down. Maybe do a couple shots of tequila first, it said, above a link to Conner Marr's blog.

He hesitated.

He didn't want to think about Con right now, not in bed with Oberon. But Oberon was asleep, while Ángel was awake and curious. And the load he'd blown against Oberon's taut abdomen was definitely the equivalent of two shots of tequila.

Wasn't it?

He tapped the link.

Hey beautiful people, (it read)

Sorry I haven't updated in a while, but I've been busy touring. That doesn't mean I'm not working on new songs though! Maybe an EP next year, we'll see!

I want to share with you some new lyrics. I'm sorry it's a little raw. But you know how a broken heart can make you feel a little raw?

—Conner

"Gabriella"
You gave me your body
When I wanted your hand
You spread your legs for me
When I wanted you to stand
Gabriella
You called out my name
But only in the dark
You played me like a game
Yeah, you left a deep mark
Gabriella
All I do is think of you
All you wanted was more
All night long I think of you
All night long you needed more
All I do is think of you
Gabriella
You took my heart
But you just wanted some
You tore me apart
But you just wanted to come
Gabriella
Gabriella
Gabriella

"Fuck you too," muttered Ángel, slapping the tablet closed and tossing it onto the floor.

He lay in the moonlight and seethed.

After a moment, Oberon stirred and patted his hands over Ángel's body. "What's wrong?" he said, muzzy with sleep.

"Nothing. Go back to sleep."

"Not nothing." Oberon dragged Ángel into his arms, one hand splayed across his chest, reading his skin. "You're angry. I've done something?"

"No." Ángel found himself smiling. "I see the limitations of your magic-code form of communication. I'm mad, but I'm not mad at you."

"I'm the only one here." But Oberon's eyes were already searching the dim room for the tablet. He let Ángel go and crawled to the edge of the bed, extending a long arm to grab the tablet, baring his ass to Ángel as he did so. He lay on his stomach on the bed and tapped the tablet to life, reading Con's blog.

Ángel took the opportunity to scramble away from him, leaning against the headboard, wrapping his arms around his knees. He wanted to remove himself from Oberon's all-seeing touch for a minute. But he didn't deny himself the exceptional view: Oberon in the moonlight, apparently unmindful of his nakedness, lying on his belly in a tangle of sheets, his ankles crossed. The shadowed groove of his spine led Ángel's gaze down to his lean waist, then over the *exceptionally* gorgeous globes of his ass.

"This song is about you," said Oberon.

"Yep."

"Gabriel is the name for an angel, feminized. It's a . . . a reference that you were intended to understand?"

"Maybe. Of course he had to make it a female name, so his fans wouldn't suspect he likes dick."

Oberon turned to gaze at him. "This song . . . this is not a gift? This offends you?"

Ángel sighed. "That's not how it happened," he complained. "It wasn't like he was in love with me and I was just fucking him. That's—" He stopped, impatient with himself. Tried again. "Oberon, the thing is this. The world is full of the exes of songwriters, and every one of us is saying, 'Hey, that's not what happened!' But nobody cares. We don't have a leg to stand on. Artists get to use whatever they want. It doesn't matter."

"A leg to stand on."

"Metaphor."

"Yes. But your feelings are hurt. It does matter."

"Yeah, well," grumbled Ángel, crossing his arms over his chest. "Not to anyone but me." He looked over at the tablet in Oberon's hands, the words there shining in the darkness, and annoyance bubbled up in him again. "It's a shitty song, for another thing," he said. "Doesn't scan. A four-year-old could have come up with those rhymes. 'You played me like a game'? You play a game, you don't play *like* a game. That is not a metaphor." He scowled, then laughed at himself suddenly. "Man, there is *nothing* that doesn't piss me off about that song."

"You could write him an email and explain to him how you feel," suggested Oberon.

It was hard to stay mad when Oberon was looking at him like that, over his shoulder, his bare back a smooth panorama of gorgeousness.

"He doesn't care how I feel." Ángel shrugged, trying to dismiss his bitterness. "He knew I'd be mad when he wrote this, but he wrote it anyway."

"Is that a violation of custom? Impolite?"

"Artists can chew up whatever they want for their art. It's fine. Con wants to be a big star. He wants to get people talking about the mystery woman in his past who hurt him." He hugged himself. "Man, what a conflict he must have right now! I'm, like, halfway famous because of the podcast, but he can't tell anyone about me, because he's in the closet. That must be torture. I bet that's really why he's mad." He brooded, his eyes drinking in Oberon's naked body as he did so. Oberon had delicious little dimples at the top of his ass on either side of his spine, and deep curved creases where his buttocks met his thighs.

"And why are *you* really mad? Because he's in the closet?"

"No, I—I never wanted to make him come out. Everyone does that when they can, if they can. Country music is not very gay friendly. I got that." Ángel rubbed a hand over his face, ran his fingers through his hair. "I guess I thought we were still friends. Oh, kind of. Friendly. I didn't think he'd take to the airwaves to call me a slut."

Oberon rolled over onto his side in a graceful sprawl, dropping the tablet onto the floor and taking up most of the king-size bed. His cock lay against his thigh. Ángel scooted away from him, maintaining his small separation.

They sat together in the dim, quiet room for a while. Then, "A slut is a person who is indiscriminate with sexual partners?" clarified Oberon.

"Or who just has to have it. Like you said. Quick to come, quick to come back for more."

"That was not an insult, Ángel."

"You didn't mean it as one." Ángel quirked a smile at him. "I don't know. Maybe he didn't either. It feels like he did."

They stared at each other for a moment, the room dark and warm, the bed a mess of crumpled sheets. The rosettes bloomed like flowers on Oberon's skin, and his cock began to grow.

"You are . . . very far away, Ángel."

Ángel launched himself across the bed and tackled him. He tried to pin him down but Oberon was far stronger, heaving him up and tossing him onto the mattress. They wrestled across the bed, ending up with Ángel on his stomach with his hair in his eyes, laughing, Oberon on top of him. Oberon purred and combed Ángel's hair out of his face, nestling his cock against Ángel's ass; Ángel's was hard as a tire iron against the sheets. True to his nature, ready for more.

"You could write a song," murmured Oberon, lips brushing against Ángel's ear. He grabbed a pillow, and Ángel lifted himself off the bed so that Oberon could push it under his hips; as he did so, he ground himself more intimately against Ángel's upraised butt. "A beautiful song with complex rhymes and perfect metaphors, all suggesting that Con is feeble and sexually inept."

"You are—" gasped Ángel. It was almost impossible to think, much less talk, while Oberon's cock was grinding gently, without lube, between Ángel's cheeks. "—super mean," he managed. "'Feeble and sexually inept' is better than anything Con ever wrote."

"You may have it for your song," said Oberon, massaging his ass, rocking rhythmically.

"Thanks." The rub of Oberon's cock against Ángel's opening was sending thrills jumping over all Ángel's nerve endings. "Baby. Do you have any stuff?"

"Am I welcome?"

"*Yes.* If you have stuff."

"Hmm." A soft spurt of something thick and slippery made Ángel catch his breath; the connection between them became slick.

"Did—did you just—"

"Just a bit, for lubrication."

"We have much to learn from your people," giggled Ángel, a little hysterically, lifting up, ready for more.

The smooth head of Oberon's cock slid through the slippery warmth, nudged Ángel intimately. "Relax, now," murmured Oberon, spreading him with his thumbs, gently breaching him with the very tip. "That's right." Whatever he was doing made Ángel's ass full of slickness, and he thrust shallowly through it, his head nudging against Ángel's rim, the tip penetrating, then popping back out again. He resumed rocking slowly up and down Ángel's crack, using his hands to squeeze Ángel's cheeks tightly around his shaft, every once in a while letting the head of his cock drag against Ángel's opening.

"Oh, fucking God," moaned Ángel. "Will you *hurry*."

"No." Oberon was clearly in a leisurely mood, kneeling comfortably between Ángel's spread legs. His big hands pulled Ángel open, exposed him, then let the head of his cock slide inside Ángel, then slipped it back out again. He kept doing that *thing*, leaking lubrication, warm and syrupy and tingling and copious, and it made soft squishing noises as he moved; it ran down Ángel's channel, dripped down his legs, pooled in the small of his back, slicked over his balls and soaked into the pillow under his dick.

Ángel, hanging onto the edge of the mattress with a death grip, arched his body. "You're killing me," he panted. "Oberon. Please."

"I know. But you'll just have to wait."

"I don't want to wait," whined Ángel.

Oberon exhaled huskily, a sound between a groan and a growl. "Oh, neither do I, really." And then he slowly slid in, balls-deep.

If he'd been bigger it would have hurt; instead, the burn was good. Ángel lifted up and pushed back, fucking himself on Oberon, mindlessly seeking pressure on his prostate and reaching for his own dick. But Oberon restrained him with his greater weight and strength, growling, "Be still, beloved."

"*More.*"

Oberon entwined his fingers with Ángel's and pinned his hands to the bed, forcing his legs farther apart with his own. "No. Be still."

"You are such a dom," muttered Ángel, obeying. He was spread open, impaled, ass up and head down. He felt conquered, helpless, and couldn't believe how much he loved it. The smell of Oberon's pleasure rolled over him like an intoxicating drug; his cock, as deep inside Ángel as it could go, throbbed palpably.

"Be still," Oberon said again, his voice warm. "Just feel it."

And Ángel could feel it: with a surge, Oberon's cock thickened and stretched inside him. Got . . . bigger.

Ángel grunted. "That thing is full of surprises."

Another surge, another pulse. Oberon's dick plumped and flexed and lengthened, opened Ángel wider, reached deeper inside him. Ángel moaned helplessly. He wanted to writhe, to fuck back on that cock, to rub against the pillow, to come.

"Let me know," Oberon said, breathlessly, "if you don't like it. If you want me to stop."

A surge. Longer, thicker. Ángel pressed his face into the mattress and cried out. He tried to move again, desperate for friction, the pillowcase on his dick, the slide of that thick penetration on his prostate. Oberon gripped him, tried to hold him still.

"Killing me," Ángel complained hoarsely.

"I hope that is a metaphor."

Oberon's cock pulsed, swelled. Thick enough now to stretch Ángel open. It was almost too much; overwhelmed, he whimpered. "Oh, Jesus."

"Is it all right?" whispered Oberon.

"Yes, yes, yes, yes."

And now Oberon began to fuck Ángel with an easy, rolling movement. He released Ángel's hands and raised himself up, lifting Ángel's hips, thrusting voluptuously.

"Oh fucking God, that is so great," said Ángel, his voice ragged with pleasure. Pleasure so wild, he didn't even know what he was saying. "Ob—*oh my God,* yeah." Hotter and more intense than anything he'd ever had before. "Oh yeah. Oh fuck. Oh yes. Oh please."

But Oberon was so *slow.* The lingering grind and slide inside Ángel was exquisite but exasperating at the same time; Ángel's heated dick and balls were brushing lightly against the pillow beneath him. "Baby," he gasped. "Please."

"I love this," Oberon said, his voice velvet in the dimness. His broad palm stroked up and down Ángel's sweating back. "It's been so long, beloved. Oh, you should see yourself." His fingers tightened on Ángel's hip, and he pulled out gradually, all the way, until Ángel could feel just the crown of his cock breaching him. "You don't look big enough," he whispered. "But look at you." He slid back in, opening Ángel, the entire length of his fat shaft dragging heavily over Ángel's prostate.

Ángel could only manage a shattered groan.

"I want to keep doing this all night," Oberon whispered, sliding out. "I know you like it faster," he said, idling. "But this." He forged deliberately back in. "*Ah.*"

Ángel's hands were helplessly grasping the sheets. He was on the edge of orgasm. At this pace, Oberon could keep him there for hours. He tried to push himself onto Oberon, to increase the tempo, but Oberon simply wouldn't let him. "You came already," purred Oberon. "You don't need to again right away."

Ángel made some kind of reply—he didn't know what. A moan. A whimper. Oberon was stuffed so big and deep inside him, stroking so slow and thorough.

"Or maybe you do," observed Oberon. He brought his hand around to stroke Ángel's abdomen, long fingers combing into his pubes and parting around the base of his dick, lifting him up and powering in at the same time. "You do need it. Now." His hot fist stroked up and down Ángel's dick. "Oh Ángel," confessed Oberon quietly. "So do I."

It was too much. It was all over for Ángel: he was coming in a hard wave of delight and relief. He bore down hard on Oberon's dick and spurted all over the bed and himself and Oberon's hand, shouting with pleasure. He felt Oberon coming too: not breathing, not moving, just coming and coming.

Ángel managed to push them both over onto their sides, and twisted around so that he could hold Oberon.

Who was continuing to come.

Ángel embraced Oberon while he shook, on and on, spasm after helpless spasm.

"I got you, baby," he whispered, resting his cheek on Oberon's sweating forehead.

Oberon seemed to prefer to be dominant during foreplay and sex, controlling the pace and the position and the dirty talk with an iron will. But during that minute-long orgasm he turned to pudding.

Face pressed against Ángel's neck, fingers flexing helplessly with every long, endless pulse. Overbearing top into mush. Just like that.

Ángel cradled him tenderly.

"We are always able to sense others, at all times," Oberon had said to him once. *"How they are feeling, what they are doing. We can always feel each other, through our skin. For us, that is comfortable."*

That meant this. Right now, as Oberon gulped for breath and collapsed quivering into Ángel's arms, he was transmitting on all channels. To Ángel, these were the most intimate, private moments of his life. But Oberon's feelings of arousal, orgasm, and orgasm's aftermath must be expressing themselves on his skin and broadcasting outward into the universe, in magic pulsations, for anyone to detect. No sense of privacy, and no sense of intimacy. *Communication.* All the time. That's what made Oberon happy.

And there was no one to pick up the magical signal.

No one but Ángel, and the best he could do was inhale the smell rising from Oberon's skin—like musk, like fruit, like cloves, like Oberon. He tightened his embrace around Oberon.

He could never hope to replace the lovemaking of other fae. He could fuck and be fucked, but he couldn't commune with Oberon the way he needed.

He cradled Oberon in his arms, stroked his skin. "Baby," he murmured, inadequately. "I got you."

CHAPTER
TWENTY-TWO

Ángel woke up to an empty bed and tangled, aromatic, crusty sheets.

He felt sore and loose-hipped. He flexed his limbs and wiggled his toes, making sure everything was still connected, before rolling out of bed. Skipping his usual treadmill run, he staggered to the shower.

This development is not going to stay a secret for long. There might not be cameras in Ángel's bedroom, but those sheets told a story. Lily would notice.

Ángel let hot water pour onto his head and run into his eyes. He was not shy. But he felt a little shy about this.

People would not understand.

Oh, who cared if anyone understood? He'd had the *most* fantastic sex, and he was happy.

He went down to the kitchen for his morning coffee and toast. Lily was there. She didn't need to see his laundry: somehow she clearly knew everything. She seized his hand and squeezed it, her eyes big and full of concern, and pulled him into the walk-in pantry. Perhaps avoiding cameras.

"Are you okay?" she whispered.

"Of course," he said, putting an arm around her shoulders. "It's fine."

She looked like she was about to cry. "It's not fine! I'm so sorry, Ángel. This isn't— I didn't think he—"

He gave her a little reassuring shake. "You know he's a good person. You told me yourself not to be afraid of him."

"Yes, but— Ángel!" She *was* crying. "He's kind, but you're—you told me about the money—"

"Oh. You're thinking it's a financial arrangement." It was a bit surprising how much that stung.

"No, but he's—"

A monster. A python. "No, he *isn't*," said Ángel sharply. "And I'm not a hustler, Lily, okay? I don't do anything I don't want to do, and I don't do anything for *money*."

She put a hand on the back of his head and pulled him down, touching her forehead to his. "I'm sorry, Ángel. I don't think that. But we're snowed in. The roads are closed. It's seventeen degrees out. You can't leave if you need to." She smiled a little through her tears. "I'm worried about you. Even though I'm not your mother."

That made tears start in his eyes too. This was crazy. "I'm okay," he said. "I promise."

"You don't have anyone here to protect you."

"I don't need protection. He's not a monster, and I'm not a victim." He squeezed her. "And you're a lot nicer than my mother." He bumped her forehead with his. "I'm just hungry."

Lily didn't look convinced, but he knew that she was incapable of letting him go hungry. She wiped the tears from her face and made him toast and a poached egg. As he ate it, he said, ostensibly to her but also to the listening air around him, "I sure hope the security team isn't getting ready to swoop in and rescue anyone this morning. Because it's *fine*."

He took the tablet and sent a quick text-like email to Marissa.

Thanks for sending me the link to Con's most recent masterpiece.

After several minutes, she responded, *I thought you'd find it interesting. Would you like me to fly to Nashville and punch him in the throat?*

Por favor.

He finished his toast and sipped coffee, then wrote, *It made me regret my life choices. I definitely should have dated Taylor Swift. She, too, would have dumped me and then savaged me in a song, but it would have been a much better song.*

Long pause. He heated milk for another cup of coffee.

True, wrote Marissa. *Taylor Swift would never have perpetrated "you took my heart but you just wanted some." On the other hand, judging from the caliber of Tay's ex-boyfriends, she's unlikely to have ever looked twice at your narrow Balsero ass.*

He grinned.

O suggests that I write a song in response calling Con "feeble and sexually inept," and that is a direct quote from the cultural envoy from the Otherworld. I'd like to work in "my narrow Balsero ass" too.

You shared this with O?

Carefully, he typed, *All of the above, yes.*

Another long pause. Maybe she was texting Chandler for confirmation. Feeling a little nervous, like he had just come out to her, Ángel finished his coffee, rinsed out his cup, washed the moka pot, and put it away. When the tablet pinged again, it said:

Don't do anything dumb, Ángel.

When have I ever given you cause to call my personal life dumb?

You are hilarious, she sent. *Remember the pool has a lifeguard.*

No need, he replied. *I can swim.*

Over canned soup for lunch, he and Oberon decorously discussed hip-hop. They listened to Nas, Tupac, Rakim, and the *Hamilton* cast recording. They talked about how in the early days of the genre, people with no money, no instruments, and no musical education had still responded to the call to create music. The conversation ranged over topics. It never touched upon the personal, though.

Ángel was starting to feel a little uncertain. Had last night been a one-time thing? Were they done?

Hamilton prompted questions from Oberon about American history, and the etiquette of interpreting historical events using anachronistic musical styles.

"I'm probably the wrong person to talk to about that," Ángel said. "I don't actually care, so long as the songs are good."

"Artists can use whatever they want?"

"Well, pretty much. If they pay for it. Maybe even if they don't."

"Really, Ángel. And you are a professional musician."

"Like you. Hey, do you pay for the songs that you send back to the Otherworld?"

"Of course I offer to," said Oberon. "That is, the DOR has intellectual property lawyers who handle it. I tell them which songs I want, and they secure the rights. Sometimes I talk to the artists. No one has outright refused me so far. Most artists allow me to send their songs to the Otherworld for free."

"Do you make artists pay for sampling yours?"

"A pittance. I don't need the money, but I'm interested in the impact of fae culture on Earth music. It's impossible to quantify, but the permissions help me keep track of direct influences."

"How much money do you have?" wondered Ángel, thinking of the ten million dollars that Oberon had paid to his father's victims.

"More than enough."

After lunch, Ángel left Oberon in the arms of Kendrick Lamar and went for a walk around the estate. He half expected Chandler to come out to talk to him, but to his relief she didn't. Plowing through the thigh-deep drifts of snow added a level of aerobic difficulty, and he was wet, sore, and tired when he made it back. He changed into dry clothes and settled in the swan chair with his guitar.

He felt a little unsettled. Anxious. He checked the tablet to see if Marissa had anything else to say. She didn't.

He began playing the repetitive, rolling guitar lead from "Jane Says" by Jane's Addiction: G, A; G, A; G, A. Again and again. It was easy to play and he liked the sound—it never changed. It soothed his nerves.

After a while, Oberon came out of his office. As he seated himself in the turquoise chair, he made a small gesture with one hand as if to say *keep going*, so Ángel continued to play. G, A, G, A, round and round. Oberon picked up the Yamaha guitar and held it across his lap, not playing, twiddling the pick between his fingers.

"Are you well, Ángel?"

"Fine."

"Do you regret last night?"

Ángel stopped playing. "Not at all. Do you?"

Oberon ran a thumb down the Yamaha's shining strings, and then quickly adjusted the tuning by ear. "No."

He began to strum "Jane Says." Ángel smiled at him and played along. Oberon's pick struck the strings with crystalline precision and Ángel said, "Relax. Let it sound a little buzzy. It's not classical."

Oberon's pick hand got looser. They played a few more bars, falling into effortless synchrony.

"This is not a very complex song," commented Oberon.

"Nope."

"You are not entirely happy, Ángel?"

Ángel shrugged. They played. Oberon began to improvise, keeping the G and A chords but adding variation. Ángel maintained the rhythm while Oberon created a new lead melody, building a new song around the cycle of G and A chords. For a few minutes the song soared like a gull, and Ángel closed his eyes, exhilarated. Then Oberon modulated up a step and Ángel tried, a beat later, to follow suit; the song tangled and went pear-shaped, and they stopped.

"You're so good," Ángel said, smiling, leaning back in the swan chair and pulling his feet up, cradling his guitar across his knees.

"It's been a long time since I played music with anyone."

"We should do it more."

"Yes, Ángel, thank you. We should. Now, will you tell me why you're troubled?"

Not going to give it up, huh? "I'm— You know, I'm actually sort of a moody person, Oberon. You don't need to come and try to make me feel better."

"I understand that," said Oberon, his voice warm and soothing.

The washy winter light slanted through the window and splashed across Oberon, shining on the yellow guitar top, on his streaky gilt-green hair, his beautiful, singular face. His skin was no longer scary-white but had gone a pale lustrous golden color, and his eyes shone like peridots.

Ángel thought about the coil of different things that were bothering him. Where to begin? "Well, for starters. We didn't use a condom."

"There are no sexually transmitted diseases in the Otherworld." After a thoughtful pause he added, "It has been centuries since any fae had sex with a human, and there are new illnesses here now."

Ángel belatedly realized that this was a question. "I don't have any."

"Then I think it's fine."

"Okay."

"Is that really what's bothering you?"

It wasn't, of course. "I'm really mad at the Otherworld. I still can't believe they sent you here alone, Oberon. That you've been all alone for eight years. Can't you tell them that you need to come home?"

"No."

"Why can't you? That poisoning thing that happened to you before—really looked like it was killing you."

"It was," said Oberon. "It probably will, eventually, if I'm not assassinated first. But the veil . . . it takes a lot of energy for things to move through the veil from the Otherworld to here. Exponentially more energy to move from this side, back. I am not strong enough—I can never go back."

"Oh. Did you know that when you agreed to come?"

"Yes."

"How could they make you do that?"

"I volunteered, of course."

"Why?" Ángel's heart was beating hard; he hadn't even realized, himself, how angry he was. "To come here and die in a cage in the mountains, so that they can understand *Hamilton*? That's just wrong."

Deliberately, Oberon plucked a complicated tune, pick flashing across the strings of his guitar, muscles playing in his left forearm as he shifted his fingertips over the strings. "Don't let it distress you so, Ángel. I was the best qualified person to come, and it's worth it to us—to me. I am a great adventurer."

"You are," said Ángel, laughing a little. "You're like Columbus, if Columbus had been by himself in a rowboat. And hadn't done anything bad to the Native Americans."

"Complicated metaphor."

Oberon seemed to be soothing him with his voice, and steering the conversation to less troubling waters. But then he added, "That's one of the points of information I'm intended to gather—how long one person can last here."

Ángel, who'd been relaxing into the sound of Oberon's voice, sat up sharply. "That is fucked up," he snarled.

"No. I knew how it would be."

"When you had sex with me, did it mess up their data?" Ángel tried to match Oberon's light tone, but it came out bitter.

"I was never given instructions *not* to have sex with a human," said Oberon, meeting Ángel's gaze, still playing. "Perhaps it didn't occur to anyone that I might. It would be considered rather kinky, you know."

"Yeah. I know."

Ángel sat back, shook the tension out of his hands, and set his fingers to his guitar again. He tried to copy Oberon's melody. Oberon slowed down, letting Ángel follow him, and they played together for a while, a sort of dueling-banjos exercise in which Oberon played a riff and Ángel copied it; then Ángel would play, and Oberon would mirror. Adapting, improvising.

"It makes me nervous that everyone knows," Ángel said eventually, chest aching a little.

Oberon stilled the strings on his guitar with his flattened palm. "Explain to me why?" When Ángel hesitated, Oberon said, "Once when I didn't understand something, you told me to take your word for it. I didn't, and I regretted it. Help me understand."

Ángel plucked his A-string, let the note resonate in the room. He said slowly, "People will think I'm a pervert. I mean, a lot of people already think I'm a pervert. My mom thinks I'm disgusting. I guess, part of me doesn't mind confirming their low opinion of me. But part of me does."

Oberon played his own A-string. "I understand that if the world knew, it would be a scandal. The fact that we are both male would be a problem for some people. And in many states, including this one, it is illegal for humans to have sex with nonhumans. The publicity might be extremely unpleasant. Of course, the world does not know."

"No," agreed Ángel, who was unaccountably blushing. "I just . . . I don't actually care what Chandler and the security team think, not really. They must be so damn bored out there, a little deviant nonhuman sex will be good for them. I just— Marissa—"

"Do you truly think Marissa will judge you so harshly?"

"I hope not," he said, disconsolately.

"Do *you* think you are disgusting?"

Ouch. "Oberon, I don't think *you're* disgusting."

In a very gentle tone, Oberon said, "I don't think you're disgusting, either."

"And it doesn't mean I want to stop," added Ángel.

"Ah," said Oberon, voice brightening. "That is what I was waiting to hear you say."

CHAPTER
TWENTY-THREE

That night, Ángel surfed the internet in bed, naked, waiting for Oberon to come to him. Eventually his eyes grew heavy, and he tossed the tablet to the carpet, wrapped himself in the peacock duvet, and fell asleep.

He woke up smiling, feeling hands on his body, fingers running over his scalp and neck. "Oberon," he said, eyes still closed, recognizing the stinging, singing magic of the fae's touch.

"You are so very sweet," murmured Oberon in his ear. He was kneeling beside Ángel's body, sliding his hands all over him. The deep purring growl of his voice resonated through Ángel. Drowsy and half-asleep, his body tingled with arousal as Oberon kissed his neck, his shoulders. "So sweet."

"I was waiting for you," mumbled Ángel, allowing himself to be rolled over onto his stomach. "Where were you?"

"Thinking about you." Oberon massaged his ass, and licked hot kisses down his spine.

"Me too. I wanted you all day," said Ángel into his pillow. His dick was hard, balls tight; he ached with want. Oberon's mouth reached his tailbone and sucked there, right above the cleft of his ass. Ángel whimpered, hot pleasure sparking through his veins. He spread his legs and Oberon headed south. The tip of his tongue swirled around Ángel's hole, and Ángel's body jerked. "Oh yeah," he moaned. "Love that."

Oberon made a muffled hum and his tongue flicked around Ángel's opening. His touch was so light it tickled, and Ángel began to giggle. "I was afraid my *mouth* was too dirty for you."

"Nothing about this is dirty," said Oberon, and then he stopped playing and buried his face in Ángel's ass, opening him with his thumbs and drilling in with his tongue. Ángel yelped. He grabbed handfuls of the sheets, raised his hips. Oberon's tongue worked him wetly and Ángel moaned, closing his eyes.

Delight and need spread through him with every silky stab. "Oh yeah." He rocked his hips almost involuntarily, trying to fuck himself on Oberon's tongue. Good, so good, but it wasn't enough. It wasn't what he needed—he wanted to be filled up, stretched, taken.

"Oh please," he begged, writhing. "Oh, Oberon, please. I want you so bad."

Oberon prowled up Ángel's body and ground his slender, hard dick through Ángel's spit-wet crack. Ángel emitted a shattered groan of need. Oberon slid up and down—and he was doing that magical thing, self-lubricating. Moisture surged intimately against Ángel's opening, trickled down his thighs, pooled in the small of his back. The smell of Oberon's lube was thick in Ángel's nostrils: musk and pepper and lush sweetness. "Please," he whispered again, aroused almost beyond speech by Oberon's cock sliding up and down between his cheeks.

"Slow or fast?"

"Fast," whispered Ángel, arching his back, spreading his legs, giving himself to Oberon. "Fast."

Oberon hauled Ángel's body to the edge of the mattress, stood between his parted thighs. He rubbed against Ángel's ass, interlaced his fingers with Ángel's, pushed Ángel's hands above his head to stretch his body out, teeth scraping Ángel's nape. Overwhelmed by the feel and smell and power of Oberon's body, all Ángel could do was beg: "Please. Come on, please."

Oberon slid inside him in one long thrust, and Ángel yelled with triumph.

"You need it fast?" said Oberon, pumping his hips, fucking Ángel in short rapid strokes.

"Yes, oh God," panted Ángel, his sweating face pressed to the mattress.

Oberon started medium-sized, but with each smacking penetration he got bigger. Ángel was distantly aware that he was crying out, his voice melding with the slap of Oberon's body against his ass. His cock was grinding into the mattress with every jab of Oberon's growing cock.

Oberon growled as he fucked him. He was everywhere at once: on Ángel and inside him and around him. Ángel's brain went blank like he'd taken a shot of Novocain to the cerebral cortex, and he came, mouth open in a silent scream, pleasure arcing hard through his body, semen streaming out of him in hot spurts.

He must have actually passed out from the power of it. When he came to himself again he was on his back, arms splayed. Oberon was on his side, tucked against him so that Ángel's legs were draped over his thighs. Oberon's cock, large and hard, was buried inside him.

"Oh, Jesus, Oberon," he managed to say.

"There," murmured Oberon, warmly. "Now you can relax." He was possessing Ángel's body completely. He ran a lazy hand over Ángel's belly, rubbed semen and lube into his skin, stroked his dick and balls.

"*Aaah*. Oberon." Ángel's body jolted, still wildly oversensitive. The big hand on his scrotum sent sparks of discomfort up his spine.

"Relax." Oberon shifted that hand to Ángel's hip, and he began to move, dragging his fat hard cock endlessly out, surging slowly, slowly back in. "Feel free to take a nap."

Ángel's toes curled. He moaned, helpless to do anything but feel, as Oberon continued to sinuously slide in and out of him, and thumbed his nipples. Oberon cupped his balls again, and his body jerked.

"Too much," gasped Ángel.

Oberon crooned, a pleased noise, as though Ángel had done something particularly skilled, and he took his hand off Ángel's scrotum and used it to hitch one of Ángel's legs higher, over his waist, opening Ángel and sinking deeper. "Better?" he murmured, stroking Ángel's belly, pulling slowly out.

"Nnngh—"

"You're very sensitive," said Oberon. He toyed with Ángel's navel and gradually thrust his hips, pushing back in. "Should I stop for a few minutes?"

"No," whispered Ángel. He dared a glance at Oberon's face; his eyes were closed, his expression peaceful. But his hands were commanding and the air was thick with an erotic thrum. Ángel closed his eyes as well, letting Oberon move his body, use him for his pleasure. This soon after climax Ángel was even more pliant than usual. Palms open, he melted into the mattress, enjoying the drag of Oberon's dick against his prostrate.

"At last you are still." Ángel could hear the tease in Oberon's voice, the playfulness. "You're like one of those little hovering birds—what are they? They fly around in the flowers?"

"A hummingbird?" Ángel huffed a laugh. "Shut up."

Oberon mouthed his neck, his shoulder, and continued to leisurely grind inside him. "Always in motion," he said. "You're always dancing or pacing or singing or jumping into swimming pools. The only time you *hold still* is when I fuck you unconscious."

"This is the worst sexy talk I've ever heard," said Ángel—which was not true. The timbre of Oberon's voice was pure sex, and the words *fuck you unconscious* made his skin flush hot all over.

"It's not criticism," murmured Oberon. "I enjoy making you jump." His fingers ghosted over Ángel's nipples, pinched them, and Ángel jolted.

Ángel's nipples stood up against Oberon's fingertips. His dick was valiantly trying to get hard again, which was ridiculous. It never knew when it was down for the count. "More," he whispered, seeking Oberon's mouth. Oberon pulled out and rolled on top of Ángel, drawing him into a voluptuous kiss that made Ángel's senses swim. Ángel moaned softly in acquiescence. Without breaking the kiss, Oberon caught Ángel's knees and pressed them up toward his chest, curling Ángel's pelvis off the mattress, and pushed back inside him. Ángel gasped and cried out against his lips.

"Mnh," said Oberon. "So good. So perfect. Ángel."

Oberon settled into a lazy, comfortable fuck, his weight on his arms, Ángel's legs draped over his shoulders.

"I can feel you getting aroused again," whispered Oberon, grinding into him, breath ghosting across Ángel's neck. "I can feel it. It feels so good."

Ángel moaned as Oberon changed the angle of his thrusts, making his dick stroke Ángel's prostate. "I cannot believe," panted Ángel, "what you are doing to me."

Oberon possessed him. Held him tight and helpless, fucked him slick and steady. His relentless touch lit Ángel on fire. His bulging shaft dragged slowly in and out of Ángel's tenderest flesh. Ángel stopped thinking and just drowned in sensation, in Oberon's scent, in the pleasure that went on and on.

Gradually Oberon's pace changed. He began giving it to Ángel in short, driving strokes that made him gasp and cry, and murmured, "*Perfect,*" as he drove Ángel to climax again. Then Oberon went rigid and came and came and came into Ángel's ass, his seed overflowing and dripping onto the sheets.

After, Oberon slept as if stunned, his head heavy on Ángel's chest, big body relaxed. Ángel rested his cheek on Oberon's shoulder, his body warm and sore and stretched in all the best ways, satisfied in a way he hadn't even known he needed to be satisfied. *You are ruining me for humans.* Ángel didn't say it out loud, but was sure it was in his skin and sweat, in his mouth, everywhere that Oberon touched him.

He couldn't sleep. Drowsily he stroked Oberon's hair, wondering why he was so restless. Unable to just be still, *like a hummingbird*—the memory of Oberon calling him that made him smile.

Then he remembered Oberon calling him *perfect*, and *sweet*, and discomfort intruded upon his contentment.

"You are so very sweet."

But Ángel was far from sweet, and he knew it. He was antsy and demanding. His moods could turn on a dime. *"You fuck like an alley cat,"* Con had said. *"But you're such a prick when you're not playing or fucking."*

Oberon, though, *was* sweet. So brilliant, so courageous, so alone. So generous, even in his need. He was so . . . He was so . . . Ángel couldn't think of words to express how much he admired him. Respected him. Loved him?

He squirmed out from under Oberon and, wrapping himself in a sheet, went over and curled up on the purple chair. He needed to think.

"So perfect," Oberon had said. But no, Ángel could never be perfect for Oberon. They were two different beings, from different worlds. Ángel couldn't give Oberon the communion he needed.

But Ángel was the only thing around. Years of abstinence, and then one willing body? Of course Oberon was happy for it, was grateful for it.

That didn't mean he loved Ángel. Not the way Ángel loved Oberon.

Loved Oberon. He loved him.

Oberon, alone in the bed, began to purr.

Ángel knew that Oberon found him attractive. He believed that Oberon liked him. He knew the fae didn't see him as an available hole, and he didn't begrudge Oberon the use of his body. Obviously. Oberon could have him whenever he wanted. Whatever he wanted, whenever he wanted it.

But he didn't want to be told that he was perfect, or beautiful, or beloved, when he wasn't. He was just a session man.

"That's okay," he whispered in the darkness. "It's okay." Oberon didn't love him, but by God he needed him. No one had ever needed Ángel before. His mother had left him when he was a boy. His father certainly didn't want a fag musician for a son. His friends were fine without him. Miami was crawling with competent guitarists.

But Oberon, this one great, strange, lovely creature, Oberon needed *him*.

"You are thinking hard, beloved," Oberon murmured.

"Bad habit."

Oberon opened his eyes and gazed at him like a lazy tiger from the welter of sheets.

"So . . ." said Ángel. "If you were home. You'd be in a house with lots of others. And when you had sex, everyone in the house would sense it?"

"Yes." Oberon stretched, then relaxed again. "Well, of course, they would probably be the ones I'd be having sex with."

"Oh." Ángel had never had group sex. "Like, five or six people?"

"Sometimes." Oberon rolled onto his back, his lean shoulders shifting. "Before I came here, all my friends came to say goodbye."

"Wow." Ángel's imagination grappled with the image of a group of fae, all as beautiful as Oberon, having sex together. "And your magic feelings would all meld and harmonize together. Like a chamber ensemble."

Oberon's eyes drifted closed. "Yes. That is a nice metaphor."

How lonely Oberon must be, stuck with just *him*.

Oberon scratched the center of his chest, drowsy. "Of course," he added, "I am getting older. Usually by my age, someone like me would have settled in with a single lover. Or sometimes two. Someone permanent. Someone who . . ." He yawned. His voice was deepening toward sleep. "Someone whose magic would suit mine so perfectly, give me so much joy, that they'd change me. And I would give them joy and change them, and over the years we would grow together and become attuned, and suited for no other . . ."

Itchy and trapped and miserable, Ángel stared out the window.

Oberon's eyes snapped open. "Ángel? What is wrong?"

"Nothing."

"No, no. It is too late for that, beloved," said Oberon, rolling over onto his stomach, resting his head on a propped-up fist. "I know you too well now."

Ángel wrapped his arms around his knees, curling in on himself like an armadillo. He was being ungrateful and wrong and stubborn. He was *supposed* to be happy. He was having great sex with a good friend who was amazing, who liked him and needed him, and he had no reason not to be happy. If anyone should be dejected and grouchy, it should be Oberon. He was the one who had lost everything, who was making do with a substitute for what he really needed.

"Why do you call me 'beloved'?"

Oberon gazed at him. "You know the meaning of the word."

"I call you 'baby,' but you aren't one."

"You have been undervalued by many. But not by me."

What was that? Evasion? Distraction? "You have to value me," said Ángel. "You don't have anyone else. I can't harmonize with you. I can't do anything with you except get you off. I'm sorry," he added. "I am not trying to be a jerk. Or to make you change. I love how it is with us. I don't want to stop. I just want to be clear."

In spite of the conciliatory words, he could hear the sadness in his own voice.

Oberon rested his chin on his folded arms. His eyes glowed. "This . . . is not the kind of conversation my species has to have. You should be able to feel my feelings in the air."

"I can," said Ángel, smiling through his sadness. "It's sort of like baking bread."

Oberon held out his hand, palm up. "And when you touch me?"

Ángel shook his head, still hugging himself.

"I am clumsy," said Oberon, dropping his hand. "But I, too, want to be clear. I do not have to value you, but I do. I have been alone for a long time, but my judgment is not impaired. I see you."

Ángel looked away.

"You are . . . you *are* harmonizing with me. I feel the magic in your skin, and your skin feels mine. Your magic is different, your taste and smell are different, but we are learning. I am learning you."

"I'm learning you too," admitted Ángel.

"There would be a process of learning between any lovers. It would be easier with a member of my own species, but . . . How do I explain? Right now you do not play the mandolin very well. Someday you will, but you need to learn it. It takes time for the music to be good. That is all."

"I'm the mandolin in this scenario?"

"Ah, it's not a good metaphor. You are my lover." Oberon's voice was unusually hesitant, though his face was unchanged. "And I am yours. Your skin changes when you are near me, and mine changes when I am near you, and soon—if we go on like this—we will have created a new kind of music that no one else will be able to hear. A new language that no one else will know."

"Oberon, I just—" said Ángel, his chest tight with anxiety, "I just want you to know that I'm here. I'm here for you, for however long you need me. Not because of what my dad did, or because of the contract I signed, but because I want to be. I want to be what you need. Even though I'm not, I'll try. You can trust me to always be here and to always try, okay? I promise." He gulped. "So you don't have to say things like that."

"Thank you," said Oberon, his tone warm, his skin fragrant, like jasmine and browned butter. "Oh, thank you. I'm happy for that, Ángel, truly. But how can you not understand? You've touched me. You know that I desire you. You are desirable. I admire you because you are admirable. I call you beloved because I love you."

Ángel's breath was hot in his lungs.

Oberon could feel it, surely: his bewilderment, his anxiety, his disbelief. He went on, "I promise you. Once we have learned each other, Ángel, and changed each other, and grown together, I will be yours, and you will be mine, in a way that no one else will ever know or understand. We are a new thing in the universe, and I love it. You are precious to me. I love you and I always will."

But Ángel didn't believe him, and Oberon clearly knew it.

"You're angry?" he asked. "But . . . No, you're not angry. You're afraid. I don't understand why you're afraid."

"Well, you don't know me very well."

Because this was, seriously, just an epic misunderstanding. It had to be. A failure to communicate of magical proportions. Born of desperation and sex and loneliness-gone-crazy. A basic inability to understand.

No one loved Ángel, not really. Not once they got to know him. And the idea that he could be transformed by Oberon's love into something lovable . . . permanently changed, unfit for anything or anyone else . . .

"Oberon," he said. "I can't. I *can't*. I will be here for you every day and every night for the rest of your life, if that's what you need, but I don't think I can be a new mandolin."

"We are saying the same thing," Oberon said gently. He extended his hand again, his voice soft. "Come to me. Let's go to sleep," he urged. "We can argue another day. Tonight, come and sleep, and don't be afraid. Sleep, and I'll keep you safe. Tomorrow you can make coffee and explain Christmas carols to me."

Ángel nodded and went into his arms.

CHAPTER
TWENTY-FOUR

"Welcome to *The Oberon Podcast*," said Oberon into the microphone the next morning. "I'm Oberon, the cultural envoy from the Otherworld. Joining me, as always, is Ángel Cruz."

"Hi," said Ángel.

They had reversed the usual format of the podcast for this episode: Oberon was interviewing Ángel. Oberon had slightly mimicked Ángel's speaking cadence, possibly not enough for anyone but Ángel to notice.

Ángel grinned at him.

He was warm and full of coffee. He'd taken a long walk in the snow after breakfast, and when he got back Oberon had kissed him. He felt young and strong and in love, and the fears and insecurities of the night felt insignificant. He loved Oberon, and Oberon needed him and liked him and enjoyed him. Everything else was semantics. They were together. For as long as it lasted.

"So, Ángel, what do you do for a living?"

"I'm a session musician."

"Can you tell us what that means?"

"Well, I sing and play guitar. Usually acoustic. If you're recording an album, or doing a show, and you need a good guitarist, you can hire me. Or maybe you're producing a TV show and you want some nice interstitial music; you can hire me to play it. Or if you're an ad agency and you want someone strumming a guitar in your commercial, you can hire me for that too."

"You're based in Miami?"

"Yes. I think you used to have to be in New York or LA or Nashville if you wanted to do this for a living, but the music industry has really decentralized. So usually I'm in Miami, but I've gone up to Nashville to play a lot too."

"What else?"

"In between that kind of gig, I like to play live music. I never want to give up live performing. It's what I first loved about music. I've toured with musicians, and I've played a lot of bars and things around Florida. I don't make a steady income that way, but playing live is fun. So if you've ever sipped a beer in a hotel bar in Fort Lauderdale or Sanibel Island, and there was a guy in the corner playing Cuban songs on the guitar, that might have been me."

"Are you in a band?"

"Sort of? Sometimes people want to hire an ensemble to record, not just one guy, and so there are musicians that I partner with quite often. Marissa Sommers and Tonio Ortiz. I guess there's a YouTube going around of the three of us playing a pretty wild party. That was before I started to get steady session work."

"We have a recording of you playing in a commercial," said Oberon. "Let's hear it."

He touched the tablet to launch the clip. A folky acoustic guitar melody filled the room, while a man with an attractive, gravelly voice said, "It's summertime in Alberta, and the oats are ripening beneath the morning sun."

Ángel was laughing when the clip came to a close. As usual, they had outlined what they wanted to talk about on this episode, but they hadn't actually scripted the conversation. "Okay, so. If you've ever seen this oatmeal commercial," he said, the giggle probably coming through on the recording, "you know there's this really handsome guy sitting in front of a barn, playing a guitar as he surveys his field of oats. That is not me. He's an actor, and they've got him wearing farmer clothes, like, overalls? But he's making that shit look *good*."

"So you enjoyed this job?" asked Oberon, his voice warm with humor. He actually sounded flirty.

"Not like you mean," chided Ángel. "I never met the guy. I was in a sound studio in Florida, and he was in an oat field somewhere. He's not playing that guitar. The guitar is me. Also, I'm pretty sure that's not him talking, either. That's a voice-over actor. So there's actually three of us, but they layered it all together to make it seem like the hot guy is playing and talking."

"I find that rather strange," said Oberon. "Why not just hire one person to play and talk?"

"I don't know. I'm glad they didn't, though, or they wouldn't have hired me. I don't look anything like an oat farmer."

"Tell us some of the other work you've done."

So Ángel talked about some of his other collaborations, and they played a few more clips. They wrapped up the interview with Oberon saying, "Ángel, why aren't you a famous recording artist?"

"Because I didn't want to take that path. Everyone pays attention to the celebrities, but the music industry is full of people like me, you know, who love to play music, but don't want to be big stars. I look at the stuff that famous people put up with, and it's too much. It's not for me."

"You mean fame."

"Fame, yes. Some people really want fame. They want everyone to hear their music and love it, and I get that. I get it. But they pay a high price too. Everyone knows their face, everyone knows their business. I never wanted that."

"Ángel," said Oberon gently, "your picture was recently on the cover of *Us Weekly*."

"I know! Isn't that crazy? I didn't mean for that to happen. I especially didn't mean for reporters and photographers to start following my friends and ex-boyfriends around, hounding them with questions." He let his voice grow serious. "Listen, if you're a reporter, could you not do that? We'd all be grateful, okay? Yes, I am gay. Yes, I am friends with Oberon. We play music together sometimes. No, I'm not going to talk about my personal life, not just because it's no one's business, but also because there are scary people out there. None of us intended to become targets. Including Oberon."

"It is my biggest concern," said Oberon. "By being my friend, you and your friends have been exposed to danger of violence. Neither of us really anticipated that, when we started this podcast. That was foolish of us."

"Last time you made a public appearance, people threw Molotov cocktails and set fire to the building you were in."

"Yes. I would like to make more public appearances—since we started this podcast we have had many invitations to do live interviews and events. I would like to listen to live music. But we get death threats too, and it's usually very dangerous. Not only for me, but for everyone nearby."

"Because people want to kill you," clarified Ángel.

"I think most people don't. There are a few people who are angry. Perhaps they are afraid. But most people understand that, like you, I am just a person who wanted to spend my life playing and studying music. When the opportunity came to travel to another land to study music— Imagine what an exciting opportunity that was! What musician, what scholar of music, would not go to learn about music from another people?"

"Not me," said Ángel. "Too scary for me."

"Well, but I did not foresee the Molotov cocktails. And certainly, I did not foresee that my friends"—Oberon purred the words—"would be in danger too."

"So we'd like to thank all of our listeners who support this podcast," said Ángel, "and who understand that we're— I mean, I know it's funny, because he *is* a magical being from a different world. But we're just people who like music. I'm not a fame-whore. He's not a monster. He's a scholar, and I'm his friend, and that's kind of the most important thing."

Oberon chimed in, "We would also like to thank those who gave us permission to play their songs on this episode, including the makers of Alberta Oats. And the Department of Otherworld Relations for making this podcast possible. And thank you, Ángel."

"See you next time, Oberon."

They turned off the recording and sat back in their chairs. Ángel felt exhilarated, his heart beating like a bird's wings in his chest.

"They will have to edit it a little," said Oberon. "You said 'shit.'"

"Oh, whoops. Can they just cut that line?"

"It was rather funny," he said, gravely. "I will suggest they keep it."

Oberon was radiating contentment, both in his voice and in the air that filled the room, and Ángel wondered, not for the first time, if it was possible to become intoxicated by the magic rising from his skin. He felt intoxicated now, flush with pleasure and anticipation.

"Can you control the security feed to this room?" he asked. "Turn it off?"

Oberon wordlessly reached for his laptop and pressed some buttons.

"The mikes too," said Ángel. "Everything off."

"Everything is off."

He eased out of his chair and crawled onto Oberon's lap, straddling him, wrapping his arms around Oberon's shoulders. Oberon's arms encircled his waist, and he rested against Oberon's body. They breathed together for a moment.

"I just came out to millions of people," Ángel said.

"You're out already?"

"Yeah, but you sort of do it again and again, with every new person you meet. I guess now that the *entire world* knows, I probably won't have to do it anymore."

"Do you want to edit that part out? Or scrap the episode?"

"No." He leaned his cheek against Oberon's shoulder. "It's fine. It's the only way to be, really."

Oberon stroked his back. "We think—in the Otherworld—that everyone is male and female both, sometimes. That it can change over time, that it's . . . It's not the most important thing about people. We are influenced by the magic of one another, constantly . . . It is not our way, to think that men must only love women, or women must only love men. Or that there's a wrong way to have sex or to love. The only wrong thing is to violate the magic. To try to force or pollute it . . . But if the magic is there and true between people—" he gently pulled up Ángel's T-shirt and ran a thumb across Ángel's bare back, making Ángel shiver "—there can be nothing wrong."

Ángel shifted a little in the chair, tightening his embrace, wanting to feel more of the magic. "I was taught that it was the *most* wrong thing."

"So was I," said Oberon, "when I first arrived here. I think the DOR was very shocked by me." His fingers caressed Ángel's back in little circles. "I was so frightened, and I needed comfort. Do you understand?"

"Did you try to touch someone?"

"I tried to touch everyone," Oberon admitted. "Oh, it took me a long time to learn not to try to touch people. But by that point everyone was horrified by me. They told me I was *too much*. They told me that I was *unacceptable*. And they were right, of course."

"They were wrong," whispered Ángel.

"Someone shot me. I almost bled to death. They told me it was partly my fault, for being so . . . so elfin. So fae. So they made me cut my hair, and they bought me clothes."

"Oh my God." Ángel pulled back, staring into Oberon's still face. "The black clothes, the short hair—that comes from the DOR?"

"They thought if I looked more like a man, I'd be safer. And they would be safer, the ones who have to protect me. So I try to look like a man. But it doesn't work."

Ángel cupped Oberon's face in his hands, thumbs stroking his high cheekbones. Oberon's face was as still and remote and beautiful as the moon, but at some point Ángel had stopped seeing it like that, frightening and perfect and strange. Maybe it was the magic, tingling in his palms as he caressed Oberon's smooth cheeks, his jaw, tunneled his fingertips into Oberon's soft white-gold hair.

"You're in the closet. You're pretending to be someone you're not to keep safe. I don't know why I never realized that before."

"I'm not as brave as you."

"No," Ángel said, "no, you're a thousand times braver than me. But I wonder if they were wrong. I wonder if they shouldn't have defied everyone and showed the world the real you."

"I don't know," said Oberon. "It's hard, when people hate you."

Ángel nodded. He knew that.

"They thought people would hate me less if I pretended. You're the only one who's ever thought they'd hate me less if they really knew me."

He thought of Oberon's room—the thick carpets on the floor, the piles of down duvets on the bed. "You like soft things against your skin," he guessed, tugging at the crisp collar of Oberon's shirt. "Not this. You like silk and cashmere. You have a blue silky robe that you never wear."

"You looked at my things."

Ángel's hands thrilled with magic. Oberon smelled peppery, and his voice had gone hot. Oberon was *delighted* that Ángel had looked at his things.

"Bring your soft blankets to my room," whispered Ángel. "Wear your pretty robe when you're alone with me. When it's just us, when no one can see you but me, you can be yourself."

"I can." Oberon was whispering too. The signs of his arousal bloomed on the white skin of his throat, and the air hummed with sex. "Oh, Ángel. How I need you."

Ángel slid off Oberon's lap to his knees, stroked up Oberon's thighs, parting them. He nibbled Oberon's stomach through the fabric of that hateful crisp black shirt, and then pushed the shirt up to press his open mouth to Oberon's flat abdomen.

"Ángel," murmured Oberon, his hands gently stroking into Ángel's hair.

Ángel licked and nibbled the lustrous suede-like skin that covered Oberon's abdomen, hairless and strange and delicious against his tongue. He undid Oberon's belt and zipper, and Oberon lifted his hips to let Ángel slide his pants down. His penis bobbed free, erect but not large.

He took the moment to examine him. The rosettes turned into red-brown ringlets on his cock, like a raccoon's tail. The skin was rougher at the base, napped like velvet, but smooth and shining-slick on the shaft and tip. Ángel nuzzled him, pushing his legs apart and licking his body, his balls, probing with his tongue, sucking. Oberon moaned. His head had fallen back against his chair, his pelvis canted up to give Ángel better access.

"You can get a little bigger, baby," Ángel whispered, and watched. Oberon's dick pulsed, swelled before his eyes. Longer, thicker through the length, while the head stayed relatively small. Silky and flushed. "Nice," said Ángel. "Right there."

Ángel sucked the tip of the cock into his mouth, then slowly went all the way down, pulling him all the way in. It was smoother than a human penis. Small roundish head, widening to a thick bulge on the shaft that opened Ángel's mouth. No foreskin, but the skin on the whole shaft was satiny and slightly loose, and Ángel moved it with his lips and tongue, up and down. Oberon liked it slow.

Moisture flooded Ángel's mouth. Not spurting from the tip of Oberon's cock—he wasn't coming—but the whole length, tip to base, flushed with slippery moisture, musky-sweet. Ángel sucked, swallowed. He could taste Oberon's pleasure, take it into himself. Ángel's mind whirled; he felt drunk, painfully aroused. The lube kept coming out of Oberon's skin, too much for him to take in, so he let it flow out of his mouth as he bobbed his head, and at the same time grappled his own jeans open. He pulled up long enough to gather a handful of lubrication from Oberon's weeping cock and began to jack off with it, sucking Oberon back into his throat while steadily working his slickened fist on his own dick.

Oberon began to pant. Ángel was barely holding on himself, his balls tight, his skin burning, his hand rubbing Oberon's sex magic right into his skin while he drank him up, more and more. More. Oberon cried out and gripped his chair and began to come, his head thrown back, seed pouring out of him in a long gush. Ángel tried to take it in, choked, pulled off, pressed his face to Oberon's belly as he came, sweet and piercing, onto the chair and Oberon's legs. Oberon gasped, come surging out of him into Ángel's hair, onto his neck and face. Ángel wrapped his arms around Oberon's waist, and Oberon collapsed forward onto him, his cock still emitting spurts of come onto Ángel. By the time he was done, Ángel was laughing.

"This is ridiculous," he said. "No one needs this much. You could fill a bathtub."

Oberon murmured wordlessly, clearly dazed.

Ángel climbed into Oberon's lap, straddling him. "This is the best part," he said roughly, and grabbed his face and kissed him, openmouthed, tonguing the taste of Oberon's come into Oberon's mouth. Their bodies ground together, tongues tangled. Oberon moaned again, and Ángel felt another pulse of semen surge out of him onto his own legs.

They stayed in the chair afterward, cuddling for a few minutes, until Ángel tried to mop the drying come off his face with his shirt, and found that it was already saturated. He began to laugh again.

"I have . . . In there . . ." Oberon gestured with an enervated hand toward a desk drawer, and Ángel opened it to find folded clean towels.

"I see," he said, pulling one out and wiping his face and hands. "What do you do in here all day, Oberon?"

"I have sometimes amused myself."

"Yeah? Well, I've sometimes amused myself too."

They tidied themselves and the chair and desk, but Ángel really needed a shower and a change of clothes. *Te amo*, he thought, kissing Oberon, before sneaking upstairs.

When he came back down, clean and de-jismed, he could feel a change in the air. Something was different, some sort of singing quality—not a sound or a smell, but a feeling, happy and electric.

"What's happening?" he asked Lily.

She was making lunch: macaroni and cheese, and a salad with apples in it. "What do you mean?"

"Can't you feel it?" he asked, bouncing slightly on his toes.

She shook her head. She'd been a little shy around him lately, probably not sure what to make of his relationship with Oberon.

"Really? You can't feel that? It's like Christmas morning."

"It's November eleventh."

"No, I mean—" What *did* he mean? Was he actually feeling something real, some magical signal that Oberon was emitting? "I think something's happening. Is he in his office?"

She nodded. "Lunch is almost ready. Wait a minute, I'll give you a tray."

So he waited while she fussed with bowls and cutlery. "What's this green stuff in the mac and cheese?" he ventured, hoping to tease a smile out of her.

"Bok choy. It's very good."

"Sure, in a salad or something. Not in mac and cheese."

"Green vegetables are good for you. You need vitamins in the winter or you'll catch a cold."

He smiled at her. "Will you take care of me if I get sick?"

"No. I'll stay away from you so I don't catch it." But her dimples had reappeared as she handed him the tray.

He took lunch to Oberon's office, where the electric hum in the air was stronger. Oberon was writing, his pen scratching swiftly across the paper; his body seemed taut with concentration.

"Is something happening?"

"A message," said Oberon. His voice thrummed like a beehive. "From the rose bush. In the middle of the day."

"Is it good news?"

"If true . . . Beloved, I cannot say. I cannot eat. Leave me, won't you? Forgive me. I must—" He waved a hand, eyes on his work.

"Okay," said Ángel, backing toward the door. "Oberon—I hope it's good news."

Oberon's gaze flickered up to him. "It might be the *best* news," he breathed.

CHAPTER
TWENTY-FIVE

Á ngel didn't find out what was going on until late that night.
He was up in his room, on the purple chair, playing his guitar,
when Oberon came in.

Oberon dropped to his knees on the carpet in front of Ángel, his
big hands gripping Ángel's thighs.

"Ángel," he said, his voice rough with excitement. "Ángel."

Ángel carefully put the guitar aside, leaning it up against the wall,
because Oberon was all but shaking him in his excitement. "It's true,
then?" he asked, smiling, putting his palms on Oberon's shoulders.
"The good news?"

Oberon yanked him into an embrace, then stood, lifting Ángel
off the ground, and spun. He was saying something in his own
language, a rapid, melodic run of syllables as he held Ángel tightly and
twirled them around the room. Ángel clung to him, gasping a little for
breath, laughing. "What is it?" he demanded, tugging Oberon's hair.
"Put me down and tell me!"

Oberon set him gently on the floor. "I almost cannot believe it.
They are sending another envoy. They are sending me another fae."

Ángel blinked up at him. "What? Really?"

"The roses gave me another box. They're pleased that I've lived so
long, so they're beginning the spell to send another. He is a biologist.
He is coming here to study *plants*." Oberon's voice was resonant with
excitement.

Ángel stepped backward, and when his legs contacted the purple
chair, he sat in it. "When will he get here?"

"Tomorrow."

"*Tomorrow*?" repeated Ángel, dumbfounded.

"They are beginning the spell tonight. I don't know if he's coming here, or to Atlanta, where I went, or somewhere else. Oh Ángel—Oh Ángel!" Oberon dropped gracefully again, kneeling in front of the chair, and Ángel found himself squeezed warmly against his chest. "What would you say? You would say, 'Oh my God.' Ángel, how will I wait?"

Ángel's hands had gone cold. "That's—" he started to say, but his voice sounded funny. *Pull yourself together.* But he was so shocked his lips were numb. "That's wonderful."

Oberon hugged him tightly against his chest. "I will have someone to talk to at last."

Ángel bit his lip.

"Will he live here with you?" His voice had gone a little high and thready, and he cleared his throat.

Oberon didn't seem to notice. "I don't know. Perhaps. At least for a while. The DOR did not know he was coming, either, so they are not prepared at all. There is already security here. Perhaps they will make other arrangements for him soon, though, because he must travel the world to look at plants, and I will go wherever he goes."

"Do you know him?"

"No, we have never met. He is younger than I. But soon we will meet. Perhaps tomorrow." Oberon cupped Ángel's face in his hands, and the touch of his skin was like champagne bubbles. He was all aglow.

"I'm happy for you."

Whether it was his voice, or the way Ángel felt beneath his hands, but something seemed to alert Oberon. "You *aren't* happy," he said. "Why?"

"I'm— No, I—" Ángel flushed, horrified, but there was no way he could lie to Oberon. "I am. But I'm very self-centered, you know. I liked having you to myself. But that's—"

"Oh, but I will introduce you," said Oberon, grasping his hands and squeezing them. "I know he will love you too."

"Thank you," Ángel whispered. "I'm sure . . . I'm sure that will be . . . That will be nice."

There was a long pause, while Oberon stared at him, and Ángel wanted to sink into the ground.

"You're weeping, beloved," said Oberon. "Why are you sad? Don't you see how good this is? The isolation, it was torture for me." He stroked Ángel's hair out of his face. "Any shock, any grief could kill me. But if I have another here, if I have a friend, I will live long. Don't you see?"

"I do. I do. I'm glad, Oberon. I really am."

Oberon ran his fingertips through the tears that, despite Ángel's best efforts, were spilling down his cheeks. "Why are you sad?" he repeated.

Ángel looked away. "It's just a big change," he said, inadequately. His voice was harsh, forced past the aching lump in his throat. "Maybe I'm reacting because it's a big change. It's okay."

Oberon kissed his eyes. "I want you to be happy." He kissed his mouth, and Ángel sobbed into the kiss.

This was humiliating. It was awful. He ached to be alone. To escape from Oberon and his gentle touch and his sweet kisses and his knowing skin, just for a while.

"Stop." He pushed Oberon away, tried to escape from his all-seeing touch. "I need, I think I need privacy tonight, Oberon."

"Why?"

"I'm sorry. Leave me alone. I'll see you in the morning."

"Are you sick?"

"No," said Ángel. "We don't get sick from emotions. Not really. We just—we sometimes need to be alone." Oberon wasn't moving. "Oberon. You know this."

"But something is wrong, and I can't tell what it is."

"And you won't," said Ángel, his grief coming out in sharpness. "You won't *ever* be able to tell what it is. Not with me." He shook Oberon off, got to his feet, and stumbled away from him. "Please," he said. "Please go away. I'll be better in the morning."

Oberon remained kneeling, looking up at him, the lamplight on his still face.

Ángel made a frustrated, sweeping gesture with his hand. "Would you just *go*?"

"All right," said Oberon, softly. "But—" He rose gracefully and stepped toward Ángel, hand extended to him again.

Ángel shrank away. He stumbled into his guitar where it was leaning against the wall. Oberon reached to catch him just as Ángel was trying to dance away from the guitar; he twisted, and the neck of the guitar seemed to rise up between his ankles.

Ángel fell. His full weight came down on the body of the guitar. There was a *crunch-snap*, the sharp singing cry of guitar strings, pain as his hip drove straight through the wooden box to the floor.

He rolled to his knees, stared down at the wreckage.

"*Ay*, my baby," he whispered, as he gently picked up the guitar: not a guitar anymore, but a collection of broken pieces of wood, held together by strings. The spruce soundboard was splintered, one curving maple side shattered, the head snapped right off the neck. Struts and braces, which should be hidden away inside the box, were exposed like broken ribs.

Hopeless. Beyond repair. Poor dead thing, like a bird struck by a car. His eyes blurred with tears. *My fault*, he thought. *Mi culpa, lo siento. I didn't take care of you, and now look at you. Pobre cosa muerta.*

Oberon crouched beside him. He drew a breath.

"Please go," whispered Ángel. "Please. Please go."

Oberon rose without a word and left, closing the door quietly behind him.

CHAPTER
TWENTY-SIX

Ángel cried easily, but it rarely made him feel better. He knew that some people felt cleansed by it, but after sobbing over the corpse of his guitar for half an hour, he just felt thick-headed and stupid and in as much pain as before.

He was a terrible person. Selfish, selfish, selfish. In the face of Oberon's uncomplicated happiness, he was bitterly disappointed.

Oberon wouldn't need him anymore.

And he'd killed his guitar. There were other guitars in the world—better ones, and he could afford to buy them. But *this* guitar, this old sweet-voiced Martin, with the cutaway and the mother-of-pearl inlay, and the cracked tortoiseshell guard and the loose pickup—now it was gone.

Sniffling, he eventually got up and went downstairs. It was the middle of the night, and the house was dark and still, but he needed to walk. So he pulled on his coat and boots and went out the front door.

It was the middle of the night, moonless, and truly cold. The wind cut right through his heavy coat. He wasn't wearing a hat, and the wind combed icily through his hair, froze on his swollen face, frosted his throat and lungs as he breathed. Not paying attention to where he was going, he slogged through the deep snow.

He'd been so careless, so stupid, so overwrought. How had he let the situation—relationship, love affair—with Oberon so overwhelm him that he failed to take the most basic care?

He trudged in a straight line until he reached the wall. He didn't know how long he stood there, leaning against it, slowly turning into an icicle. Too upset to go back to the house.

Oberon was there. Oberon, who was brave and radiant and gorgeous and so, so alone. Oberon said he loved Ángel, and maybe he did. But Oberon was about to not be alone anymore.

Would Oberon and the new envoy be lovers? Would they communicate with touch, making beautiful magic together as they stroked one another's skin? How soon would Oberon realize—if he hadn't already—how pitiful a substitute Ángel was? How inadequate Ángel was at giving him the companionship he needed?

What he and Ángel shared could never compare with what he could share with a member of his own kind. And Ángel would be discarded again.

His mother hadn't wanted him, and his father had thrown him away in disgust. His brothers were friendly but distant, his lovers temporary. Even the ones he thought liked him ended up writing angry songs about him. The Church certainly didn't want him back. Oberon, too, would find that Ángel was just not good enough.

Ángel was crying again. He was being self-indulgent, self-pitying. *Drama queen.* He promised that he would be brave tomorrow. Tonight he would give himself over to wallowing, and then tomorrow he'd be brave and considerate and happy for Oberon. And welcoming and polite to the new envoy.

Or, oh God. Maybe he was expected to have sex with the other fae as well? Oberon had promised to *introduce* him. They were a polyamorous species. They lived in colonies, and made love together, and their magic combined like symphonies.

But no, Oberon and the other one, the only two fae on the planet, they would grow together. Oberon had even described the process. There could be no need, no room for someone like Ángel in that union.

Tears were freezing on his eyelashes, inside his nose. It was gross and uncomfortable. The sky was empty; the wind cut like a knife. He should go in.

No one was around. No one for miles. No one knew he was here.

So what was that noise?

It sounded like voices. In the woods, on the other side of the wall. Voices, the rustling crunch of footsteps in the snow. A metallic *chink*.

Ángel watched, numbly, as four men in helmets and goggles appeared at the top of the wall, about twenty feet to his right. They crouched on the wall like gargoyles, silhouetted against the windblown sky.

Four goggled faces turned toward him.

Fuck.

Was he in the security blind spot that Chandler had shown him? He was. How had they known to come over the wall right here?

They rappelled down the wall on thin lines, like bad guys in a James Bond movie, and, while he stood frozen and watched, two trotted through the snow toward the house, and two came toward Ángel.

Ángel spun and ran.

Someone shouted.

He didn't look back. He ran toward the gatehouse. Toward the security team.

He was in pretty good shape from running on the treadmill and walking the estate, and he ran like a deer: that is, in a clumsy, leggy, too-slow scramble through deep-drifted snow. A darted glance over his shoulder showed that they were chasing him. He ran, stumbling through snow, his legs burning. Hair and snow were in his eyes, cold air bit his lungs, and the sound of his pursuers was loud in his ears.

It was too far. He'd never make it.

He veered and ran back toward the house—toward the pool. Chandler monitored the camera by the pool.

It was like a bad dream: chased by an unknown enemy, and he couldn't run fast enough because the snow weighed him down, clung to his legs, slid beneath his feet.

He could see the floodlights around the pool, and the nude statues, transformed into inhuman shapes by the mounded snow, silhouetted against the light.

He'd reached the edge of the patio when two fists struck his back—and then he was facedown in the snow, convulsing, screaming as agony ripped through his body. He thrashed and tried to get up, but his legs had gone rigid, muscles locking up, *useless.*

Chandler. Help.

But maybe Chandler was the one who told them where to come over the wall.

He might have passed out for a moment. When he came to himself all he could see was the booted feet of two strangers, who were having a semi-panicked argument about what to do with him. He ached in every joint and muscle, and the snow was painfully cold on his hands and face. Trying not to draw attention to himself, he flexed his arms and legs while listening to the argument going on above him.

"The fuck did you tase him for?" whisper-yelled one of the guys.

"He was gonna raise the alarm." This guy's voice was a deep rumble, and despite his correct defense, he seemed unsure. "Needed to buy Logan and Tommy time to finish the job."

Ángel rolled onto his side, to get his face up out of the snow. It hurt, and a little groan escaped him.

"Stay down," said the deep-voiced guy, prodding him sharply with a foot. Ángel collapsed back into the snow.

"So what do we do with him now?"

"Leave him."

"He'll die out here."

"What the fuck do we care?"

"Guys," called someone. "Come on. We gotta go."

The voice was familiar. It belonged to one of the security team— Logan the goon, the one who'd strip-searched him ages ago. The one who'd said Oberon gave him the willies.

"Is it done?" asked the deep-voiced man, and his companion added, "Where's Tommy?"

"Come on," said Logan, striding toward them.

Ángel curled his shoulders and ducked his head, hoping to not be recognized. Hopeless. "Is that the boy toy?" demanded Logan.

"No," said Ángel into the snow.

"He was going to give us away, so Aaron tased him."

Logan rubbed his face. "Jesus Christ. Shoot him and let's go."

There was a moment of shocked silence from everyone. Ángel shrank down into the snow like a rabbit, his heart stuttering. Then the deep-voiced guy said, "Fuck you, Logan. What happened, and where the fuck is Tommy?"

"Tommy's dead," snapped Logan, a ragged edge to his voice. "The elf killed him. We're fucked, and this little fag knows my face. So we need to kill him and get out of here. That okay with you, Aaron, or do you want to stay and talk about it some more?"

Ángel lay folded in on himself, trembling so hard his teeth chattered, waiting for death.

Then Aaron said, "I don't kill fags. I'm only here to kill elves." He yanked the taser's prongs out of Ángel's back, and a high whine escaped Ángel's lungs.

Aaron hoisted Ángel over his shoulder in a dizzying swoop that almost made Ángel vomit.

"Thanks," whispered Ángel, as they began to head back through the snow toward the wall.

"Shut up."

Give the guy credit: he had to be in damn good shape to lug the twitching Ángel through knee-deep snow. Ángel didn't struggle. He was no match for these guys, and at least one of them was willing to murder him. He forced himself to breathe, to stay limp, to not antagonize Aaron by throwing up on him.

Buy time. Stay alive. Get back to Oberon.

Oberon, he thought. *Save me.*

CHAPTER
TWENTY-SEVEN

They hauled Ángel over the wall with ropes. That *did* make him throw up, though he managed not to spray anyone with vomit. He felt pathetically grateful to Aaron for not shooting him. Down-to-murder-elves-but-not-fags Aaron.

They had snowmobiles. Aaron straddled the seat in front of him and said, "Hang on." The machine jolted to life, and his empty stomach heaved again. He was so nauseated and dizzy that he could barely sit upright and, as the machines lurched and began to move through the trees, he tightened his fingers on Aaron's parka. In the interests of not pissing off Aaron, he tried not to cling to him. This was rural Montana. They might not kill homosexuals up here, but they probably didn't want to be cuddled. But as they picked up speed, Aaron growled, "This is a single-man sled. Hang on." So Ángel wrapped his arms around Aaron's torso.

They were going to kill him. They had already tried to kill Oberon.

Oberon had been betrayed by someone he trusted. Oberon would definitely be upset. Oberon had killed a man. Oberon might be injured. And Ángel wasn't there to help him.

He needed to get back to take care of Oberon.

Miserably, he debated the wisdom of throwing himself off the snowmobile. But they were going really fast now, flying through the trees. He was shivering constantly and uncontrollably, from fear and stress and the icy air in his lungs. Plus he didn't want to be tased again. Or shot. Or left to freeze to death.

He hung on.

Hours passed. The world brightened, and then abruptly a sunrise ignited half the sky, burning gold and bronze and pink, sending golden rays between the black trunks of the trees, bathing the white snow in bands of flamingo light. Ángel's tears streaked out of the corners of his eyes and froze on his temples.

He hadn't prayed in a long time, not since the priest told him he would die unloved even by God. *Lord, I am not worthy to receive you*, he mentally recited, gazing at the golden light. *Please help Oberon. Please let Oberon be okay.*

Gray clouds rolled over the beautiful sky and the snow started to come down again, stinging his face. By the time the snowmobiles pulled up at a little cabin, he was numb with cold and fear and exhaustion. The silence, when the engines turned off, rang in his ears. Aaron climbed off the snowmobile and gave Ángel a little tug as if to help him rise, but his muscles had locked up, and he fell to his hands and knees in the snow. Aaron roughly hauled him up and dragged him into the cabin, which was heartbreakingly warm. He was shoved into a chair near a woodstove. While the men shucked off their snow-caked outerwear, he extended trembling red hands to the heat.

He timidly looked around while he warmed his hands. There were four guys. Logan the traitor, who wanted to kill him. Aaron, black-bearded and deep-voiced, who didn't. The third guy: a skinny weaselly dude not much more than eighteen, whose name he hadn't caught, and whose stance on killing Ángel he hadn't yet determined. And a fourth: midfifties, with piercing blue eyes and an air of authority, who'd presumably stayed behind in the cabin.

"I already know this was a clusterfuck," growled the old guy, folding his arms over his broad chest. "Where's Tommy?"

"Probably dead," said Logan. He and the others seemed to defer to the older guy as though he was their leader. "The elf wasn't asleep. We went up to his bedroom, but he wasn't there. He came up behind us and killed Tommy."

"How?"

"He threw him down the stairs." Logan's voice was husky with horror, and Ángel shivered too. "Broke his neck. I ran."

"Did he recognize you?"

"I don't know." Logan jerked his chin at Ángel, who was huddled by the stove, his thawing hair dripping. "This one knows me, though. He was outside for some reason, and spotted us going in."

The leader's blue gaze clicked over Ángel, who shrank deeper into the chair and said nothing.

Logan went on, "I'm not expected back from leave for a week, so if the elf didn't make me, the DOR won't know I was there."

Aaron said scornfully, "Dude, you think they won't figure out that the guy on vacation was involved?"

The leader asked, "Why wasn't Oberon asleep? Was he warned?"

"No way," said Logan.

"Bullshit." Aaron seemed to be Logan's chief opposition in all things. "You gave it away somehow. You did something stupid and tipped someone off, and the elf was ready for you."

"Fuck off," said Logan.

"You fuck off. You came to us saying this was a sure thing, and now Tommy's dead and we're going to have the DOR all over us, because of you."

"They were supposed to be asleep," whined Logan. "No one was where they were supposed to be."

An argument ensued, during which Ángel learned that weasel-face's name was Ron and he was the older guy's son. Ángel gathered that Logan had sought out the local anti-elf cell and sold them on his foolproof plan, and that now he was in deep shit.

"*He* must have figured it out somehow." Logan waved a hand at Ángel. "Dumbass little cocksucker."

There was so much venom in his voice that Ángel was unable to control a cringe.

"If he's such a dumbass, how'd he figure it out?" Aaron, his new best friend, stood like a rock, arms folded across his big chest. "Unless someone even dumber tipped his hand. Huh, Logan? How do you think that happened?"

"Enough." The leader's voice was sharp and cold. "None of that matters now. Tommy is dead, the elf is alive. We have to decide what to do next—are we safe here, or do we run? And what do we do with him?"

They all looked at Ángel.

Ángel frantically tried to think of something to say—some reason they should keep him alive. Dizzy and ill, he couldn't think of anything.

They argued some more. Ángel strove to keep from hyperventilating with terror. Eventually they decided they'd "put him on ice," and he squeezed his eyes shut, stomach clenching with fear. He opened them again when Aaron grabbed him by the collar of his coat and hauled him outside. Ángel couldn't quite control a high cry of alarm; he struggled and Aaron punched him in the kidney. His legs gave way and he collapsed, gagging. Aaron unceremoniously dragged him through the snow to a small wooden shed. He threw him in, and Ángel sprawled on the concrete floor, staring at Aaron's silhouette in the doorway.

"Listen up. You stay here while we figure out what to do. If you piss us off, we'll shoot you, and we know where to put your body where no one will ever find it. Got it?"

"Yeah," whispered Ángel.

"Good." Aaron paused. "There's a space heater and some blankets. Piss in the bucket, please. Don't set the shed on fire. We'll come get you when we decide what to do with you."

Ángel nodded. Aaron slammed the door, and Ángel heard him lock it.

Ángel bowed his head in despair. Tears dropped onto the concrete floor, and froze there.

After a few minutes, he forced himself to teeter to his feet. He tugged a chain to turn on the light—a single bulb hanging by its cord from the ceiling—and looked around.

The shed was, like most sheds, dusty and stale, a small box with one door and one high, cobwebby glass window. There were electric power outlets in the walls, and tidy shelves and cabinets. In the summer it was probably home to spiders; now it was bitterly cold, far too cold for anything to live. The light bulb was giving off a bit of heat, but not enough.

He dug in the cabinets, where he found some folded wool blankets, some sleeping bags, the promised bucket. And—"Oh yes, thank you," he breathed—a small electric space heater.

But there was no food or water. He was thirsty and, to his surprise, queasily hungry.

Nose wrinkling, he used the bucket, then covered it with a folded tarp. He swathed himself in blankets, positioned the space heater to blow on him, plugged it in, and turned it on. Its elements glowed red, and for several minutes he huddled in front of it and bathed in its warmth.

Then there was a *snap*, and both the space heater and the overhead light died.

Hmm. He'd blown a breaker. He heard his father's voice in his head: *"Old wiring. Too much load on the circuit. You should have turned the light off before you turned on the heater."*

No problem. He stood up, wrapping a blanket around himself like a shawl, turned off the light switch and unplugged the heater, and began hunting for the circuit box by the sunlight slanting in through the dirty window.

He didn't find the circuit box. It was probably in the cabin.

"Fuck." His voice was shivering. "Oh, goddamn it. Oh, motherfucking shit."

Now he was in real trouble.

It was extremely cold. This shed was uninsulated and unheated, and he'd just blown the power. With nothing but his damp coat and some blankets to protect him, he could die out here. He *would* die out here, unless he located a source of heat. The kidnappers wouldn't have to kill him; they'd find him frozen like an ice cream bar.

For a moment Ángel wavered, on the brink of collapsing to the floor again. He was too scared, too cold. It was too much. A vicious cycle, like when Oberon grieved, and couldn't stop grieving.

No. He clenched his jaw.

"Don't set the shed on fire," Aaron had commanded.

I will burn this fucker down.

He hunted through the cabinets. To his frustration, he found everything you might possibly need for a camping trip *except* something to make a fire: air mattresses, tents, backpacks, snowshoes, skis. No lighters, no matches, no flint and steel, no batteries, no cans of gasoline, no bullets. Nothing he could use.

His fingers grew bright red and clumsy, and his feet, in their boots, went totally numb. His breath was steaming, and he was shivering constantly.

"If I ever get back to Florida, I am never going to leave," he vowed through chattering teeth, wrapping a blanket around his right fist. Then he flipped the bucket over, stood on it, and, with all his strength, punched the window.

It shattered. Ángel fell backward off his makeshift stool and landed on the ground, clutching his hand between his thighs in agony. After a few minutes of silent breathless cursing, he crawled to his feet, unwrapped his right hand. He flexed his fingers, which didn't want to straighten all the way—cold, or broken?

That was his pick hand. If it was broken . . . He remembered his crushed guitar and almost started crying again. *No, come on, Ángel.* He needed to get out now, before someone noticed the broken window. If they hadn't noticed already.

Keep going. Pushing past his fear and pain, he climbed back up onto the bucket. He used his left hand to clear the shards of glass out of the window frame. No one was around, thank God—he still seemed to be undetected. Then he hoisted himself up and crawled out the window. He got snagged on a hidden chunk of glass, clawed himself loose with the sound of tearing denim and a sharp stabbing pain in his hip, and then he was out, rolling in a snowbank.

From the watery sunlight streaming through the trees, it seemed to be midafternoon. He staggered to his feet and limped stealthily toward the cabin, unhappily aware that he was leaving a trail of footprints in the snow that an idiot could follow. But the woods were silent. He didn't see anyone around.

There was a large, well-used-looking blue pickup truck parked in front of the cabin, but two of the snowmobiles were gone. He crept around the cabin, peeping in windows, scalp prickling with fright. He saw no one.

Had they left? Could he have gotten that lucky?

He tried the front door—it was unlocked. Quietly he let himself into the cabin and closed the door behind him and stood listening. The cabin seemed to be just three rooms, all of which he could see from where he hovered in the doorway: the kitchen/living room where he stood, one bedroom, and one bathroom. All empty. He relaxed. Maybe he could find a phone, or—

The pile of afghans on the couch shifted and mumbled, and Ángel nearly had a heart attack. Ron, the weaselly young guy, was there on the couch, buried in blankets. Ángel didn't breathe while Ron rolled over and sighed, apparently fast asleep.

Ángel removed his boots, and, in his socked feet, throbbing hand squeezed into his armpit, he searched the cabin. Fast and silent, hoping to find a weapon, or incriminating evidence, or a way to escape. Kitchen cabinets. Bathroom vanity. Bedroom dresser, shelves. Ron did not stir. In the bedside table Ángel found a roll of cash—three hundred dollars—which he pocketed.

Passing silently back through the main room, he spotted, hanging on a hook behind the wood stove, a set of keys.

Ángel stared at the keys, then the pickup, then the man in the sleeping bag, who still slept peacefully.

He grabbed his boots and the keys, and slipped outside.

He had to use his injured right hand to start the truck, which made pain radiate up his arm. The truck was a diesel and he worried that it would be hard to start in the cold, but it roared to life loud enough to wake the dead. Clenching his teeth, as if he could keep weasel-face Ron from waking up by will alone, he executed a clumsy three-point turn in the driveway—thank God it was an automatic—and pointed the truck's nose down the mountain.

For the rest of his life Ángel would revisit the terrifying white-knuckle drive from the cabin in his nightmares.

He had never driven in the snow before. This road was nothing more than a pair of tire ruts in snow, winding steeply down through the trees. Constantly clenched for disaster—for pursuit, for the truck to slide into a tree, or to jam itself in a snowbank—he found himself praying again. *Don't get stuck, don't get stuck, don't get stuck.*

He didn't get stuck. He eventually came out onto a lonely paved two-lane road, plowed and sanded, which surely meant it lead somewhere. At random, he turned left.

He was still shivering a little. The truck had a powerful heater which, cranked up to the max, warmed him but could not thaw the ice around his heart. He was dizzy from fatigue and hunger and pain, too, and was worried that he would fall asleep and drive right off the road. So he turned on the radio. It was tuned to the local NPR station playing *All Things Considered*.

The man on the radio said, "Audie, security was extremely tight here in Missoula this morning when the new envoy from the Otherworld arrived in a maple tree not far from the University of Montana campus."

Ángel braked hard, steered the pickup onto the shoulder of the road, and stopped with a lurch. He turned up the volume.

"The tree began to glow early this morning," said the radio man, "giving the DOR time to arrive and secure a perimeter for his safety."

"Tell us about the new envoy, Larry," said Audie.

"Well, the press was kept in a sort of corral pretty far away," said Larry. "But from what I could see he looks just like Oberon. He was greeted and given a robe by the mayor of Missoula, because like Oberon he arrived without any clothes. And Oberon was there. Due to the last-minute announcement of the new envoy's arrival, the governor of Montana was unable to attend."

"We've seen some very moving photographs of the two elven envoys greeting each other," said Audie. "Tell us what that was like."

"It *was* very moving, Audie," said Larry. "Oberon approached the new envoy and I thought he was going to shake his hand, but instead he threw his arms around him. He—" Larry's professional demeanor seemed to slip a little. "He really fell into the new envoy's arms, and they embraced for a long time. Of course I couldn't tell what was said, but the scene appeared quite touching."

"And where are the envoys now?"

"Audie, we don't know the answer to that question," said Larry. "Security around the envoy has always been tight, and it's even more so now. As we said, no one knew that the fae were going to be in Missoula at all, and at the moment, no one knows their whereabouts except the DOR."

"Do you think that's in part because of the recent assassination attempt?"

"That's right. As you know, in the early morning hours last night, assassins broke into Oberon's compound in northern Montana and made an unsuccessful attempt upon his life. Oberon was not seriously injured in that attack, but one of his assailants was killed and several others escaped. During the night Oberon's friend and podcasting partner, Ángel Cruz, vanished. The DOR is still investigating, and seeking clues as to Cruz's whereabouts and his possible involvement."

"*What*," yelped Ángel.

"Thank you, Larry," said Audie. "Larry Mandalay from KUFM, Montana Public Radio in Missoula, is covering this surprising story."

Ángel turned off the radio and sat in the truck, trembling.

His *possible involvement.*

Until now, Ángel's one driving thought had been to be reunited with Oberon as soon as possible. It had never occurred to him that he would be under suspicion. But he had walked straight out of the house and into the security blank spot, into the assassins' arms. He had accompanied them to their cabin. He was driving their truck, he had a pocket full of their cash.

Could he prove that he *wasn't* involved? What was his defense? *I was outside in the snow because I was upset* sounded spectacularly stupid.

"I don't know what to do," said Ángel aloud. His voice sounded ragged, even to himself. "What do I do now?"

He might get arrested. He might go to prison.

Oberon wouldn't let that happen. Would he?

Ángel's stomach growled. He hadn't eaten since . . . was it the day before? The day before yesterday? His sense of time was all messed up.

He might be able to come up with a rational plan if he had some food. Shaking, he pulled the truck onto the road again.

Just at sunset he passed a green sign that announced: Entering Cascade: Population 939.

There was not a lot going on in the town of Cascade: a tackle shop that was closed for the winter, a grocery store, a US Forest Service office. Ángel stopped at Auntie's Homestyle Restaurant (*Come Hungry, Leave Happy!*) and went in, hoping that the local cops weren't on the lookout for dirty, sweaty, frightened Cubano fugitives.

Auntie's was blissfully warm. The hostess seemed friendly and too busy to be suspicious; she told him there would be a wait for a table, but that he could sit at the counter right away. He perched on a stool at the counter and tried not to be obvious as he glanced around. The place was full of white people, mostly older couples and families. But one corner table hosted five brown people, quietly speaking Spanish to each other. *Probably Mexican*, thought Ángel, illogically but instantly a little more comfortable.

He ordered coffee, soup, a cheeseburger, and a side of tater tots. As he waited, the guy next to him paid and left, leaving behind a newspaper. The *Idaho Statesman*.

Ángel ate the huge quantity of hot food that appeared before him and read the paper. They must have rushed to print. The photograph on the front page showed Oberon and the other fae envoy with their arms wrapped tightly around each other. Oberon's face was buried in the other fae's shoulder, and their identical green-and-ivory hair blew around them. The new envoy had a slender hand cupped around the back of Oberon's head.

They were communicating with each other. Through touch.

The article confirmed that the DOR was *very* interested in Ángel's whereabouts. There was a toll-free tip line and everything.

Oh God.

Staring at the picture, he wondered if Oberon thought Ángel had betrayed him too. The cheeseburger was suddenly a cold and greasy wad in Ángel's stomach.

He didn't have a home. He didn't have a family. His best friend was now friends with a DOR agent.

Oberon was his lover. Oberon was his love. He trusted Oberon. But Ángel had run away. He hadn't been there when Oberon needed him. And now, *right now*, Oberon was being comforted by someone else. Someone who could communicate with him better than Ángel ever could.

"You okay, hon?" asked the waitress.

He deliberately fisted his sore right hand, letting the pain wash through him and clear his whirling mind. Did the waitress seem suspicious? Did she know they were looking for him? Was one of his fellow diners at Auntie's going to call the cops on him?

"Yeah," he said, huskily. "I'm okay. It's been a long day."

"You want more coffee?"

"Just the bill. Thank you."

He paid and put on his coat, making for the exit. No one seemed to be paying him any attention. No, someone *was* watching him—one of the guys at the corner table met Ángel's eyes. He gave an infinitesimal head-tip. Did he recognize Ángel? Or was he just greeting a fellow Latino? Ángel returned the nod and went outside.

It was full dark out, but the sodium streetlights washed the parking lot in an unnatural pinkish glow. There wasn't as much snow here as up at Oberon's estate, but the wind was whipping through town, laden with fragments of ice that stung the skin and worked into his coat.

He didn't know what to do. The food and coffee had not cleared his mind. He did not have a clever plan. He felt just as trapped and frozen now as he had in the shed.

Aimlessly he walked across the parking lot toward the truck, with no better idea than to get in and keep driving.

His eyes fell on the handsome green-roofed building across the street.

In front of it, improbably, was a payphone.

CHAPTER
TWENTY-EIGHT

He stumbled up to it through the punishing wind, fed it all the change from his pocket.

He didn't even think about it: he dialed the number he'd memorized when he was six years old, the number he'd been told would get him to safety, no matter what.

"*Bueno.*"

"Papá," said Ángel.

There was a long pause. Ángel squeezed his eyes shut, wondering if Victor was going to hang up.

But then his father said, "Ángel. Are you all right?"

"I'm lost," Ángel said. Another pause, and Ángel added, "I'm sorry. I don't know who else to call."

"You always can call me, Ángelito," said Victor gruffly.

"I didn't do it." Ángel hugged himself against the cold, the phone wedged between his shoulder and jaw. "I didn't sell him out."

"No one thinks you did that. We were scared you was dead, Ángel. Are you hurt?"

"I hurt my hand. They tased me. I can't stop shaking. But maybe that's the cold. It's so cold here, Papá, you wouldn't believe it."

"Tell me where you're at. Someone will come get you."

"Can you get a message to Oberon? Tell him I didn't do it."

"Ángel," said Victor, slowly. "Tell me where you at."

"Idaho," said Ángel, sliding to sit on the sidewalk. "I think Idaho. The town's called Cascade."

"Someone's coming, Ángel. Hold on."

"I'm really cold. So cold."

He rested his forehead on his knees, the telephone cradle icy against his cheek.

"Tell me what you see."

"A Forest Service building, with a green roof. A Shell station. There's a sign—it says there's a senior center."

"Go on," said Victor, softly. "Tell me what else."

So Ángel talked, describing what he could see of the town of Cascade in the pinkish glare of its streetlights. They'd been cut off by the time the DOR helicopter landed in the parking lot.

In a featureless office building in Atlanta, Ángel was questioned for hours by a team of DOR agents, led by Neil Jeremy, the red-haired man he'd first met in Jacksonville.

They didn't seem angry. Ángel didn't seem to be in trouble.

A medic had looked at his hand, and they'd given him dry clothes: socks, tighty-whities, a light-blue DOR T-shirt, and a navy sweat suit, all slightly too big. Under the soft clean clothes, his body was still dirty and rank with sweat and blood.

His mind felt frozen. He hadn't been able to nap on the plane, and he was numb with exhaustion.

"How long were you on the snowmobile after you left Oberon's estate?" asked Jeremy.

"I don't know." Ángel had answered this question already. Jeremy's secretary had written it down. He'd already told them everything, everything. "I was really out of it. But I think it was around midnight when they caught me, and it was daylight when we got to the cabin. So it must have been several hours."

The only thing he hadn't told Jeremy was his reason for being outside in the middle of the night at Oberon's estate. That last conversation with Oberon—Oberon had been so happy, and he, Ángel, so selfish—burned his memory.

He'd discuss that conversation with Oberon, and no one else.

"And you think you went south?"

He remembered the gold-and-flamingo sunrise filling the sky to his left. "At least some of the time we were going south."

"But maybe not the whole time?"

"I don't know."

"Tell me about the men again. Everything you can remember."

He told them. He ratted out Logan the goon with relish, and put in a good word for Aaron the not-a-fag-killer. Jeremy seemed to think Ángel had some variety of Stockholm Syndrome when it came to Aaron, but what could he say? Aaron had tased him, had hoisted him over the wall, had put him in the shed to freeze, but he could have just shot him in the snow. He hadn't.

"They were armed?"

"Yes."

"What kind of guns were they carrying?"

"I . . . I didn't see any guns. But they talked about shooting me, and they didn't seem like they were fucking around."

"You didn't see the guns?"

Ángel closed his eyes. "No."

"What kind of snowmobiles were they?"

A single-man sled. Hold on.

"Ángel? Did you notice the make of the snowmobiles?"

"No," he said, not opening his eyes. He'd already told them he didn't know anything about the snowmobiles.

"And what direction did you go?"

"Sleep," he said. "I think we went south. I need to sleep."

"Ángel." The voice was gentle, insistent. "One more question, and you can sleep. Okay?"

Let me sleep, he said. Or thought he said.

"The day before the attack, you told Oberon to turn off the cameras and microphones in his office. What did you talk about?"

Ángel's exhausted mind struggled to wrap itself around this question.

"You were off mike for about twenty minutes. Why did you do that? What did you and Oberon have to talk about? Did you argue?"

What?

"You were upset when you left the house. Did it have something to do with what you talked about off-mike? Did Oberon break your guitar?"

Ángel forced his eyes open. "*What?* No."

Jeremy's eyes were blue and innocent. Ángel frowned at him. That question made no sense. He was so tired, and none of these questions seemed to make any sense.

Deliberately, Ángel said, "I told him to turn off the mikes, and then I sucked his dick."

Jeremy's eyes widened, his nostrils flaring.

"That what you wanted to know?" demanded Ángel, his voice ragged. "Here I thought you were trying to find out who attacked Oberon, but really you just want to know whether we were fucking? Well, we were. What else? You want to know if he tops or bottoms?"

Agent Jeremy's fair skin flushed, his eyes now downcast. "I wrote your employment contract. It made no mention of—of sexual—"

"Oh, fuck off."

"It was never our intention—"

"Am I free to go?" Ángel stood up and swayed alarmingly. "You're not arresting me or anything, right? I can leave?"

"Ángel—"

"Okay then, I'm leaving." He went to the door, fumbling with the knob.

Agent Jeremy stood up and opened the door for him. "Emma," he said to his secretary, "take Mr. Cruz to a hotel. Make sure he has everything he needs. Ángel, we'll talk more when you're rested."

"Can't wait," snarled Ángel.

CHAPTER
TWENTY-NINE

At the hotel Ángel thought he'd sleep like the dead, but he was restless, plagued by dreams that he wasn't safe, that he was lost, that he was missing something vital. He bolted awake near dawn gasping Oberon's name. Tunneling beneath the sterile-smelling hotel-bed blankets, he tried to calm his mind and sleep again. He couldn't seem to get warm.

He was still tired when a knock on the door dragged him out of bed at eight thirty. Expecting Agent Jeremy, he shuffled to the door and opened it, and was nearly bowled off his feet by Marissa, all curves and curls and a powerful hug. He put his arms around her, resting his cheek on her head, and watched with dawning bewilderment, as Chandler Evanston and Victor Cruz stepped into the room.

"How did you get here?" he demanded.

"We drove all night!" Marissa's strong arms tightened, and then she pulled back to scrutinize him. "We picked up your dad in Jax on the way. You look like *shit*."

"You look amazing." She was big and beautiful, wild hair and lush mouth, radiating health and joy, just like always—even after the grueling ten-hour drive from Miami to Atlanta.

Then Victor was there, and, awkwardly, Ángel accepted his hug too. "*Mijo*." Victor cupped Ángel's face in his hands, brows crooked with concern. "They hurt you. They treat you bad?"

"No, I—" Suddenly overwhelmed, Ángel felt his eyes fill with tears. His father despised displays of emotion, so he swallowed them. "They— No, it was okay. Until it went bad."

"It wasn't okay," said Chandler. She had seated herself at the hotel desk while the other two crowded around him. She was in civilian clothes—jeans and an Oxford shirt. "None of it. You were a virtual prisoner there. You had no avenue for escape or opposition to anything that happened to you. No ground to stand on for resistance."

He blinked at her, and saw, to his surprise, that she had cut her hair: the long sleek braid had been lopped off above the shoulder, and her dark locks waved softly around her face. It made her appear disconcertingly young. "I resigned from the DOR the morning of the attack," she explained.

"It wasn't your fault."

"That's debatable. I hired Logan." She cocked her head, ice-blue eyes assessing him. "You really don't look so good."

"*And* you stink," said Marissa. She gave him a little push toward the bathroom. "Shower and shave, Angela. When's the last time you ate?"

He shook his head, wonderingly. "I think I was in Idaho."

"I'll order breakfast."

When he emerged from the bathroom, Marissa had turned the bed into a lavish room-service buffet: eggs, ham, fried potatoes, cheddar grits, sliced tomatoes, biscuits, sausages, orange juice, and coffee. Good Southern food. He accepted a cup from his father and a plate from Marissa. "Can we eat all this?"

"It's on the DOR's bill," said Marissa, with rancor. "I'm thinking of ordering more. Talk, Ángel."

"I was upset," he said. "So I went outside for a walk . . ."

Marissa let him lean on her as he ate and told the story, and by the time he was scraping cheese off his plate with his fork, he felt physically better. His heart still ached, though, with a palpable pain, so after he set his plate down he said, "What I really need to do is talk to Oberon."

"Why?" said Chandler, bluntly.

He and Chandler were the only people here who knew Oberon, who knew what it was like in that house in Montana. "You know why. He was worried when I disappeared."

"He was, but I'm sure the DOR has told him that you're okay."

"That's good," he said. "I still need to talk to him."

"I listen to your podcast," said Victor, who'd been quiet.

"You do?" Ángel said.

Marissa put in, "Everyone listens to it. People talk about it on the bus, in the grocery store. It's good."

"Everyone likes the elf-lord," said Victor. "Made him seem like a nice guy."

"That was the idea." Ángel felt shyly pleased. Victor had never come to listen to Ángel perform, so far as he knew. He disapproved of his career as a musician.

But he liked the podcast, and in spite of the years of anger between them, a little flower of pleasure opened in Ángel's heart.

"I'm sorry I sent you there, Ángel," said Victor. "It was weak. It was wrong. I never should have done it."

"It wasn't so bad there, though," said Ángel. "I like him. He's extraordinary. I wouldn't have met him without you. So it's okay."

"It's not okay," interrupted Chandler. "Ángel. Oberon is not your friend."

He scowled. "Yes, he is. You *know* what he is to me."

"I know that he used you," she said. "And God help me, I and the rest of the DOR abetted him. He put you in an impossible position. He played with your mind. He made you think he needed you—"

"He does need me!" cried Ángel.

"He needed a warm body," said Chandler. "To survive, he needed someone. If it hadn't been you, it would have been someone else—Lily, or me."

"That is such bullshit," said Ángel. "If you think that, you don't know him."

"I've known him for years," she said pitilessly. "I know what he is. He's a creature that needs touch to survive. When he first arrived, he wanted to touch everyone—he tried to touch *me*—I know how awful it was."

"No—"

"He procured you, and he took what he needed. And on one level I can't blame him, because that's what he needed to live.

And maybe to live with it you need to pretend you had some kind of special relationship with him. But it's time to wake up, Ángel."

"He didn't *procure* me," spat Ángel. Both Marissa and Victor drew back.

Chandler faced him down. "He manipulated you!"

"He closed himself in his room and quietly started *dying*, all by himself. He didn't ask for anything. I went to him."

"You were groomed—"

"I'm not a child!" Ángel shouted. "I *am not a victim*. I did it because I wanted to. That make you uncomfortable? You feel better about it if you think of me as a poor innocent kid? Okay! I get that. But my eyes are open, Chandler. I do what I want. *I have always done what I want*, even if other people don't like it."

"Okay," soothed Marissa. She wrapped her arms around him from behind, holding him, putting her chin on his shoulder. "Okay, Ángel."

"What I see," Chandler said, gently but implacably, "is someone who is strong, but who was caught in an impossible situation. I see how independent you are. I do. But do you see the contortions you're turning right now, to convince yourself that what happened was okay?" She ticked off points on her fingers. "You were imprisoned. You were under constant, *constant* surveillance. He watched you sleep. When you disabled the cameras, he made you feel guilty about it. Anytime you asserted your independence, he made you feel bad about it, like it was hurting him. He used your estrangement from your family. He used your loneliness. How could any of that be acceptable?"

Ángel was silent.

"You were fucked by the elf-lord, Ángel! And I'm culpable for that," Chandler said. "I'll regret it for the rest of my life."

"So will I," said Victor humbly.

"God*damn* it," said Ángel. He looked at Marissa. "Do you think that too? Do you think—"

"I don't know what to think." She rested her forehead against his. "I don't ever want you to feel ashamed of anything, baby. But I know you sometimes do impulsive things, and regret them later."

"He needed me," whispered Ángel. "No one ever needed me, Marissa, not once in my whole life. Is it so bad to be with someone who needed me?"

"I don't know," she said. Then: "Yes, of course it's okay to help someone. But maybe it wasn't okay for him to make you feel like you had to help."

"*It wasn't like that.*"

She pressed her lips together. "I love you no matter what it was like, okay?"

But she didn't believe him. They were twisting everything, taking the loveliest thing that had ever happened to him and turning it inside-out, into something disgusting. They were wrong. In that moment he ached for Oberon to hold him, to tell him again that he was safe.

"I just— I just need to talk to him, okay?"

"Then do it," Marissa said simply.

He got up, fumbled in the pocket of the too-big sweats for a business card: Agent Neil Jeremy. He went to the phone on the bedside table and called the number.

He got Jeremy's secretary. She put him through, and the DOR agent immediately asked if he was rested and well enough for another meeting and more questions.

"Sure," said Ángel, picking up the hotel pen, doodling on the hotel pad. "But first I want to talk to Oberon. What's his number?"

"Oberon's been really busy," said Jeremy. "What with the arrival of the new envoy."

Ángel paused. Then, politely, he said, "Excuse me, but that is not true. I know that Oberon was upset when I went missing. I know that he will want to hear from me that I'm all right."

"Of course, we told him immediately when we learned you were safe," said Jeremy. "We've been keeping him posted. He is reassured that you're fine."

Ángel wrinkled his brow. He put a palm over the phone and said to Chandler, "Is there a reason the DOR would be keeping me from talking to Oberon?"

She shrugged. "I can't think of one, but I don't work for them anymore."

Ángel spoke into the phone again. "I know that Oberon will want to hear from me. I would like you to put me in touch with him. Better yet, I want to go see him. Is he still at the Montana house? Or are he and the new envoy somewhere else?"

"I'll leave him a message and ask him what he'd like to do," said Jeremy. "But as I said, he's been very busy."

"I don't get this." Ángel stabbed the pad with the pen, frustrated. "You hired me to keep him company, right? Now you don't want me to do that? What changed?"

"It's really not up to me," said Jeremy. "Oberon makes his own decisions about who he wants to talk to."

"Neil, did I do something wrong? I haven't been fired, have I?"

"Definitely not. Your contract with the DOR is in good standing. You're still drawing a salary. But I'm not able to put you directly in touch with Oberon. I can certainly pass along your message, though."

"He'll want to talk to me."

"Then don't worry. I'll tell him, and if he wants to talk to you, I'm sure he'll call. In the meantime, why not relax? Take a vacation day from Oberon and the DOR."

He hung up. Ángel tossed the pen down and looked around at the others: sympathetic Marissa, cool Chandler. His father, uncomfortable, silent.

"Well," Ángel said. "I don't have any clothes, or a phone, or anything, but I do have some money. Who wants to go shopping?"

They walked to a shopping mall near the hotel, where Ángel spent the better part of an hour buying a new phone while Chandler and Marissa went to get him some clothes. Then he and Victor bought sweet tea and sat in the food court waiting for the women, and Ángel bent over his new phone, connected to the mall's wi-fi, and began to set up apps.

He heard Victor take in a breath to say something, and he braced himself: would it be disapproving? Pitying? Both?

Instead, Victor said, "Father Dennis died in October. He had a stroke."

"Oh." *Good fucking riddance.* But Father Dennis had been Victor's friend for years. "I'm sorry for your loss."

Victor sighed. "He regretted it, you know. He always felt he drove you away from the Church."

"Well, *yeah.* He totally did. He meant to."

"No, Ángel. He knew he shouldn't have told me about you," said Victor. "That was wrong. But he believed you could choose another path. He thought we could help you."

"Papá. I know you liked him, and I don't want to fight with you. But he was *not* trying to help me. If he'd known the word, he'd have called me a *cherna* to my face."

Victor winced. Not a big fan of the gay, he also deplored name-calling. "Sometimes," he said, "people are helping you, and it looks like something else. If you look at it from their point of view you can see."

"Sure."

Victor sighed, nodded. "I know. And sometimes people are wrong, and they regret it, and they wish they could make it up to you."

Ángel disagreed, but he didn't want to wrangle about this with Victor. This was the longest conversation he'd had with his father in years, after all. Why ruin it?

"I was wrong to send you there," said Victor.

Ángel studied his father. Victor had rarely, if ever, admitted fault before. But he seemed different now, less hard. He was thinner too, and browner; maybe he'd been spending more time in the sun, since he'd lost his business. "Was it Mom?" he asked. "The Ponzi scheme?"

"Your mom and Bill. They used my name. I didn't know about it at first, not until it was big." Victor paused. "I couldn't let her go to prison."

Ángel snorted softly. "I notice she's not here."

"No, she—she was embarrassed. By the publicity. You know."

"Yeah, Papá. I know." She had already been embarrassed by him—and that was before he'd gotten a reputation for being an elf-fucker. Victor was here, though. No doubt he was embarrassed by the publicity too; not to mention that he'd taken the fall for something he hadn't done. But here he was. "I'm glad you came."

"I'm glad you called me," said Victor. "I knew I was wrong the minute you signed that contract. I was scared, and the DOR made it seem like the best thing. But then I saw you were so angry. I knew you'd never forgive me. I tried to make it right. I wrote him—Oberon—I wrote and apologized to him. I asked him to let me take your place. He . . . he said he was happy to have you there. But I knew it was wrong, Ángel. I'm sorry."

"Oh, God. It's okay. Don't feel so bad." Ángel tried to smile. "One time I asked Oberon why he came here, and he said, 'I am a great adventurer.' That's me too, no? I mean it. I had a great adventure."

Victor nodded, not meeting his eyes. "Look. There are the girls."

Marissa and Chandler were approaching, carrying shopping bags, and Ángel and Victor watched them from a distance. Marissa was bouncing, laughing, chattering, gesturing with her hands. Chandler, just as straight and military as usual, was gazing at Marissa with an expression of dumbfounded fascination that made Ángel smile. "Now *that's* a relationship I didn't see coming."

"She was Oberon's security chief?" asked Victor.

"Yes, and a giant pain in my ass."

"Sometimes," said Victor, "we thought you and Marissa would be together."

By *we*, Ángel knew Victor was referring to the community of Cuban family and neighbors and fellow-parishioners who had helped to raise him. Who he had mostly lost. He scratched his head, pushing his hair away from his face. "I let you think that sometimes," he admitted. "Sometimes I got tired of being the talk of the town. But no."

"Don't you think you could ever—"

"Papá, *look* at them," said Ángel, gesturing at the two women. Marissa had taken Chandler's hands and was now dancing in the middle of the courtyard, swiveling her hips to make her skirts flare out and her hair swing, eyes locked on Chandler's. "Forget about me for a second, and see the way Marissa's looking at her. I don't know Chandler so well, but Marissa could never look at any man like that. It's not a choice. It's just how it is."

Marissa's face was bright with admiration as she twirled Chandler around. Oberon's face would never brighten that way when he looked at Ángel. Or anyone. But he'd called Ángel his love.

He tapped his new phone's screen and dialed Neil Jeremy's number. This time Emma the secretary didn't put him through: "I'm sorry, Agent Jeremy is in a meeting for the rest of the afternoon."

"I wanted to give him my new phone number, so that Oberon can call me."

Was there an infinitesimal pause on her end? "Okay, that's great. What's the number?"

He gave it to her. "It's really, really important. You'll make sure he sees it as soon as he's out of the meeting?"

"Of course."

"Or, you know, you could just text my number straight to Oberon; how would that be? That way, he can call me directly, and we wouldn't have to waste Agent Jeremy's time."

"I'll check with Agent Jeremy as soon as he's free," she promised.

He sighed and hung up, and got up to go see what the women had bought.

After that they all trooped off to the shoe store, since Ángel only had his heavy snow boots. And then Marissa saw that, somehow, there was an ice rink in the mall, and wanted to go skating. (She was *definitely* treating this excursion as a date with Chandler.) Ángel couldn't get into the spirit, so he sat on the sidelines and watched as Marissa, Chandler, and, surprisingly, Victor, glided around the ice.

The waiting was killing him. He *ached* to talk to Oberon. Where was he? How did he feel about what had happened? How did he feel about Ángel?

Ángel called Neil Jeremy again. Again Emma put him off.

Was it that Oberon, alone and bereft, had turned to the new envoy and didn't need Ángel anymore?

Or maybe it was as Chandler believed: Oberon had *never* loved Ángel, had just manipulated him and used him, and simply no longer required his services?

No. Oberon cared about him. Oberon was his friend. Ángel just needed to talk to him.

After skating they were hungry, so they went to a restaurant and ordered a feast: shrimp and grits, chicken and waffles, crab cakes. Ángel could barely eat. He watched, interested, because Marissa was not fucking around here: she was aiming a firehose of sparkling charm at former DOR goon Chandler Evanston, and Chandler was visibly thawing. Chandler accepted a bite of bourbon pineapple upside-down cake from Marissa's fork, her cheeks flushing red, and Ángel found himself exchanging a knowing glance with Victor.

"You should come back with me to Jacksonville, *retaco*," said Victor.

Ángel smiled at the old childhood nickname. "Thanks. I'll think about it."

"Or just come home to Miami," said Marissa. "Your apartment's still there, isn't it?"

"I think I have a sublet," Ángel said listlessly. "The DOR arranged it."

"Well, the DOR can un-arrange it."

"I can't leave," he said. "I signed a contract."

"Yeah, but things have changed, and they don't seem to know what to do with you right now," she said. "You don't have to keep hanging around here while they figure it out. You have a life. You can come back to it."

"I can't."

She leaned across the table, waggling her eyebrows. "I heard Kinsley Halliday's going to be recording an album in January."

"Really?" Kinsley Halliday was a young country singer-songwriter who had Kickstarter-produced a bunch of very good songs. He heard she'd been picked up by Sony. "In Miami?"

"In Nashville, but they're scouting Miami musicians because she wants to do an island sound." Marissa smiled at him. "Interesting, yes?"

It would be a great gig—to get in on the ground floor with a promising up-and-comer. A year ago he'd have fought for that gig.

"I can't," he said again. "I have to talk to Oberon."

She put a hand on his. "You were kidnapped, and I know you're still recovering. But remember that it's over. You can come home."

She didn't understand. It wasn't over at all. It was like he was still helpless on the back of that snowmobile, swiftly getting farther and farther away from Oberon.

They walked back to his hotel, discussing whether they could get the DOR to pay for a room for Victor. (Victor was broke. He hadn't gone to prison, but he'd apparently gone bankrupt, his shop had closed, and no one would hire him because everyone knew he'd pled guilty to fraud. He was living off food stamps and handouts from friends.)

"You can stay in my room," said Ángel. "There's two beds."

"Thank you."

"I'm in the one by the window."

"I prefer the one closer to the bathroom," said Victor. "Because of my age."

Ángel grinned at him. "Oh, please. You're not *that* old."

The *real* question, as they entered the hotel lobby, was whether Chandler and Marissa were going to be sharing a room. As the women made their way to the front desk, he pulled out his phone and saw that, during diner, Neil Jeremy had left a message. Cursing himself for missing it, he played it back:

"Ángel, this is Agent Jeremy. I wanted to let you know that I passed your message on to Oberon. He said that he's been spending so much time with Mendel—that's what they're calling the new envoy—that he doesn't have time to talk to you right now. But he says he's glad you're okay. Call me tomorrow and we'll discuss renegotiating the terms of your contract—"

"What?" Ángel had stopped walking, not noticing that the others had gone on ahead. He stood in the middle of the busy hotel lobby, pressed his fingers to one ear, and listened to the message again.

". . . he doesn't have time to talk to you right now . . . he says he's glad you're okay."

"What?" he whispered. He listened to it again.

Oberon doesn't have time *for you.*

"Hey."

He was sitting on the floor now, replaying the message again. Marissa was there, kneeling in front of him, prying the phone out of his cold hand. He leaned into her, rested his head on her shoulder, and they listened to the message together. Victor was kneeling too, his hand steady on Ángel's back. Marissa handed the phone to Chandler, so she could hear it too.

"I thought—" said Ángel, breathless with pain. "He said— He told me he loved me."

Chandler turned off the phone's display decisively. "Ángel. I'm sorry, but—"

"Don't," Marissa said sharply, her hands in Ángel's hair. "Now's not the time, Chan."

He opened his eyes and looked into Marissa's. "She's wrong, you know," he breathed. "I never believed him. I never really believed that he loved me. But I believed that he— I believed that he *liked* me. I knew he needed me, and I thought—I thought, when he realized he didn't need me anymore, that he would be kind."

He was crying. He was making a giant scene in a hotel lobby, on the floor, surrounded by strangers, but he couldn't stop crying. His heart hurt so much.

Marissa held him. Victor wrapped his arms around his shaking shoulders.

"I hate crying," he sobbed into Marissa's neck.

"I know."

"Why do I always cry? It doesn't help."

"I know," she soothed, stroking his hair. "I know."

CHAPTER THIRTY

"So, are you coming home?" Marissa asked him over breakfast the next morning.

Ángel's head still felt clogged with grief, but Marissa wasn't letting him wallow. She'd harassed him out of bed, made him take a shower, and was now sitting cross-legged on the floor of his room, tapping a reggae beat on her plate with her fork.

"I guess I should," he said, cutting up his pancakes into small pieces, not eating them.

His unlikely family—Marissa, Victor, and Chandler—was all assembled, along with a mountain of room service food. Victor had found a local NPR interview program on the hotel's clock radio. It was soothing. Victor always listened to NPR during breakfast.

She put an arm over Ángel's shoulder and gave him a little shake. "Come on," she said. "Let's blow this popsicle stand. We can be in Jacksonville by lunchtime."

How can I just leave? He stared at his mutilated pancakes, his eyes blurring with useless tears. *But how can I stay?*

"I need to call the DOR," he temporized. "I need to . . . end my contract, I guess. Get paid. Find out if I have a place to live."

"You can do all that from the road."

"Yeah." He tried to think ahead. "I guess . . . I should update my website too. Call people and let them know I'm open for business again."

"You'll be in huge demand," she said encouragingly. "Everyone's gonna want Ángel Cruz on their record."

He smiled at her weakly. "You're an optimist."

"I'm really not. You're going to be so hot, you might need to hire an agent to filter out the lookie-loos." She jostled him again. "You're going to be *busy*. You'll make good music, and meet lots of people, and you won't have time to be sad."

He leaned on her. He couldn't imagine not being sad. The idea of leaving without even speaking to Oberon, just because of a secondhand kiss-off on his phone—it felt wrong.

He opened his eyes and saw Chandler watching him.

She said, "I would walk away, Ángel. This is a bad scene, but you can leave it behind."

"That's what you did?" he asked—not challenging her, just wondering. "You left it behind? Isn't it hard?"

She smiled a little, a one-sided twist of her lips. "It's hard," she said. "But all you have to do is start walking. Keep walking until you're free."

"Free," he said disconsolately. He rubbed his chest, as if the pain there was a physical bruise that could be massaged away.

"Come on," Marissa said, ruffling his hair. "Gather up your stuff."

"Yes. Okay."

He put his few belongings into yesterday's shopping bags, pocketed his new phone, and checked out of the hotel. As though from a distance, he listened to the others make plans: with luck they'd hit Jacksonville by one, where they'd have a bite to eat and drop Victor off at home. They'd hit Miami that evening—right at rush hour, but that couldn't be helped. Chandler was coming too. She needed to find a job, but she had some savings and didn't have anywhere in particular to be. Ángel averted his eyes, sick with misery and envy, as Marissa and Chandler held hands on the way down to the parking garage.

Ángel stood and watched as they all piled into Marissa's little car: Marissa and Chandler in the back seat, where they could cuddle; Victor in the driver's seat, because *naturally* Victor wanted to be in the driver's seat. He looked happy, adjusting the seat and the mirrors, fiddling with the radio to find an NPR station. He leaned over and pushed the passenger-side door open. "Get in, *retaco*," he called.

Ángel didn't get in.

Oberon, where are you? He shoved his hands into his pockets, staring blindly at the car's waiting passenger seat.

If Ángel could just find out where he was, he would go to him. He would see him, see that he and the new envoy were happy. Maybe he would wish him well, and say goodbye. The thought of it hurt unbearably, but the thought of getting into that car and driving away without doing it was far worse.

Marissa rolled down the back seat window. "Come on, Angela, what's the holdup?"

He wasn't getting in that car.

"I can't leave," he said. "Not without talking to him."

"Why?" demanded Chandler, leaning over Marissa.

"I can't. No. I promised him I'd stay. As long as he needed me."

"But he—"

"I know, Chandler." He ran his hands through his hair, desperately. "I *know* he doesn't, anymore, but I still have to talk to him. Just once. To say goodbye, I guess. I have to get them to let me see him."

"Ángel," said Marissa, with exasperation. "Why?"

"Because I love him." They were all staring at him. "I know you don't get it. And maybe he doesn't feel the same way. But he said he did, and I do. So I have to see him, that's all."

They stood at an impasse. The only sound was the voice coming through the car's radio, echoing in the quiet parking garage. "My real name is difficult for you to pronounce."

Ángel's heart clenched. The voice was almost familiar. He stepped toward the car.

"Turn it up," he said to his father. Victor blinked at him, startled, and Ángel repeated, gesturing to the radio, "Papá. Turn it *up*."

It was a fae voice. A rich, expressive, beautiful voice, a voice created by a nonhuman larynx, a voice like a musical instrument. But it wasn't Oberon's resonant bass-baritone; it was higher, poised between tenor and alto, soft-toned. That voice made a tremble thrill through Ángel's body. He braced himself on the car's frame and leaned in.

"They wanted to call me Caliban, after a famous Shakespeare fae. As they called Oberon after a famous Shakespeare fae. But actually, Patrick, neither Oberon nor I like the Shakespeare fae very much, because they are rather cruel."

It was an interview on Victor's beloved NPR. The host asked, "So why did you decide on Mendel?"

"Well, I asked for a famous gardener instead. Someone who liked plants," said the second envoy from the Otherworld. "And they told me about the famous scientist Gregor Mendel."

"He founded the study of genetics," said Patrick.

"By growing *peas*," said Mendel. His lovely voice expressed delight. "I have never seen a pea, but I looked it up, and they are the *most* beautiful plants. I would love to see a pea someday."

"I'm sure that can be arranged," said Patrick, who sounded utterly charmed. "We have wonderful botanical gardens here in Atlanta."

"Are they here in Atlanta?" murmured Marissa.

"I suppose they must be," said Chandler.

Weak-kneed, Ángel sank into the car's passenger seat. Mendel told Patrick how he longed to study plants where they lived in the wild, not just in gardens. He wanted to go to tropical atolls and frozen tundras and to every seashore, to study how plants adapted to different Earth environments.

"Oberon's study of music allowed him to remain in a secure place," Mendel was saying. "Although I know he would have preferred to go out and see musical performances, security concerns kept him indoors, away from people, and music was sent to him. But my study of plants will not permit that. I must go where the plants live in order to study them. That seems to be a problem for the DOR. But there is no point in my being here if I am not allowed to study."

"That makes sense. The DOR must be concerned about keeping you safe. We heard that Oberon was recently attacked. How is he doing?"

"He isn't very well, Patrick."

Patrick, clearly an experienced radio man, had a voice that was almost as expressive as a fae's. "I'm sorry to hear that," he said sympathetically. "Will he be all right?"

"I don't know."

Ángel glanced at Chandler, who shook her head. She obviously didn't know about this. This was *news*. Victor reached over and pulled Ángel's finger away from his mouth—he'd been chewing a cuticle.

Mendel said, "My species—Oberon tells me that you are different from us, in this. If we suffer a very great emotional shock, a very great emotional pain, we can fall ill. On my world, when someone dies unexpectedly or violently, sometimes their family can comfort each other, but other times they cannot, and then they might die. The attack on Oberon, and the disappearance of Ángel Cruz, these have been a great shock to Oberon. He has grown ill."

"We heard that Ángel Cruz was unharmed," said Patrick.

"Yes. We heard that too. But we have not seen him or spoken to him." Mendel's soft voice had gone even softer. "I don't know why. I suppose lovers sometimes quarrel."

Patrick's hesitation was palpable. This seemed like a pretty classy show, but Mendel was handing him a celebrity gossip scoop that he could hardly ignore. He asked delicately, "Oberon and Ángel Cruz are lovers?"

"Yes. Oh, was that not generally known?" asked Mendel. "Oh. Well. They were. But now they are parted, and Oberon . . . I cannot comfort him. I cannot help him. Oberon is dying."

"That's terrible. Is there anything anyone can do?"

"I don't know," said Mendel again, sounding helpless. "I cannot help him."

Patrick wrapped up the interview by asking his listeners to send their thoughts and prayers to the bereft first envoy from the Otherworld, said farewell to Mendel, who was "calling in from somewhere here in Atlanta," and then moved on to his next interview.

Ángel turned off the radio. They all sat in silence for a moment, but Ángel couldn't keep still; he leaped to his feet and began to pace. He heard the others get out of the car and turned to face them: sympathetic Marissa, worried Victor. Chandler, whose blue eyes were blazing with anger. Her response was the closest to his own, so he spoke to her. "They lied to me."

"Yes," said Chandler.

"They lied to *him*."

"It sounds like it."

Ángel and Chandler saw eye to eye on almost nothing, but there was one thing he knew about her: she hated lies. She was furious now; not, probably, because she cared about Ángel and Oberon's relationship. But she'd worked for the DOR for years, given years of her life for them, risked her own life for the envoy's out of loyalty to them. She was fundamentally honest, and they were liars.

"Why isn't Mendel helping him?" he demanded. "He told me another fae would prevent this from happening!"

"I don't know," said Chandler.

He rubbed his mouth with a trembling hand. "What do I do?"

"What do you want to do, Ángel?" Chandler asked. "Do you want to be free of all this? Or do you want to go to him?"

"I have to go to him. Chandler, I *have to*."

She nodded sharply. "Then maybe you need to start by kicking Neil Jeremy's ass."

Ángel told Marissa and the others to stay at the hotel, and walked to the DOR headquarters alone.

It was about six blocks, and he needed the time to clear his mind and ready himself for the confrontation. Just as he needed to spend a little time alone before a live performance.

Besides, while they were supportive, they didn't really understand why he needed to do this.

At first, lost in mentally rehearsing what he was going to say, he didn't notice all the people on the streets. They were streaming from all directions toward the Olympic Park. He was headed that way too—the DOR headquarters was across from the park on Marietta Street—so he saw that the park was full of people, and more were arriving.

The trees and grass were winter-brown, but the sun was bright, and at first Ángel thought there must be some festival or party happening. Food trucks were doing brisk business. Someone seemed to have set up art or craft projects: they were passing out big sheets of cardboard, drawing on them with markers.

They were making signs. Ángel saw two women, talking and laughing, comparing signs: *MONSTERS GO HOME* read one. *NO MORE ELFS* said the other.

They were getting ready to march, he realized. They'd heard the NPR interview too, and they were going to protest. Across the park, he could hear a guy with a megaphone talking about how they were going to assemble in front of the DOR headquarters.

Ángel walked faster.

It was utterly disorienting. He remembered the riot in front of the Tiepolo Ballroom, the flying glass and fire and screams, all because Oberon had been accepting an award for donating money to schools. How much more enraged was Atlanta, to discover that there were now *two* fae among them? What kind of murderous violence were they capable of?

But they didn't seem angry at all. They seemed like people waiting for a concert, excited and smiling.

How dare they have fun. They had gathered to chant hate and wave signs of rejection, in an effort to wound the bravest and loneliest man Ángel had ever known, and they were treating it like a party.

Furious, he jaywalked across Marietta and went into the high-rise that housed the DOR. The guard in the lobby clearly recognized Ángel. "Sir. Do you have an appointment?"

"You see the crowds gathering in the park?" Ángel said. "They're ready to rumble. Headed this way. Are your guys ready?"

"Oh—" The guard looked out the window, glanced at his phone.

Ángel walked right past him and pushed through the big glass doors into the DOR offices.

It was one big room, a cubicle farm, full of people. They all stopped what they were doing and stared up at him.

Last time he'd been here, he'd been exhausted and hurt, dirty and ashamed. Now he stood and glared at them, letting everyone look their fill. Ángel was not large, and he didn't take up much psychic space. He avoided trouble, ignored people who were rude, smiled at everyone else. He knew how to use charm and pleasantness to slip under people's radar, and as a result those who did notice him sometimes tended to see him as weak.

But he had performed his heart out before thousands of people. He had *presence*, when he wanted it. He knew how to command attention, and as he walked slowly past cubicles and file cabinets toward Neil Jeremy's office, he was *on*.

He was so angry, he felt like he was seven feet tall.

These people had evaded him, manipulated him, lied to him. Worse—much worse—they had manipulated and lied to Oberon. Ángel let his eyes roam over the employees of the DOR, feeling his heartbeat.

Oberon was worthy of their respect, their admiration. He was worthy of love, and Ángel loved him. And he was done being pushed around by the DOR.

People throughout the big room fell silent as he walked by. They stood up in their cubicles, eyes drawn by him. As he approached Neil Jeremy's office, the agent's secretary, Emma, stood up too. She backed away, not blocking his passage.

The door to Neil Jeremy's office opened when he reached it. The red-haired agent looked pale.

"Ángel," he said. "Hi! Come on in and sit down—"

But Ángel wasn't going to relinquish this audience.

"Did you tell him I didn't want to see him?" He pitched his voice, not loud, but ringing like a bell, so that every person in the room could hear it.

Jeremy blanched further, but maintained his calm tone. "Let's not do this out here."

"I think we should," said Ángel. "I think you should explain to all of us why you told me Oberon didn't want to see me, which was a lie, and why you told him that I didn't want to see him, which was also a lie."

The room was so silent, he heard someone drop a pen.

Jeremy said, "This is private business."

"Yeah, it is." Ángel stalked closer. "But Mendel just announced my private business on NPR. My private business is probably going to be on the front page of the *New York Times* before morning, and I'd like an explanation."

"That—that should never have happened." Jeremy seemed to abandon his effort to get Ángel into his office and came out into the main room, hands spread placatingly. "Mendel's phone has been taken from him. Listen. None of this should have happened. Oberon asked us to find him someone who would be willing to go up there and be his friend. That's all. We had no idea that he—that he expected—"

"What are you even talking about right now?" demanded Ángel.

"There's going to be an outcry about this." Sweat shone on Jeremy's forehead. "People are going to want to know why the DOR procured—"

"'Procured'?" repeated Ángel. "Do you mean *pimped*?"

The word rang through the room, and all around him he heard people gasp.

"Let's get one thing straight," said Ángel, deliberately keeping his voice slow and low, and his audience leaned in a little to hear him. "The DOR did not pimp me, because I am not a sex worker. I am not some boy the DOR picked up off the street. I have sex with who I want, when I choose, and my decision to have sex with the cultural envoy from the Otherworld was *mine*, and it had fuck-all to do with the DOR or with you. But you made a decision to lie to me, to lie to Oberon, in a misguided attempt to protect the DOR's public image, and that decision made Oberon sick."

"No!" cried Jeremy, lifting his hands in a warding gesture.

"No what? You didn't lie? You didn't cause Oberon's illness?"

"No, I— *We*—we weren't trying to protect the DOR's public image. We were trying to protect you."

Fucking spare me.

He didn't say it, but his exasperation rang in his voice anyway. "Great. Thanks for that extremely patronizing explanation."

"Anyway, now he has another elf to be with, so you don't have to be with him," said Jeremy.

The guy was not listening. He was so committed to his idea of Ángel as a victim that he couldn't see him any other way. Ángel let that go and said, "Except it's not working. Mendel said himself that he can't heal Oberon."

"They just need time—"

"No," said Ángel. "Now. I need to see Oberon. You are going to get me a car to wherever he is. Right now."

Jeremy didn't say anything. His eyes were bright and hectic, his mouth firmly closed.

Emma appeared at Ángel's elbow. "Here." She handed him a plastic card.

It was blank. He turned it over to see the magnetic strip on the back. "What's this?"

"You need it to access the top floor. Just tap it to the pad in the elevator, and it'll take you to the fourteenth floor."

He stared at the card. "He's *here*?" he said. "In this building? He's been right here all along?"

She nodded.

Ángel directed one last livid glare over her shoulder at Neil Jeremy. "I don't care about your good intentions," he said. "I promise you, if Oberon dies, it will be *me* on the front page of the *New York Times*, telling the world how you killed him."

He turned, and walked out toward the elevator bay.

CHAPTER
THIRTY-ONE

T he elevator opened up on a silent indigo-painted hallway. There was one door, and when Ángel touched it, it swung inward. Not just unlocked, but ajar.

He stepped in and was slapped in the face with wrongness.

The air, the *feel* of the air, was somehow dissonant and terrible. His heart pounded, and the hair on his arms and scalp prickled. It was like someone was screaming, though he couldn't hear a sound.

He was in a large, glossily modern penthouse apartment, dimly lit and dark in spite of the bright afternoon sunshine outside. He barely noticed the clean modern furnishings as he made his way through the large, dim apartment. The feeling of horror increased as he crossed the foyer, past the kitchen and dining room, down a hallway to a bedroom. There he found two fae: an unfamiliar one, sitting on a chair with his long legs drawn up, feet tucked under his body, and Oberon, who was naked on the bed, face to the wall, loosely covered by a sheet. Ángel's lover was curled in on himself, the knobs of his spine visible on the back of his neck, the wings of his scapulae bladelike and vulnerable beneath his eerily blue-gray skin.

The strident horror was radiating from Oberon.

"Ángel Cruz," said Mendel quietly. "You're here."

Ángel tore his gaze away from Oberon. "The door was open," he said, stepping hesitantly into the room.

"I leave it open in case anyone wants to come in," said Mendel.

Your security team must love you.

Mendel seemed, at first glance, very much like Oberon: tall, white, with a haunting, expressionless face and wide dark green-gold eyes. His hair was a long silky hank of platinum streaked with mint, tied at his nape in a purple ribbon, but he'd acquiesced to a no-doubt DOR-mandated uniform of charcoal pants and a white cotton button-down shirt. Where the angles and planes of Oberon's face made him look sinister and mocking, something about Mendel's slanted brow ridges and curved cheekbones gave him an air of harmless innocence.

Both impressions were probably equally misleading.

Mendel was stroking Oberon's bare shoulder, and the sight of it made the breath in Ángel's lungs feel hot. He wanted to tell Mendel to take his hand off Oberon, and at the same time, demand why Mendel wasn't doing more. Why wasn't he in bed with Oberon? Why wasn't he holding Oberon in his arms, why wasn't he making Oberon better?

He dropped to his knees beside the bed. The emotions Oberon was emitting were scorching his skin, the inside of his nose, gathering bitterly at the back of his throat and making his eyes water. Even if Oberon hadn't turned the color of skim milk, Ángel would know that he was dying.

"They told me he didn't want to see me," whispered Ángel, gently using a fingertip to push Oberon's hair out of his still, distant face.

"They told us you didn't want to see him," said Mendel. "He was doing all right—I mean, he was very anxious, and very sad, but he was not like this, until they told us that you didn't want him anymore."

Oh, Oberon. "And—" Ángel looked up at Mendel. "And you can't do anything? He said— He was so happy when he heard you were coming. He said, with you here, he would be safe. From, from this."

"I tried. I am trying." Mendel ran a hand over Oberon's shoulder, and this time Ángel saw Oberon flinch and shiver. "But we never got a chance to know each other, you know. And he will not permit very much from me."

The magic of Oberon's grief was radiating out into the air. Were he surrounded by trusted friends, they would grieve together by touching, and their magic would meld, and change, and sing out for all to feel, and somehow this change would comfort them. But Oberon wasn't permitting Mendel to share his grief. So Oberon was trapped in this excruciating song. A vicious cycle, he'd called it. A cycle that would just get worse and worse, until someone interrupted it.

Ángel stripped off his shirt, then stood up to toe off his shoes and socks, saying, "Well, I'm not going to give him any choice." His voice was trembling a little with fear and bravado. "I am not putting up with this passive-aggressive dying-of-a-broken-heart horseshit."

And he crawled into bed with Oberon, wrapping his arms tight around Oberon's bare torso, pressing his chest and belly to Oberon's back, his cheek to Oberon's neck.

It was awful. Everywhere their skin touched, Oberon's magic penetrated Ángel's body, filled him up with greasy, sick despair.

"Oh, God," he moaned, tightening his grip, hanging on for dear life as hot pain and fear and grief shocked through him. "Oh, God, Oberon. I'm here. I'm here." Oberon shuddered, and the motion seemed to send waves of awfulness through Ángel's body. "Oberon, please," he begged. "Please stop. Oberon, stop, please."

"He might not be able to," said Mendel. "He is very ill. Sometimes people don't come back." He paused. Sounding worried, he added, "If he dies, you mustn't let it kill you too."

Can that happen? Of course, neither of them knew. "He won't die," whispered Ángel, starting to weep. "He's going to come back to me." He sniffed, wiping his tears on Oberon's cold, clammy skin. "I hate it when I cry," he complained. "Come back to me, Oberon."

He stayed in bed with Oberon for an agonizingly long time, rubbing his chest, stroking his face and neck, twining their legs together. Oberon, for his part, sometimes shivered, sometimes gasped, sometimes seemed to struggle weakly, but mostly lay still as the dead. Ángel took to singing his fae name: nine alternating 16th and 32nd notes, with a 32nd rest after the seventh note and a slur connecting the third, fourth, and fifth. Again and again. Sometimes Mendel sang with him.

And, later: "Oberon, please come back," cried Ángel, exhausted, not sure how much longer he could bear it. "Oberon, I'm here. I'm here for you. Oberon, can't you hear me?"

"He hears you," said Mendel.

"Don't you trust me?" Ángel hugged Oberon tightly. "Oh, baby, I'm sorry. I told you I'd be with you as long as you needed. I'm sorry. I tried. I tried to come back as soon as I could. I'm sorry."

Eventually, he slept. He dreamed of a fairy tale: a witch, and a castle, and a forest. An evil spell, a princess, a talking clock. When he woke up he was groggy, his skin clammy with sweat and strange magic. He rolled Oberon onto his back, lying on top of him.

Oberon was awake. His eyes were open, but glassy, some sort of yellowish crust accreting in the corners. Ángel wiped his lids gently with the corner of a sheet, and Oberon closed his eyes.

The dream still in his mind, he said, "Oberon, do you remember how you were afraid to kiss me? Because kisses are important to my people, you said. All our stories about magical kisses that transform beasts to men and heal sleeping princesses. Remember?" He cupped Oberon's face, stroking his dry lips with his thumb. "This is one of those magic kisses," he whispered. "This kiss will wake you up, and heal you, and bring you back to life, if you'll let it." And he pressed his mouth to Oberon's.

Oberon shuddered violently. Then with a spasmodic lurch he wrapped his arms around Ángel, clasping him, opening his mouth and returning the kiss. They both moaned—Ángel felt like he was being *injected* with Oberon's illness—but at the same time he felt a desperate hope, that as he took Oberon's emotions into himself, he somehow eased Oberon's agony.

Oberon was speaking now, a fluid melodic stream of incomprehensible syllables, hands in Ángel's hair, gripping him tight enough to drive the air from his lungs. After a moment, he regained enough control to switch to English: "Forgive me, forgive me, forgive me—"

"Oberon," gasped Ángel. "Shhh, baby. It's okay."

"Ah, I am sorry," cried Oberon softly, against Ángel's neck. "I am sorry, but I want to live—"

"Yes. Live. Live."

They clutched each other, murmuring pleas and reassurances, Oberon's hands roaming roughly all over Ángel while Ángel cradled him.

"You're going to be okay now?"

"Ángel—"

"You'll get better now, yeah?"

"Don't leave me again—"

"No, no, no. I never left you." He caught Oberon's face in his hands, threading his fingers into Oberon's hair, made him look into his eyes. "They took me from you, and I couldn't get back. And you *do not get to die* if something like that happens, Oberon. You have to stay alive until I can get back."

"I wanted to. But it was hard."

Oberon's skin, still grayish, had gone dappled with lust. While Ángel was grappling with surprise, Oberon slid his hands down Ángel's body, pushing them into his pants to palm his butt. Ángel gulped in air as Oberon sucked on his throat and pressed his legs apart with a thigh. The movements were blatantly sexual, but the magic coursing through Oberon's skin continued to speak of wrongness. Fear and desperation, mixed with the desire. Ángel squirmed, caught between arousal and discomfort.

"Baby—you don't—"

"You still want me?" Oberon growled, his breath hot in Ángel's ear, his hands kneading the cheeks of Ángel's ass, making Ángel's hardening dick rub rhythmically against Oberon's thigh.

"Ah, yeah," Ángel moaned, needing to surrender to Oberon's need, his legs falling open.

"Is this what's called a pity fuck?" asked Mendel.

Ángel startled, going rigid in Oberon's arms. He turned slowly to glare at Mendel, who was sitting in a chair near the bed.

He had completely forgotten about the second envoy, had not imagined that he was still in the room.

"This is not," Ángel said, "a *pity fuck*."

He felt, rather than heard, Oberon gasp for breath.

"You didn't come back until you heard he was dying," said Mendel. "You want to comfort him."

Mendel's face and voice were all innocence, but his words cut.

"How about you," snarled Ángel, furious, "go the fuck away and leave us alone?"

"Oh," said Mendel. "I would rather stay."

Ángel opened his mouth to tell Mendel what he could do, and Oberon squeezed him. "Your *anger*," he murmured. "I'd forgotten." To Mendel he said, "I think the phrase is offensive."

"'Pity fuck'?" asked Mendel. "But if he is having sex with you because he feels sorry for you—"

"*Get out*," said Ángel, attempting to struggle free of Oberon's clasp, "before I break your fucking face."

"Privacy," Oberon said to Mendel, hanging on to Ángel. "Do you remember? You learned about privacy."

"Yes," said Mendel. "I know. But there's no one else here, and I don't want to be alone."

"You'll have to get used to it," said Oberon. "Go on." Mendel made a meow of acquiescence and left the room.

"Close the door!" yelled Ángel.

Mendel closed the door.

Ángel flopped back on the bed, panting, torn between laughing and punching something. Oberon lay beside him quietly. They just breathed for a while. Then Oberon began to smell like rain, and he slowly drooped his head and rested his forehead on the center of Ángel's chest.

Ángel felt his sorrow.

"No," he said. "No. Don't think that."

"You *didn't* come back until you heard I was sick," said Oberon.

"They told me you didn't want to see me."

"You believed them?"

"So did you," said Ángel.

"Because you never believed in my love," said Oberon. "You didn't believe in me. You only wanted to get away from me—"

"Shh, no," said Ángel, wrapping his arms around Oberon's shoulders. "Don't, please." He held him, his cheek against the top of Oberon's head. "Can you feel me?"

He closed his eyes and called to mind the moment he fell in love with Oberon: the music room. The swan chair. Guitar and mandolin. Ángel's sad melody, and Oberon: harmony, consonance, a perfect musical melding, a moment of perfect emotional understanding. And then Oberon had deepened the song, transformed it, infused it with hope—sweet, impossible, fragile hope. Ángel remembered, and the memory took his breath away, filled him with awe and admiration and helpless love.

True love, for this strange and singular individual. Impossible love, undeniable, unworkable, but powerful and aching and true. Ángel knew he'd feel this way forever.

Oberon shivered.

"Yes," whispered Oberon. "I feel you."

"I was scared," said Ángel. "I'm still scared. I couldn't believe you would love me, especially because I'm not fae, and I don't have magic—"

"You are overflowing with magic."

"Am I? Then it's the wrong kind—so I was scared. And when they told me you didn't want to see me, I believed it. For a minute. But oh, Oberon. Can't you feel how I feel?"

Oberon stroked Ángel, reverently. His skin color was coming back—pale taupe, only lightly tinged with gray. "You love me? You love me?"

"I love you," said Ángel. "Even if you—even if you decide Mendel is the one you love, I'll still feel this way. It's not pity, Oberon. I'm just not very brave. But I love you."

Oberon began, softly, to purr. "I am *not* going to decide that Mendel is the one I love. I only love you."

He cuddled Ángel close, rubbing his face against Ángel's chest. The signals coming from his skin tingled, became warm, soothing; he began to smell faintly like ginger. They lay together, legs entangled, for a long time.

"I read this magazine story," said Ángel, after a while, "about penguins. That's a kind of bird. They lived in a zoo, so, like, an artificial environment, but the zookeepers tried to make it as natural for the penguins as possible. And in the spring all the penguins mated and started laying eggs, and the zookeepers noticed that two boy penguins had mated and were trying to incubate a rock."

Oberon murmured, "How sad."

"Yes, but then there was an orphan egg, so the zookeepers gave it to the boy penguins, and they adopted it and they were like a little family. Total happy ending, right? But the article said it only happened because there were more boy penguins in the zoo enclosure than girl penguins. In their natural environment, they would have sought out female mates. And later, when there were more girl penguins available, the boy penguins broke up and mated with females, because that's what's natural for penguins to do."

"I am not a penguin," said Oberon. He raised his head. "Ángel, you are not a penguin, either. This planet has *millions* of available human mates for you. Do you think you will find a human man you love better, and stop loving me?"

"No." Ángel was certain of that.

"Why do you have faith in your own love, but not in mine?"

Ángel gazed at him. "I guess that's a good question." He touched Oberon's face, his lips. "I don't know. Maybe because no one ever loved me before without wanting me to change." He paused. "Although I think my dad is trying."

"I want *you*." Oberon kissed Ángel's fingertips, touching one with his tongue, and the sensation sizzled down Ángel's nerve endings. "Only you."

Ángel smiled. "How can you be ready for sex so soon when you've been so sick?"

"I was last time too," said Oberon. "Remember?"

The memory of Oberon's couch made Ángel weak. "I remember I left you hanging." He stroked his face. "Baby, you've kind of got a *residue* on you. Want to shower first, and then see?"

Under dual showerheads of streaming warm water, they stroked each other, kissing softly. Ángel poured shower gel into his hands and massaged the lather over every inch of Oberon's body, rinsing away the coating of spent emotion, burnishing the dappled golden-white skin. They stroked lathered hands through each other's hair, drank running water off each other's bodies. Oberon, clearly still a little sluggish after his illness, tasted Ángel's neck, his jaw, his shoulders. They could feel each other's desire through their skin, a feedback loop of pleasure fizzing in Ángel's blood like champagne. He closed his eyes and arched his throat, rubbing against Oberon's wet body, humming.

"I missed you so much."

"Ángel." Oberon nuzzled into the crook of Ángel's neck. "When they told me you were gone, I was so afraid."

"I was terrified. The whole time, I just wanted to get back to you. God, Oberon—"

They kissed. Oberon's hands roamed, as if memorizing Ángel's body. He ran his hands over the place on his back where the taser's prongs had gone in and Ángel flinched; he opened his eyes, and Ángel felt the bitter wash of his surprise. "They told me you were undamaged!"

"I am." Ángel leaned against him, trying to preserve the mood, not sure how fragile Oberon's recovery was. "I'm fine."

"You're *injured*." Oberon said the word with horror, brushing a gentle finger around the healing punctures. "Did the kidnappers do this to you?"

"Yes, and it really hurt. But it's okay now."

"And what is this?" Oberon traced the scabbed gash on Ángel's hip.

"I cut myself on some glass when I was escaping."

"You'll tell me the whole story." Oberon's hands mapped Ángel's body, finding every bruise and ache. His tone was grave, angry. "I want to know everything they did to you."

"Yes," said Ángel. "But not now." He went on his tiptoes and kissed Oberon, pushing them both back under the shower, cupping his butt and pressing his body close.

The distraction worked.

Oberon carried him out of the bathroom and laid him down on the thick rug in the bedroom, ravished him with hands and mouth, slicked his entrance and teased him to full panting arousal. And then Ángel was captured in Oberon's strong embrace, his legs draped over Oberon's big shoulders, and his ass nudged by Oberon's cock.

Oberon hesitated.

Moaning, Ángel arched up, hands grasping Oberon's arms, hips twisting. But Oberon, smelling cool and green, of snow on trees, didn't move.

Ángel looked into his face. Their gazes locked for a still, breathless moment. But as always, Oberon's face told Ángel nothing. So he closed his eyes and felt his magic, breathed Oberon's scent, palmed one curving bicep, cupped his face, ran a thumb over his lips. Ángel felt Oberon's love and desire, thrumming like a musical note through his skin. Felt, too, his hesitation.

Love, and desire, and fear. Because for Oberon, this moment was irrevocable. He was changing, the magic in his skin was tuning itself to Ángel's, so that he could never communicate this way with any other. Ángel was, unintentionally, marking him, making him his own, in a way that could never be undone. And Oberon loved him, loved the change.

But with his eyes closed, Ángel could smell and feel Oberon's fear so clearly, he could almost put it into words: *This has never happened before. This is something new, in all the universe. Would Ángel always love him? Did Ángel understand that this change was permanent, that Oberon would belong to him forever?*

"Yes," Ángel whispered, pressing his hands to Oberon's skin, hoping he could feel him as well as hear him. "I will. I do."

He felt Oberon's joy, then, and his awe, and a little warm wash of something that tingled and tickled: Oberon thought he was *cute*.

Ángel laughed. "Are you going to fuck me, or just admire me?"

"Both," said Oberon, and did.

They got back in the shower to rinse off, and as they were toweling themselves dry Oberon opened the bathroom door and sang out in his own language. In a moment, Mendel came in without knocking. Ángel made a stifled yelp of protest and covered his groin with the towel, glaring as Mendel handed the naked Oberon some clean clothes. The second envoy leaned against the sink while Oberon began to dress.

"Are you just going to stand there?" demanded Ángel.

Mendel gazed at him. "Yes?"

Oberon nudged Mendel. "Go see if there's any food."

"There isn't," said Mendel forlornly. "The food they brought all has meat." He looked at Ángel. "They won't let me leave." As he spoke, Mendel unselfconsciously reached out to stroke Oberon's shoulder and neck. "And they're afraid of me, so no one ever comes here. And since I did the NPR interview without their permission, they took my phone away. It's very boring, and I'm hungry."

Ángel took a deep breath. He was going to have to get used to Mendel touching Oberon. He was going to have to explain appropriate boundaries.

But first, he was going to have to take care of these fae.

"Go away," he said, gently, to Mendel. "Because I don't want you here while I'm getting dressed. But then, if you like, I'll call my friend and she'll bring us some food. Do you want to meet my friend Marissa?"

"Yes, please," said Mendel.

"I would like that too," agreed Oberon.

"You like vegetables?" Ángel remembered Oberon's preferred diet. "Do you like noodles?"

"Yes!" said Mendel. "What are noodles?"

CHAPTER
THIRTY-TWO

Á ngel would always remember that afternoon like a sort of strange party. People kept arriving, and then stayed, and talked, and ate, and played music.

First he called Marissa and told her what to bring, and then he had to call the DOR and tell them to let her in. They'd erected a security cordon around the building in response to the growing protests on the streets of Atlanta.

"It's *crazy* out there," she said when she arrived, greeting Ángel with a cheek-kiss, her arms laden with shopping bags. "There are protests, and there are counter-protests. 'We hate elves' on one street corner, 'We love elves' on the opposite corner." Then she saw the two envoys and shrank back, uncharacteristically timid.

"This is my friend, Marissa Sommers," said Ángel, grabbing her hand. "Marissa, here is Oberon—" her gaze was flickering between the two fae— "the one in the black shirt. And Mendel is the one in the gray shirt."

"Hi," she said.

"Thank you for coming. It is very nice to meet you at last," said Oberon. "I have heard so much about you, I feel that I know you already. I enjoyed your letter that was made of MelodEye lyrics."

Marissa dimpled at him. "Oh, well, it's always nice to meet a fellow MelodEye fan."

Mendel was quiet, and Oberon added, "Mendel is a little nervous, but he is happy to meet you too."

"Is he?" Marissa's eyes widened. "Uh. So am I. But, look, um, Mr. Mendel. I heard your radio interview. I brought you a gift." Of course she had. In spite of all her rebellion, she was a Southern girl to the core. "To welcome you to, um, our world."

She bent to put down her bags and pulled a potted orchid from one of them. Its green-white flower nodded as she approached Mendel with the plant.

"Oh," breathed Mendel, reaching for the pot. Marissa snatched her hands back and dropped it, but the fae caught it adroitly. "How lovely. Thank you."

Marissa bit her lip. She was staring at Mendel's expressionless face, her eyebrows crooked uncertainly. Ángel nudged her. "He really does like it," he said. "He's not making fun of you."

"No," agreed Mendel. "I love it. I have had so little opportunity to see Earth's plants." He turned and showed the potted plant to Oberon. "Look, I think it is called dendrobium. I have seen pictures of them."

"Did you also bring lunch?" asked Ángel. "Because the DOR goons who have been shopping for these guys run to Hot Pockets and canned stew, and they need some real food."

She'd brought a smorgasbord of vegetarian Thai takeout. They crowded the dining room table with cartons and shared, and Mendel asked Marissa about the orchid. Marissa admitted that she didn't know anything about orchids, so Mendel eagerly told her about them, their habitat and range. Ángel noticed that Oberon was only picking at a container of spicy papaya salad and growled, "Stop stirring it around and put it in your mouth."

"I'm not very hungry."

"I don't care. You've been sick and you need to eat. Do you want soup instead?"

"No." Oberon ate.

Marissa stared at Ángel, her dark eyes huge and glowing. "*Sassy,*" she murmured.

"Shut up, bitch."

She laughed, then smiled shyly at Oberon. "I guess he really likes you," she said. "He's pretty polite to people he doesn't like."

"His manners were excellent when we first met," agreed Oberon.

Recalling those times reminded Ángel to ask: "I miss Lily. Is she okay?"

"She is well. She was in the gatehouse when the assassins came in. I miss her very much too—I don't know if I'll ever see her again.

She and John work for the DOR, and they're keeping us here. They won't let me call her."

"What is going on with the DOR?" demanded Ángel. "What was their plan? Lock you up here by yourself with no plants and no music, and not give you anything you can eat, and wait to see if you died?"

"There was cheese and lettuce." Mendel touched Oberon as he spoke, petted him, and Ángel was beginning to recognize the smell of hero-worship. "But I ate it all. I'm sorry. I don't like the Hot Pockets."

Oberon patted Mendel's hand. "The DOR seems to be in considerable disarray," said Oberon. "No one expected Mendel, of course, and he arrived right at the moment of greatest chaos, when I had been attacked by a member of my own security team, and Ángel had vanished. I think they had no idea what to do. I don't know why they tried to keep us apart, though."

"Neil Jeremy seems to have felt guilty about me. Like I was an innocent lamb who had been corrupted to evil ways by you. He said he thought that since Mendel was here, I could go."

"It's not the same at all," said Mendel.

"No, and even if his intentions were good, he could have talked to me. I'm able to make decisions; I don't need to be shielded." Ángel glanced at Marissa. "Not by Chandler, either."

"I didn't think Chandler liked you," said Oberon.

"I don't think she likes either of us."

"Adult child of an alcoholic," said Marissa. "Overdeveloped sense of responsibility. It's easier for her to try to control other people's lives than to deal with her own issues."

"Wow," teased Ángel. "All that and pretty too."

"I know, right?" She glanced at Oberon. "She doesn't understand you. She's afraid of you. But she doesn't hate you."

"I'm glad. I am very fond of Chandler. Is she well?"

"She's okay," said Marissa. "It was painful for her to quit the DOR, but—"

"What?" said Oberon. "Did she quit? Why?"

"She felt responsible for the attack on you," said Marissa. "She was ashamed that you were hurt, and Ángel was kidnapped, on her watch. When she heard that Ángel had been found she cried with relief."

"She was not responsible."

"She hasn't been held responsible, really, but she's pretty hard on herself."

"I would like to see her," said Oberon. "I would thank her for all her years of working to keep me safe. I would tell her that I, at least, do not blame her."

"She's here in Atlanta," said Marissa. "I can call her."

"Will you ask her to bring me a plant?" said Mendel.

So they called Chandler, and she arrived with bottles of chilled wine and iced tea. She was accompanied by Victor, silent with shame, who brought a platter of fruit and a paper bag of guava pastelitos. Chandler, prompted by Marissa, gave Mendel an asparagus fern, and Victor gave him a Christmas cactus. Mendel glowed with delight. Both Victor and Chandler apologized to Oberon, who forgave them with his usual earnest courtesy. Then Oberon sat at the piano in the parlor to play, and as the first flat notes rippled through the apartment, he and Mendel froze in shock.

"They put you in an apartment with an out-of-tune piano?" demanded Ángel. "Really, were they *trying* to kill you?"

So the two fae opened up the piano and poked around in its innards while Victor retreated to the kitchen to make coffee and listen to NPR, and Marissa passed around the fruit and pastries. Oberon explained to Mendel and Marissa the parts of the piano. "If we had the right tools, we could fix it."

Ángel asked Victor for his multi-tool, which he never left home without, and offered it to Oberon. "Will this work?"

"Perhaps."

So the two fae tuned the piano. Mendel sat on the bench and touched the keys and sang the notes at the true pitch, while Oberon adjusted the pegs. Meanwhile, Chandler and Marissa retired to the couch to cuddle and whisper together about whatever it was they had to whisper about. Victor handed around cups of coffee. It was sweet and strong and foamy, and tasted like home—Victor's coffee was always better than Ángel's.

"Neil Jeremy just resigned from the DOR," said Victor. "I heard it on the radio."

"I called him while Oberon and Ángel were in the shower," said Mendel. "I told him that Oberon was better. I told him that we knew he had lied to us and that we didn't trust him anymore."

"I wonder who will take over," said Oberon.

"Mendel, you should hire Chandler," Ángel said.

"Why?"

"Well, you don't actually have to do what the DOR says, do you? You want to travel. The DOR wants to keep you here, but you could leave, right?"

"Wait until the protests stop," said Victor.

"I mean, you have money of your own, don't you?" persisted Ángel. "It's not controlled by the government or anything?"

"I'm not sure."

"Yes," said Oberon, emerging, dusty, from inside the piano. "We have money."

"Well, off you go, then. Tell the DOR to fuck off and hire Chandler to provide security and handle logistics, and go look at plants. I know Oberon would like to see some trees."

"Ooh, you should go to Corkscrew Swamp," said Marissa. "Over by Naples. Huge old cypress trees, and wild orchids. It's very cool."

"That sounds interesting." Mendel turned to Chandler. "Do you want to do that? When could we leave?"

"Mendel," said Chandler, "respectfully, Oberon was nearly murdered by one of my employees just a few days ago."

"Chandler protected me for years," said Oberon. "She foiled several assassination attempts. I am still alive because of her. And Ángel, of course."

"I can't guarantee your safety," protested Chandler.

"I understand," said Mendel. "But I'm not expected to live. No one thought Oberon would still be alive when I got here. I need to send back good data before I die, that's all."

"This is a suicide mission?" said Victor, incredulously.

"Not really," said Mendel. "But we know we aren't going back. We will be in your world for the rest of our lives. The information we discover is what's important, not us."

Victor looked appalled.

"They're great adventurers," said Ángel.

"I would like to go," said Oberon. "I would like to see the trees."

"If Oberon's going, I'm going," said Ángel. "And then we can go to Miami. I know some bands who would sell their grandmas for a chance to play for Oberon. Chandler, I hope you're taking notes. Oberon has also been asked to teach a class on fae musicology at Colombia, so that would be another challenge."

"I . . . I'll look into it," said Chandler, clearly dazed.

"You are a great adventurer too, Chandler," said Oberon, resuming fiddling with the piano pegs. "So are all of you. Look at us. This has never happened before."

Marissa grinned at Ángel, and he smiled back at her. "I wish I had my guitar."

"I regret your guitar very much," said Oberon, from the interior of the piano.

"What happened to your guitar?" asked Chandler. "The DOR is dying to know if Oberon attacked you with it or something."

"Oh my God, no," said Ángel. "No, it was my own fault." He glanced unhappily at Oberon, remembering the fight they'd had.

Oberon said, "I am sure there is a music store in Atlanta. Why don't we ask them to bring some guitars here? Victor will give them coffee."

"There's protests," Victor reminded them.

"Oh, man, are you kidding me?" piped up Marissa, pulling her phone out of her purse. "Atlanta music store employees would fight through *actual war* to bring Ángel Cruz a new guitar. Can you even imagine better publicity?"

She was right. Two salespeople, Shawn and Caitlyn, arrived from Maple Street Guitars, pushing a wheeled cart stacked with black cases. They were smiling when they arrived, but as soon as they saw the fae, they both visibly flinched. Ángel thought the woman was going to run away.

"It's okay," he said. "They're totally harmless. Come in. They're busy tuning that piano, so we'll go into the dining room. You don't have to worry about them."

They stacked the cases on the dining room table, clearly nervous but gamely sticking to their sales pitches while ignoring the sound of piano tuning from the other room. Marissa and Ángel opened them and lifted the guitars from their velvet-lined shells. He immediately rejected a fancy Ovation that had hardwood inlays in the top.

"That one's pretty," said Victor.

"Don't like a fancy soundboard," said Ángel, closing the case and putting the Ovation aside. He played all the others, one by one, chatting with the salespeople about the features of each guitar.

He kept returning to a cutaway Taylor whose strings seemed to spring like live things under his fingertips. Medullary rays fanned across the spruce top, shining like silver under the lacquer. Its tone was warm, golden, surprisingly loud for a smaller instrument.

"That one keeps calling your name, doesn't it?" asked Caitlyn with a smile.

"Yeah." He smiled back at her and played a few licks of "Guantanamera." The notes rang out, filling the apartment effortlessly. Shawn grabbed another guitar and played along. Marissa found wooden spoons and tapped out the rhythm on the back of a chair.

From the other room, the piano responded with the old Cuban song's simple rhythmic counterpoint. Ángel grinned, closed his eyes, and played. Invisibly, from the parlor, Oberon accompanied them.

"This is so cool," whispered Caitlyn. "It's just like *O-Pod*."

After "Guantanamera," Oberon began playing something exquisite and soft on the now perfectly tuned piano.

"That's— Is that Mozart?" said Shawn.

"Would you like to meet Oberon and Mendel? They're nice. You'll see."

"It's true," said Marissa. "I met them today, and look, I'm still alive."

So the guitar store employees met Oberon and Mendel, and they gave Ángel a deep discount on the Taylor, and then they stayed and drank wine and played a few songs on the guitars together. Mendel, who knew none of the words, la-la-la-ed along unselfconsciously, his lovely alto voice forging harmonies on the fly.

Then Oberon began to play something shining and staccato. For a moment Ángel listened with drawn brows, trying to place it. Then Shawn said, "It's 'Take On Me.'"

Marissa laughed first, her big infectious laugh, and pretty soon everyone in the room was cracking up. Because the cultural envoy from the Otherworld was playing A-ha on a grand piano.

Oberon lifted his hands from the keys. "People often laugh at songs," he remarked to Mendel. "I've never been able to pinpoint why, or which ones."

"Okay, wait, wait," said Marissa, through her giggles. "I know this one. Oberon, from the top."

With wooden spoons on a pot, she played the drum intro. Oberon launched into the keyboard riff. Ángel began to sing the chorus, and the rest of the humans—except for Victor and Chandler—sang along. They killed it until they got to the verse, when not one of them could hit the high notes. The song fell apart again as they all collapsed, laughing.

Victor waved his hands urgently. "Listen!"

He turned up the NPR broadcast.

"The anti-elven protests began in Atlanta at about noon," said the radio newscaster, "when word leaked that Oberon and Mendel were housed in the DOR building on Marietta Street. But then something new happened: counter-protesters filled the streets of Atlanta."

"I'm on Washington Street near the State Capitol," said a reporter, "and I estimate that there are tens of thousands of people here, waving signs and chanting. I've seen signs that read 'No Hate' and 'We Aren't Afraid.'"

"Is it peaceful?"

"Oh yes," said the reporter. "It's joyous. It's like a festival atmosphere. I haven't seen any violent acts at all, and the counter-protesters outnumber the original protesters on a scale of something like ten to one."

"What's that I hear in the background?" asked the newscaster.

"The most amazing thing," said the reporter. "Several local church choirs have come out onto the streets, and they're singing Oberon's name."

"What?"

"His elven name," repeated the reporter. "It's kind of a little song. He sings it on every episode of the podcast, and these choirs have come out on the streets and . . . and they're *singing*."

Ángel stared at Oberon. Then he got up and went to the balcony and threw open the sliding glass window.

The sound of the crowd rose up to them: the loud, chaotic cacophony of tens of thousands of people. Chanting, shouting, singing. Church choirs, identifiable by their matching robes, had gathered in the street, swaying as they sang, belting out the nine syllables of Oberon's name. Harmonizing, improvising, *riffing* on his name, and the crowd was swaying, chanting along. As they stood and listened, a compelling mezzo-soprano voice rose above the crowd, unamplified and powerful, drawing out the nine notes into a hymn of welcome.

Oberon stood still, listening, thunderstruck.

"They're changing it," whispered Ángel, standing beside him. "The pitch isn't right . . . the cadence . . . is it okay for them to do that?"

Oberon's eyes glowed. He took Ángel's hand, and his awe and joy thrummed through his skin.

"They're making it something new," he said.

Dear Reader,

Thank you for reading Jenya Keefe's, *The Musician and the Monster*!

We know your time is precious and you have many, many entertainment options, so it means a lot that you've chosen to spend your time reading. We really hope you enjoyed it.

We'd be honored if you'd consider posting a review—good or bad—on sites like **Amazon, Barnes & Noble, Kobo, Goodreads, Twitter, Facebook, Tumblr,** and your blog or website. We'd also be honored if you told your friends and family about this book. Word of mouth is a book's lifeblood!

For more information on upcoming releases, author interviews, blog tours, contests, giveaways, and more, please sign up for our weekly, spam-free newsletter and visit us around the web:

Newsletter: riptidepublishing.com/newsletter
Twitter: twitter.com/RiptideBooks
Facebook: facebook.com/RiptidePublishing
Goodreads: tinyurl.com/RiptideOnGoodreads
Tumblr: riptidepublishing.tumblr.com

Thank you so much for Reading the Rainbow!

RiptidePublishing.com

RIPTIDE
PUBLISHING

ACKNOWLEDGMENTS

I owe a debt of gratitude to, among others, Elizabeth, Ann, Amy, Kay, Mike, and Alexis.

ALSO BY
JENYA KEEFE

Relationship Material

ABOUT THE AUTHOR

Jenya Keefe was born in the South. She has an advanced degree in European history, and has spent much of her life working the kinds of jobs a history degree qualifies you for: gift shop employee, lumber grader, classifieds clerk, hot glass artist. She currently lives in the Seattle area, where she works at a library. She has always written stories.

Website: jenyakeefe.com
Twitter: @JenyaKeefe
Tumblr: tumblr.com/blog/jenyakeefe

Enjoy more stories like
The Musician and the Monster
at RiptidePublishing.com!

www.ingramcontent.com/pod-product-compliance
Lightning Source LLC
Chambersburg PA
CBHW060608030726
47498CB00005B/1595